"Do you always ride alone?"

The image of him riding beside a beautiful woman flashed in her mind and the green monster reared its ugly head. That was ridiculous. She and Hank were only friends. Not one inch of his six-foot-plus body belonged to her. Until she'd run into him at the reunion, she hadn't spoken a word to him in years. Sure, she'd thought about him a lot when she'd first moved to California. She'd missed him. But over time, thoughts of him became fewer and farther apart.

He shook his head. "No. Part of being a sheriff is keeping kids out of trouble. So I have an unofficial program where I bring some of the kids to the ranch and I teach them how to care for horses. They love it. And it helps keep them on the path that leads to a successful future."

"Wow." Hank was an even better man than she'd imagined.

No matter how many times she reminded herself that they were only friends, she couldn't quite keep herself from drifting into *what if* territory. Like...what if she kissed him?

Or what if she proposed having a short fling while she was in town...?

Dear Reader,

Have you ever gotten exactly what you wanted and then wondered if it was worth the cost? Did you wonder if it would be wrong to change course? Those are the questions Shayna Givens is dealing with. A superstar singer, known all over the world, Shayna needs a quiet place away from her awful parents and the paparazzi to think about what she wants out of the rest of her life. What better place to do that than in Aspen Creek, Colorado, her hometown?

Sheriff Hank Morrow is surprised when his old high school friend shows up on his ranch. A former NFL star, he understands Shayna's need for time away from the limelight. As they spend time together, they begin to wonder if they could become more than old friends. Perhaps romance is in their future.

I hope you enjoy *Her Cowboy Lawman* as much as I enjoyed writing it.

I love to hear from my readers, so feel free to drop by my website, kathydouglassbooks.com, and drop me a note.

Happy reading!

Kathy

HER COWBOY LAWMAN

KATHY DOUGLASS

SPECIAL EDITION

ISBN-13: 978-1-335-18046-9

Her Cowboy Lawman

Harlequin Enterprises ULC
22 Adelaide St. West, 41st Floor
Toronto, Ontario M5H 4E3, Canada
www.Harlequin.com

HarperCollins Publishers
Macken House, 39/40 Mayor Street Upper,
Dublin 1, D01 C9W8, Ireland
www.HarperCollins.com

Printed in Lithuania

1 2 3 4 5 6 7 8 9 10 LIT 28 27 26 25

Kathy Douglass is a lawyer turned author of sweet small-town contemporary romances. She is married to her very own hero and is mother to two sons, who cheer her on as she tries to get her stubborn hero and heroine to realize they are meant to be together. She loves hearing from readers that something in her books made them laugh or cry. You can learn more about Kathy or contact her at kathydouglassbooks.com.

Books by Kathy Douglass

Montana Mavericks: Legacy of Tenacity

Roping the Maverick

Montana Mavericks: The Trail to Tenacity

That Maverick of Mine

Harlequin Special Edition

Aspen Creek Bachelors

Her Cowboy Lawman
A Reunion to Remember
The Cowboy Who Came Home
Wrangling a Family
The Rancher's Baby
Valentines for the Rancher

Visit the Author Profile page
at Harlequin.com for more titles.

This book is dedicated with love and appreciation
to my husband and sons. You guys are the best.
I love you with my whole heart.

Chapter One

Shayna Givens sat in her luxury car at the edge of the gravel driveway, second-guessing her decision. Now that she was actually here, dropping in on Hank out of the blue didn't seem like such a good idea. Sure he'd told her that she was always welcome at his ranch, but that had been months ago at the high school reunion and goodbye party for their former principal. They hadn't spoken since. Besides, wasn't that always what people said even when they didn't mean it? That night everyone had been in high spirits, happy to be reunited with people they hadn't seen in years. Decades in some cases. Invitations to get together had been tossed around like the helium-filled balloons forming arches around the gym where people had posed for countless pictures. She doubted that many—if any—people had followed through on the promised gatherings.

As she looked at the snowcapped mountains in the distance, her second thoughts turned into third and fourths. What had she been thinking? She couldn't just intrude on Hank like this. For all she knew, he had a girlfriend who wouldn't appreciate Shayna just popping up without any warning with the expectation of staying for a while. She was shifting from Park to Drive when flashing lights appeared behind her. *Great.* A police car. And not just any car or any officer. It was Sheriff Hank Morrow's official vehicle.

Putting the car back into Park, Shayna chided herself for being so indecisive. If she hadn't been waffling, as had become her habit of late, she wouldn't be trying to come up with a reason for why she was currently sitting at the end of his driveway. But then, if she could actually think straight, if she didn't always feel like she was on the brink of losing it completely, she wouldn't need to hide out at Hank's. She rolled down her window and watched in the side mirror as Hank drew closer.

"Can I help you?" he asked as he leaned down. His eyes widened and his polite smile grew warm as he recognized her. The huge ball of dread in her stomach began to shrink until only a small knot remained. "Shayna. What a surprise."

She forced a bright smile and tried to speak casually. "Hi. I hope you don't mind. You said I could drop in anytime."

"I remember. And no, I don't mind. I just wasn't expecting to see you here today. I thought you were on a world tour to promote your latest album." His voice was more than a little puzzled and she doubted that he was as cool with her showing up without notice as he appeared to be. The knot of dread expanded.

"My tour wrapped up a few days ago." Maybe it was a week now. She'd lost track of time. It was hard enough to focus on the necessities like eating regularly and reminding herself to stop driving when her vision blurred. She didn't have the mental capacity to worry about insignificant matters like the passage of time.

Shayna knew Hank must have dozens of questions,

but she didn't have answers now. At least none that she could share without breaking down. And right now, it was doubtful that she would be able to pull herself together again.

"I see," he said even though she doubted he truly did. "But why are you sitting way down here? My house is up there."

She searched for an answer. Unsurprisingly, nothing came to mind, so she shrugged.

"Never mind. You're probably tired from driving. Follow me around to the garage, okay?"

She nodded again, wondering why her ability to hold up her side of a conversation had abandoned her. She'd been performing since she was a child. Her string of number one albums had started when she was sixteen and hadn't stopped in nearly twenty years. Television and print interviews had been a regular part of her life for just as long. She had a reputation for being a witty and entertaining conversationalist. Yet, when faced with Hank's questions, she hadn't been able to string two words together.

Hank pulled his car in front of hers and she followed him up the driveway. It was early evening and as the sun set, it cast lovely orange streaks through the sky. Squirrels and rabbits scampered across the vast lawn before vanishing from sight as if playing a game of hide and seek. Birds chirped in the trees, their songs creating a beautiful melody that humans couldn't rival. It felt so peaceful and happy. So *foreign*. The loneliness that had been her constant companion over the past year became even more pronounced. Shayna had convinced herself that coming back to Aspen Creek would heal what ailed her, so her reaction was unsettling. What if Hank's ranch didn't hold a magical cure?

The garage door rose and Hank pulled his car to the side of the driveway and waved her inside. She parked beside a shiny blue pickup, got out of her car and leaned against the door. Getting to the ranch had sapped all of her energy and now she was too tired to stand.

Hank gave her a long look, then spoke in a gentle voice. "I'll get your luggage."

"Thanks." She handed him her keys. "It's in the trunk."

Mustering the last of her strength, she followed him to the rear of the car. He raised the trunk, revealing three large suitcases and a smaller shoulder bag that she'd shoved inside.

"I've always been an overpacker," she blurted out. "Don't worry. I know the rule."

He grabbed the handles on her wheeled suitcases and looked at her, one eyebrow raised. "What rule would that be?"

"Three days for fish and houseguests."

He chuckled and his eyes danced. "That rule doesn't apply when the guest is a close friend."

Shayna didn't know if she still qualified as a close friend after all this time, but she wasn't going to quibble. "Thank you."

"No worries."

Hank led the way out of the garage, pausing momentarily to lower the door before they crossed a brick path and small patio leading to the back door. Two bushes on either side of the back stairs composed the entirety of the landscaping. Of course, this was a working ranch— not a posh Beverly Hills estate like the one she owned with perfectly manicured acreage and trees that had been sculpted within an inch of their lives, or the cavernous house that she'd bought for her parents. Shayna appreciated the way Hank was letting nature be free rather than trying to shape it to please him.

He unlocked the door, pushed it open, then stood aside. "After you."

Murmuring her thanks, Shayna stepped into the kitchen and looked around. The walls were painted an off-white and the cabinets were red oak. The farm sink beneath the window overlooked the backyard. A large round table set beneath a ceiling fan dominated the space. An old-fashioned Crock-Pot was on the counter beside the stove. It all felt so homey. She inhaled the delicious aroma of roast beef.

"Are you thirsty? I have iced tea, beer and water. Of if you'd prefer something warm, I have tea and coffee." He sounded unbothered, as if he'd expected her to show up tonight.

"I don't want to put you out."

"You aren't. The roast has been cooking all day. It's just about ready. The makings of a salad are in the refrigerator. I'll microwave some potatoes and heat up some rolls and we'll be in business."

"Do you need help?"

"No. You just get settled."

Shayna nodded. She was pretty exhausted. The decision to come to Aspen Creek had been more of an instinct than a well-thought-out plan. She'd only been home two days after completing an exhausting six month tour and wanted a few days of peace and quiet to decompress.

It was stressful knowing that she was responsible

for the livelihood of the three hundred plus people who worked on her tour. Her fans paid good money to see her perform. Sick or well, happy or sad—how she felt didn't matter. They deserved to see an excellent three hour concert and she'd done her best to make sure that was what they got.

And that was just the tour pressure. Harvey, her manager, wanted her to consider doing a Broadway show. A song that Shayna had written for a movie had won an Oscar. Now Harvey had an EGOT on his brain. Apparently winning the most Grammys of any artist wasn't enough of an accomplishment.

She hadn't been able to think of that. She'd been in need of a break. Time when she didn't have to worry about anyone or anything. Of course, she should have known her mother wouldn't allow that. Wendy had been self-centered and demanding all of Shayna's life. She'd never cared about how Shayna felt before. Why would that day be any different? But Shayna had reached the end of her rope. She couldn't take any more pressure and she'd snapped.

One minute she was holding her telephone, listening as her mother droned on yet again about something that she wanted Shayna to buy for her. The next, she was rushing around her room, grabbing lingerie and nightclothes from her drawers and pulling pants, skirts, dresses and blouses off hangers, tossing them willy-nilly into suitcases. Other random clothes also made their way into the luggage. She could still picture herself sweeping her arm across her bathroom counter, knocking her makeup and facial products into her bag. It had taken a couple of trips for her to load everything into the trunk. Then she'd sped down her paved driveway and out of the electric gate. It had taken her two days to get here. Two days when she hadn't even considered calling Hank to let him know that she was on her way. Now she realized just how lucky she was that he'd been home and welcoming.

Hank insisted on carrying her luggage into the guest bedroom, which was directly across the hall from his. "I hope you'll be comfortable."

"I'm sure I will be."

"Great. Holler if you need anything," he said, then left her alone.

Shayna looked at her suitcases, lined neatly against the wall. After telling herself she'd unpack in a minute, she slumped onto the queen bed, lying on her back, her feet on the floor. After a moment, she slipped off her shoes and pulled her legs onto the plush mattress. She covered her eyes with her forearm and blew out a long breath. "Five minutes. I'll get up in five minutes."

She heard movement in her room and jerked up, wide awake. Looking around for an intruder, her eyes landed on Hank, who was backing toward the door. It all came flooding back to her. She was on Hank's ranch. In his guest room to be specific. Where she'd fallen asleep. She expelled a breath and her tense muscles relaxed. Gradually, her heart stopped pounding.

"Sorry. I didn't mean to startle you. I called you for dinner a couple of times, but when you didn't answer, I figured you didn't hear me. I didn't expect you to fall asleep so quickly."

"How long has it been?"

He shrugged. "Fifteen minutes, give or take."

"I haven't slept well for the past couple of days." Years

would be more accurate, but she wasn't ready to spill her deepest, darkest secrets to Hank just yet. Though they'd been good friends once and had reconnected at the reunion, they were closer to being strangers than friends.

"Then I feel even worse for waking you up. Go back to sleep. Dinner will keep."

Shayna swung her legs over the side of the bed and stood. "If only it was that easy. I don't think I could fall asleep again if I tried. Besides, I'm hungry."

"Then let me escort you to the kitchen." Hank held out his arm and she took it, holding it as they walked down the stairs and through the house. Clearly he was doing everything in his power to ensure she felt at ease in his home. Though she appreciated the gesture, it was completely unnecessary. Just being around him made her feel comfortable.

He'd set the table with plain white plates, silverware and paper napkins. A platter holding the roast and two baked potatoes was in the center. Two bottles of salad dressing were beside an unexpectedly colorful salad.

Hank held out her chair. Smiling up at him, Shayna sat down and placed her napkin on her lap.

"The rolls are store-bought," Hank said apologetically as he pulled a pan out of the oven and sat it on a trivet. He slathered butter across the top of the rolls and then placed them into a wicker basket.

"And they smell heavenly. Everything looks and smells good."

"Thank you. Help yourself."

"You don't have to tell me twice," she said, filling her plate. She'd barely eaten while traveling and her mouth watered in anticipation.

Hank sat across from her and added a healthy serving of everything to his plate. "Ranch or Italian?"

"Italian." She took a bite of the roast and sighed. It practically melted in her mouth. "You're a good cook."

"Lots of practice."

"Really? I would have thought the women in town would be lining up on your front porch with hot meals and baked goods for the handsome sheriff." Shayna heard the word *handsome* slip from her lips and her face heated. Even to her ears, she sounded flirtatious. Over the years, she'd grown used to using flattery with reporters and fans alike to keep them from getting too close while letting them believe that they had. But that wasn't her intent here. She wasn't using flattery to keep Hank at a distance. He actually was good-looking. Too good-looking for her peace of mind if she was being completely honest.

Hank laughed. "That kind of stuff only happens on old TV shows. If I want to eat, I have two choices. I can cook or pick up something at one of the restaurants in town. I confess to buying lunch—and even breakfast—more often than I should. But I prefer to eat dinner at home."

"Why is that?"

"I deal with the public all day. Sometimes I feel like a clerk at the complaints department." He grabbed another roll. "I don't know how much of the town you had the chance to see when you were here for the reunion-slash-goodbye party for Mr. Watson, but Aspen Creek has changed quite a bit over the past seventeen years."

"I didn't see much while I was here," she admitted. She'd flown into Denver where she'd hired a car to drive her to town for the reunion. Once it was over, she'd been driven back to Denver and taken a flight out early the next morning to Atlanta where she'd had a concert that night. But nothing could have kept her from coming to Aspen Creek for the party. Mr. Watson had been more than her principal. He and his wife had been two adults she'd depended on during her teen years. They'd been the parents she'd wished she had.

"When we were kids, the place seemed sleepy, if not quite dead. Now it's a thriving town. Tourists are here year round, although the warmer months aren't as crowded as the winter ones. But as businesses add more summer attractions, that gap is closing."

"Is there a lot of crime?" The very thought appalled her. She liked to think of Aspen Creek as the safe haven it had been in her childhood. Everything about the town had seemed picture-perfect back then, a stark contrast to her dysfunctional home life. She smiled as she recalled how the kids used to save their coins so they could buy homemade ice cream at the parlor. More often than not she'd been short, but Mr. Johnson had always given her a treat anyway, telling her that she could make up the difference next time. They both knew that *next time*, she wouldn't have any more money than *this* time, but they continued the face-saving pretense. Once Mr. Johnson found out Shayna could sing, he'd taken a song for payment, refusing to take even one of the few coins she'd managed to scrounge up.

"No more than any other town of this size." Hank ate a bite of baked potato before continuing. "Every once in a while a couple of folks get into a skirmish or a wealthy tourist who thinks the rules don't apply to them steps out of line. My deputies and I quash that pretty quickly."

"I imagine seeing your imposing physique puts the

fear of God in them pretty fast." There she went again, bringing the conversation back to his appearance. But she couldn't help it. Was it her fault that he was over six feet of solid muscle? Though he'd retired from the NFL years ago, he looked fit enough to play professional football now.

"It's not so much me as it is the power of the badge. When the citizens remember that the town comes equipped with fully operational jail cells—or when vacationers learn that fact—they usually pause and consider whether they want to continue their unlawful behavior."

"But that still doesn't explain why you choose to eat dinner alone."

"I suppose it's the tranquility. The quiet. Don't get me wrong, I like the people of Aspen Creek and that includes the ranchers who live nearby. And most of the tourists are fine. But interacting with the public can be draining. By the time my shift is over, I've had my fill of people for the day. If they spot me at a restaurant, they have no problem stepping up to my table to talk. Dinner at home prevents that."

Shayna blew out a breath. "And here I am, intruding on your solitude."

Hank shook his head. "You are not an intrusion. You're a welcome guest. An *invited* guest. I'm happy to have you spend time with me."

The warm look in his eyes matched the tone of his voice and Shayna relaxed. Perhaps she had made the right choice when she came here. Maybe she'd found a soft place to land. At least for now.

Hank kept his voice gentle and focused on keeping the conversation light. Though she was doing her best to mask it, it was clear to him that Shayna was teetering on an emotional cliff, dangerously close to falling off. The stress he'd picked up on months ago at the reunion seemed deeper and more intense now. Back then, she'd done her best to disguise her fragile mental state by pasting on a broad smile. Now, as he had back then, he saw right through her.

He didn't know what had brought Shayna here, but he had a feeling it wasn't anything good. He wasn't going to interrogate her though. That might only scare her away. As eleven-year-old kids, they'd sworn they would always be there for the other no matter what. He meant every word of that vow just as much today as he had back then. He would be here for her in whatever way she needed. Right now it was a place to lay her head. Later it might be a listening ear.

"Well, if you're sure," Shayna said, "then I'm happy to be here."

"I'm positive."

Shayna smiled again. This time it was filled with a hint of relief and the sweetness that he remembered from their childhood.

While they ate, Hank told her about the changes that had taken place in Aspen Creek during her absence. He also peppered the conversation with funny stories and was rewarded by her sincere laughter.

"Are the people who bought my parents' property still around?" Her parents had inherited a small house sitting on four acres from Shayna's maternal grandfather. They'd sold it when Shayna had hit it big and the entire family had moved to California.

"No. They moved two years ago—after their last kid

graduated from high school. The house has been sitting empty ever since. I hate to tell you this but the place has seen better days."

"Not that it was ever much to look at." Shayna's voice was bitter.

That was only partly true. Her grandfather had kept the place up until his illness had made that impossible. Her parents were the ones who had let the property fall into disrepair. Not that she needed to hear that from him. "It had its charm."

She ate some of her salad. "Ah, I see you're just as diplomatic as ever."

"It takes a lot of time, money and effort to keep a ranch going. Even a small one like mine or the one you grew up on."

"And my parents were allergic to work."

Scott and Wendy Givens had to be the laziest people he'd ever met. But he wasn't going to criticize Shayna's parents to her face. "Ranching isn't for everyone."

"You seem to like it."

He pushed his empty plate to the center of the table and pulled his coffee mug closer. "It's funny. When I was a kid, I would dream of the day I was old enough to leave this place behind. I was going to move to the biggest city I could find and make a life there."

"You weren't the only one."

He remembered how Shayna had also dreamed of escaping Aspen Creek. Looking back, she'd had a good reason. Her home life had been a mess. Unfortunately, her parents had gone with her, foiling her attempted escape. "No, but I didn't become a one-named superstar."

"Maybe not. But you were a college and NFL star quarterback. You led your team to victory at the Super Bowl."

He held up two fingers. "Twice. But who's counting?"

"Apparently you are." She refilled her water glass and took a long drink. He'd offered her coffee but she'd declined. Even so, he caught her looking longingly at his. He considered offering again but thought better of it. Maybe she was concerned the caffeine might keep her awake. That had never been a problem for him. "So what happened to living the high life in the big city and never coming back to this hick town?"

"I never called it a hick town," he clarified.

"I stand corrected. That was me."

He nodded. "It was nice for a while. Great even. But it turns out that fame and fortune isn't all that it's cracked up to be. Or at least the fame part. I wanted to enjoy the city and all that it had to offer, but fans and the media wouldn't let me. I couldn't eat dinner at a restaurant without someone interrupting my meal to ask for a picture or an autograph. It was a little bit easier after I retired, but not by much. Luckily, I don't have that problem here. Here I'm simply Hank Morrow, rancher and sheriff. As sheriff, people do their best not to attract my attention."

"Do you ever miss football?"

"No." His answer was quick and unequivocal.

"Wow. There wasn't a bit of hesitation in that answer."

"You're not the first person to ever ask me that question, so I've had plenty of time to think about my answer."

She nodded. "Even so…"

"Football is a brutal sport. I endured more than my share of broken bones and strained or torn muscles over the years. After my second concussion, I decided that the juice wasn't worth the squeeze."

"So you just walked away." It was as much a question as a statement.

"While I still could. After a few years, I moved back to the ranch. My parents wanted to move to North Carolina to be near my sister and her family—there are grandchildren to be spoiled—so I bought it from them."

"That makes sense." She ate her last piece of roast. "How did you become the sheriff?"

"Nobody else wanted the job."

She laughed. "Come on, Hank. I'm serious."

The sound of his name on her lips appealed to him more than it should have. "So am I. Sheriff McLauren wanted to retire and there was nobody else to take his place. There was only one deputy at the time and he had one foot out the door. Somebody had to step up."

"And that somebody was you."

He nodded. "It was only supposed to be for a short time. Just until they found someone else to fill the position. Before I knew it, four years had passed. It turns out that I like the job. And the people must approve of my performance because I was just reelected."

"Wow. It's funny how that turned out."

"Life has a way of taking twists and turns that we aren't expecting." He waited a couple of beats, hoping that she would say something that would help him understand why she'd dropped in out of the blue. When she only nodded, he simply finished his coffee.

They sat in silence for a while, but it wasn't uncomfortable. In fact, it was quite nice. When Shayna yawned for the third time, Hank decided it was time to bring the evening to a close. He pushed to his feet, grabbed their plates and put them in the sink.

She yawned again, then stood. "I know I should offer to help clean before letting you convince me it's not necessary, but I'm too tired to put up a token protest. But I will cook breakfast in the morning."

"That's a deal. If you want anything else, please help yourself. My home is your home."

The sweet smile she sent him before she left the kitchen struck him in the heart. Shayna needed him. Until she told him what was bothering her, he would be her friend. He just hoped it would be enough.

Chapter Two

Shayna stretched and inhaled a deep breath, holding it before slowly blowing it out. She repeated this several times before opening her eyes. A feeling of peace slowly settled over her as she looked around Hank's guest room. Despite the fact that it held minimal furniture, the room was warm and cozy. Inviting and comforting. Like a warm hug. It reflected Hank's personality. He wasn't one for putting on airs. He was straightforward and open. What you saw was what you got. As a person who spent her days around people who were more concerned with appearances than reality, and who believed that image was everything, she appreciated his genuineness.

She checked the time on the old-fashioned clock on the nightstand and reluctantly sat up. It was earlier than she was used to getting out of bed, but she had been around ranchers long enough to know that their days started in the wee hours. She didn't know what time Hank started his shift as sheriff, but if she wanted to keep her promise to cook breakfast, she needed to get a move on. Wrapping a pink silk robe around her matching nightgown, she quickly made the bed, grabbed her body wash, and opened her bedroom door.

Hank's door was still closed and she immediately pictured him in bed. Did he sleep in pajamas or was he a commando guy? Did he stretch out across the entire mattress or did he pick a side and stay there? Not that it was any of her business. He was her friend. A friend that she'd always been able to rely on. She wasn't going to risk ruining that relationship by crossing a line she shouldn't.

Though she and Hank had been close as kids, there had never been anything vaguely romantic between them. He'd always been the best looking boy in school and his status as a star football player had made him even more popular with the girls in high school. He'd dated quite a few of them. As a poor girl in secondhand clothes, she wouldn't have stood a chance of competing with them. Not that she'd ever tried. She'd known that a successful singing career could change the trajectory of her life and she'd spent every free moment working toward that goal. Even if she had wanted to become more than friends, she hadn't had the time. After her first single had become an unexpected hit, she'd had to travel to promote it. Then she'd had to work twice as hard to ensure that she didn't become a one-hit wonder. After she graduated from high school, she'd moved to California and she and Hank had lost touch.

But the work hadn't stopped once she'd released a second and then third record. A tour had followed. Though she'd been the opening act, she'd spent hours in rehearsals, making sure that her performance was perfect. Every moment onstage had been scripted down to the second, including the seemingly ad-libbed comments that she made every show. Traveling had been grueling. It had gotten to the point where she was never sure where in the world she was.

Once she returned home, she hadn't gotten the rest she'd hoped for. The rest she'd needed. Instead, the cycle started all over again. Over time, she'd gone from being an opener to a headliner to the only act. With each passing year, the responsibility and the pressures increased while her personal time decreased. Everyone wanted a piece of her. Her manager wanted her to take advantage of every opportunity that came her way. And, for the longest time, she'd tried. But she knew now that kind of lifestyle wasn't sustainable. Something had to give if she was going to hold on to her mental health.

Pushing the thoughts aside, Shayna walked into the bathroom. Hank had set a bath towel, a wash cloth, a bar of soap, a toothbrush and toothpaste on the unexpectedly large counter. Her heart was warmed by his thoughtfulness. After she brushed her teeth, she stepped into the shower. The water hit the tight muscles of her back and shoulders and she shrugged, doing her best to ease away the tension that clung to her. Though she'd left the worst of her stressors behind in California—her parents—she wasn't able to shake the shadow of their presence. It would take more than warm water and a change of scenery to do that. Short of finding a magic elixir, she would have to focus on her breathing and positive thinking to cope. Of course, letting their calls go to voicemail also helped.

Shayna finished washing up and then got out of the shower. She hadn't brought her clothes with her, so after drying off, she hung the towel on the rack and then put her robe back on. After taking one last look around to make sure she'd left the bathroom as orderly as she'd found it, she opened the door and headed for her room. She'd taken two steps when Hank climbed the stairs and stepped into the small hallway. She took one look at him and her mouth dropped open.

He was dressed in faded jeans that hung low on his hips and was holding a plaid shirt in his hands. His bare chest glistened with sweat. Obviously he'd been working. His broad chest was more muscular than she'd imagined and it tapered down to a trim waist and six-pack abs. His shoulders were huge, as were his biceps and triceps. His physique was evidence that although he had retired from the NFL, he still kept in shape.

"Good morning," Hank said.

"Good morning." Shayna tore her eyes away from his physique and forced herself to look into his face. With a strong jaw, deep dimples that flashed when he smiled and intelligent eyes, he was masculine perfection. She knew it would be all kinds of foolish to start something with Hank, but she couldn't make herself continue walking to her room. "I thought you were asleep. I was doing my best not to wake you up."

He shook his head. "I've been awake for a while."

"Did I throw you off your schedule? Were you waiting to get into the bathroom? Should I have waited until you had taken your shower?" The words poured out of her at an incredible clip, but it was hard to think straight when they were standing close enough for her to feel the heat radiating from Hank's body.

"Take a breath," Hank said, his voice gentle. "You didn't wake me up nor did you slow me down. I'm right on schedule."

She inhaled and then blew out the breath. "That's a relief."

Hank nodded and she noticed that he didn't make a

move to go into the bathroom. Instead he stared at her. She was acutely aware that her robe, which stopped mid-thigh, was clinging to her damp skin. When he glanced at her legs she was glad for the hours she spent in dance rehearsals. She'd never been vain, but she knew that men found her sexy. It never mattered to her before, but now she was hopeful that Hank liked what he saw.

As if aware that he was staring, he blinked and took a step toward the bathroom.

"What time do you want breakfast?" Shayna asked.

"Whenever it's ready. Don't stress about it. I have plenty of time to get to the office."

"I just don't want to make you late for your shift."

He pulled his cell phone from his back pocket. "I'm the sheriff, so unless I'm on vacation, I'm reachable twenty-four-seven. Not to mention my deputies are top notch. Our schedules overlap so there's always coverage. Okay?"

Shayna nodded. "Then I'll get dressed and get cooking."

Hank smiled and Shayna's heart skipped a silly beat that she told herself to ignore. He stepped around her and walked into the bathroom before closing the door behind him. Shayna sighed. Suddenly her knees felt weak and she leaned against the wall for support. This attraction to Hank wasn't good. She needed to get a handle on it before she was swept away. They were friends and she couldn't afford the messiness that often accompanied romances. Especially now when she was trying to straighten out her life. That decided, she hustled into the guest room where she quickly dressed before heading to the kitchen. Though Hank acted as if he had all the time in the world, Shayna was determined not to throw him off his schedule. She wasn't going to do anything to make him regret letting her stay here.

Hank stepped into the bathroom, closed the door, then sagged against it. Alone, he exhaled a pent up breath. He'd heard the sound of the shower when he'd come back into the house. Images of Shayna standing naked beneath the pounding water had instantly filled his mind, stirring desire that under the circumstances was totally inappropriate. Shayna was his guest. His friend. Given what he'd seen recently, she was in need of a friend, not a lover. Distress rolled off her like waves. What kind of friend— no, what kind of *man*—would he be if he acted on his attraction? He'd seen the way her eyes had traveled over his body and known that she'd felt…something. It was a cross between desire and admiration. But that didn't make it okay to pursue her, even if the attraction was mutual.

When he'd been a star college athlete with a promising NFL career, the girls had chased him ceaselessly. Initially he'd been flattered by the attention and he'd let them catch him. He'd indulged in quite a few one-night stands. One day, his father had sat him down and talked to him about respecting women. He'd reminded Hank how important it was to treat them with the same kindness he wanted to receive. That lecture hadn't gone in one ear and out the other, but it had been close. His father's words had only gone so far. It was his mother who'd made him rethink his behavior. She'd pointed out the possibility of getting a woman he barely knew pregnant and being tied to her for the rest of his life. He hadn't wanted to become someone's future financial plan. By the time he was an NFL star, he was wise enough to know the dangers that meaningless flings held and avoided them.

Not that he thought Shayna was after him for his money. That notion was so ludicrous it was laughable. She had sold hundreds of millions of records in her career. The tickets to her concerts were ridiculously expensive, yet she consistently sold out arenas and football stadiums. Shayna's makeup and lingerie lines were worth more millions than he could ever dream of making. Though he had invested wisely, his wealth was only a fraction of hers. So no, she didn't need his money.

But did she think he wanted hers? He imagined that over the years she'd encountered more than her share of users. Men who were interested in her money—and her body. He needed her to know that he wasn't one of them. The only way to be sure of that was to keep their relationship strictly platonic.

It would be easier to do that if the scent of her flowery body wash wasn't currently lingering in the air, teasing his senses. She'd left the bottle on the shower shelf, and he opened it and inhaled. Shaking his head at his foolishness, he set it down, picked up his bar of soap, lathered a cloth and began to wash up. Though he enjoyed long, hot showers, today's would have to be quick. Shayna was cooking breakfast and she expected to see him sitting at the table while the food was hot. No doubt, she would be watching the clock until he stepped into the kitchen.

He didn't remember her being this nervous when they were kids. But life had a way of throwing challenges a person's way and changing them. He wondered what had happened to make her so jittery. Though he had never been one to watch celebrity gossip shows and he avoided tabloids like the plague, he tried to keep up with Shayna. If her picture was on a magazine cover, he'd pick it up and skim the article. Lately the articles had been limited to pictures of her in concert or at a red carpet event.

That was the Shayna he grew up with. She'd always been private, not wanting anyone to know about her home life. She'd kept her innermost thoughts to herself, so it wasn't surprising that she gave very little of herself to the press. He admired her for that. He'd never been one to share the intimate details of his life with his fans either. He'd never been on social media and had only done press when required by his team.

He finished his shower, wrapped a towel around his waist and returned to his bedroom. He dressed quickly in his uniform, grabbed his Stetson, then headed downstairs. The tantalizing aroma of frying bacon and brewing coffee floated on the air and he followed the scents to the kitchen. Shayna stood at the stove, her back to him and a spatula in her hand. Her phone was on the counter and a podcast played. He listened as a woman talked about the value of a positive attitude while he stared at Shayna's body. Although she was on the thinner side, she was curvy in all the right places. Not that he was looking. Much.

She scooped scrambled eggs onto a plate and then spun around. When she spotted him, she jerked in surprise and froze. Then she smiled and set the plate on the table beside a stack of golden brown waffles. It had been so long since he'd made waffles that he'd forgotten that he owned a waffle iron. But since he preferred to grill or throw something in the Crock-Pot, he was probably the owner of lots of forgotten appliances that his mother had lovingly stored for him.

He rubbed his hands together. "Looks like I'm just in time."

"You are."

"Do you need me to do anything?"

"No. Just take a seat."

Instead of sitting down, he walked around the table and pulled out her chair for her.

"Thanks." Her voice was soft. Sexy. She'd tied her hair into a ponytail on the top of her head and she wasn't wearing a speck of makeup. Even so, with clear brown skin, high cheekbones and luscious lips, she was stunning. He wanted to kick himself for noticing. Noticing how gorgeous she looked was the complete opposite of keeping things between them strictly friendly.

"No worries," he replied, although the way his body reacted to her nearness gave him plenty to worry about. He reminded himself that he was a grown man used to exercising self-control. He was the boss of his body, not the other way around.

"I couldn't find any syrup," Shayna said.

He grinned ruefully. "I suppose this is the part of the conversation where I confess that I don't actually own a bottle."

Shayna laughed as she put eggs, waffles and three strips of bacon on her plate. "It's not a crime so I don't know if a confession is necessary. But to be on the safe side, do I need to read you your rights?"

He laughed. "If you want, I can pick up a bottle of syrup at the store today."

"Only if you want it. I'm perfectly content to eat my waffles with just butter."

"Good enough." He put a forkful of fluffy eggs into

his mouth, chewed and then swallowed. "These are quite delicious."

"They're your eggs. I just took them out of the basket, added butter and a bit of water. Voila. Scrambled eggs."

"Well, you've got the magic touch. These are even better than the ones I get at the diner."

"Flattery will get you everywhere, Sheriff. Just for that, I'll cook you a delicious dinner tonight."

"Wow. That really wasn't my goal at all. I was being sincere." He had a feeling that she could use a bit of sincerity in her life. If not from an old friend, then from whom? He ate some waffle and then continued. "How about I take you to dinner tonight? We could go to the diner or one of the fancy new places in town. Your choice."

She shook her head, her downturned lips marring her lovely face. "I would rather not. Remember what you told me about how it was when you were playing football? The way people wouldn't let you eat in peace? Multiply that by a thousand. That's what it's like when I go out in public."

"But this is Aspen Creek. You grew up here. You were just back for the reunion. That went well."

"Yes. With you by my side running interference."

"I'll be with you at dinner. Remember, these are people you know."

"But you just said that the town is filled with tourists. They don't know me so they won't remember when I was just the little girl who would literally sing for my supper. To them I'm Shayna Givens, celebrity. If it's all the same to you, I'd rather eat here tonight."

"In that case, I'll look forward to enjoying whatever you cook today. I have a stocked freezer, but a limited number of spices. Let me know if you need me to pick up something at the grocery store and I'll swing by and grab it."

"Thanks."

He picked up their dishes and placed them in the dishwasher.

"You don't have to do that," she protested.

"And you didn't have to cook breakfast either. I'm a firm believer in teamwork."

She smiled. "Me too."

He glanced at the clock. Time really did fly when you were having fun. "And now I need to get going."

"Time to join your other team?"

"Yep." He paused and looked at her. "I hope it goes without saying, but just in case you need to hear it, I'll say it anyway. Feel free to do whatever you want. Eat what you want to eat. Walk where you want to walk. Nothing is off-limits. My home is your home. Okay?"

"Okay."

Hank whistled as he got into the squad car. He started the engine, then glanced in the rearview mirror. Shayna had followed him outside and was standing on the back step watching him. His heart was unexpectedly warmed by the gesture. As a single man, he didn't get to experience the pleasure of having a woman send him off to work with a kiss and a smile. Of course, Shayna hadn't kissed him goodbye. But there had been a moment in the kitchen after he'd straightened his tie and set his hat on his head that he'd been tempted to brush a kiss against her full lips. Only the fact that he'd already decided that they could only be friends had stopped him.

He blew the horn and then waved. The image of her raised hand and wide smile stuck with him as he drove down the highway to town. As sheriff, he was responsible for the safety and security of the ranches and resorts that were a part of the county but not a part of Aspen Creek proper. Though not officially part of the town, the ranchers and resort owners contributed greatly to the town's success and were valued members of the community.

The sun was climbing in the sky and the temperature was rising with it. Today was going to be a scorcher. Though he personally liked the heat, as sheriff, he knew that tempers tended to be shorter in hot weather. That made his and his deputies' jobs more difficult as they worked to cool conflicts before trouble erupted and keep the peace.

There were more cars on the highway than usual, many with out-of-state license plates. Hank made a mental note to alert his deputies to the possibility of getting calls out to the mountains. Though the resorts offered guides for hiking and had well-marked trails, it wasn't unusual for a man—and nine times out of ten it was a man—to wander off the trail in the misguided belief that he could always find his way back to the resort. It was the rare person who actually could. More often than not, he or his deputies would have to search for them, often finding them huddled somewhere or wandering in circles. Hank had nothing against city folk. He'd been one for quite a while and had met many good people and made several great friends. He just wished they had more respect for nature. That would make his job significantly easier.

When he reached town, he slowed as he drove down the streets. The walkways had been swept clean of debris and flowers overflowed from the beds that were strategically placed along them. Shop owners called greetings to him and each other as they opened their businesses for the day. A young couple steered two young children into the diner for breakfast. The low hum of conversation filled the air as the town stirred awake.

Hank's heart swelled with pride. This was his town. Years ago it had experienced rough patches as had many other small communities across the country, but the struggle had only strengthened the bonds between the citizens. They'd stood together, sharing what they had instead of hoarding, confident in the knowledge that their neighbors would do the same.

With strong leadership and good investments, the town survived the challenging times. Now Aspen Creek was a popular tourist destination.

But Hank wasn't naive. He knew that the added prosperity and popularity came with a cost. Though most of the people were simply looking for a good time, there was always a scoundrel or two looking to make trouble. It was his job to make sure they didn't succeed. In his experience, trouble could come at any time and he had to be ready for it. These were his people and he took his job to serve and protect them seriously.

When he reached the redbrick building that housed the police station, he pulled into the lot behind it and parked in his designated spot. This building hadn't always been the police station. Thirty years ago, it had been a storefront dime store. Hank's parents used to bring him and his younger sister here after church on Sunday afternoons and let them buy a treat. Talia had debated for what seemed like hours. Should she get the pink sucker or should she get chocolate covered peanuts? Even now, he didn't know why she'd argued with herself. Each week she'd asked for the same thing—Lemonheads.

Smiling at the memory, he stepped inside the renovated building. Dana Long, one of his deputies, was at her desk, tapping away at the computer while Christopher Ingram, his newest deputy, was sweeping the floor. They looked up as he entered.

"Good morning," he said, removing his Stetson. "How were things last night?"

"Quiet," Dana said, "just the way I like it."

"Boring," Christopher added. "Practically dead. But Mr. Robinson set off his alarm as he was leaving his shop, so there was that."

"I suppose you were looking for a little more excitement," Hank said.

"Yes. Not like a shoot-out or a bar fight or anything so dramatic. Or deadly. Just something more than walking down the street and seeing a bunch of nothing."

"All that excitement you crave has a dark side you don't think about," Dana said, looking directly at Christopher. Dana had spent over a decade in the military. She rarely spoke about her experiences, but Hank knew she had seen some things. "I like the quiet. It's evidence that the people I'm supposed to be protecting are safe for the night. I can't ask for more than that."

With that final pronouncement, Dana logged out of her computer, grabbed her purse from her desk drawer and stood. "I'm going to grab some breakfast at the diner and then I'm going home. I'll have my phone on in case you need me."

"We've got it covered," Hank said as Dana walked out the door.

"I don't think she likes me," Christopher said when he and Hank were alone.

"She likes you just fine," Hank said. "It's just that she has more life experience than you do. She didn't take this job for the excitement."

Christopher gave him a sheepish look. "Don't you want more excitement?"

Hank filled a coffee cup, then added a spoonful of sugar and a dollop of cream before answering. "I like things the way they are. But I suppose busting a diamond smuggling ring or capturing an international spy could make my shifts more interesting. The paperwork would be a nightmare though."

Christopher stared. "Are you mocking me?"

"Maybe a little. I didn't become a sheriff just to give out parking tickets and judge pie contests. But my main responsibility is to keep the peace in this town and protect the citizens."

"That's just it. There's nothing to protect them from."

"You'd be surprised. I know that Aspen Creek seems like a sleepy little town, but there is lots going on under the surface." Hank took a swallow of his coffee. It wasn't as good as the pot that Shayna had brewed this morning. He added another teaspoon of sugar before continuing. "You've only been on the force for three months. How about you give Aspen Creek a little more time before you make any decisions. If it turns out that our town is too quiet for you, that's okay. Small-town policing isn't for everyone. I have friends in law enforcement all over the state. If you're willing to move, I know that I can find a department with all of the excitement that you crave."

"That sounds like a plan." Christopher grinned. "Of

course, if I decide to move, you have to be the one to tell my grandmother."

Hank laughed. "You're willing to take on hardened criminals but you're scared of your grandmother?"

"You know how she is."

He did indeed. Carol Rodgers was well known in town. She and the other senior ladies knitted booties and blankets for newborns. If someone fell sick, they were there with hot meals and helping hands. But they were just as likely to cause a ruckus in the bowling alley as they were to help someone in need.

"Go home. Get some sleep."

Christopher straightened his shoulders and grinned. "I'm a young man. I don't need sleep."

Hank shook his head. He remembered being that young and energetic once. He'd also had a thirst for excitement. Now he liked the solitude of his ranch. Although he had to admit that he was looking forward to having a little less solitude and a lot more excitement with his unexpected houseguest.

Chapter Three

Shayna watched as Hank's car traveled down the long gravel driveway, growing smaller and smaller until it was out of sight. Not ready to go back inside, she sat on the back stoop and looked around. The sun had risen, giving her the opportunity to view the ranch in the clear light of day. Although there wasn't much by way of landscaping, the ranch was still quite charming. There were numerous mature cherry, apple, peach and pear trees growing on the edge of the expansive lawn. The stable and barns were painted a deep blue with white trim that matched the house. The fence enclosing the corral was a bright white and a few horses roamed around. Several chickens pecked at the ground in a smaller fenced area. The entire ranch was well cared for. Loved even. No wonder Hank had come back here after retiring from the NFL. This was his own slice of paradise.

She lifted her face to the sky, enjoying the feel of the warm sun on her skin. The entire day stretched ahead of her and she had absolutely nothing to do. There were no rehearsals, costume fittings or meetings to attend. No ad campaigns to review or brainstorm. And best of all—no unexpected and unwanted visits from her family. For the first time in years, she was free to do whatever she wanted. For as long as she wanted.

Over the years, she'd taken the occasional vacation. But even then, her parents had been able to reach her. And they had—bombarding her with calls and texts and threatening to show up at her hotel until she'd given in to their demands. Now she was totally incommunicado. Not even her agent knew where she was. That thought made her feel a bit guilty. Paula had represented her well for over ten years. She'd shown herself to be trustworthy and loyal. Perhaps Shayna would reach out and let her know that she was okay. Later.

Shayna breathed in the fresh air and then slowly expelled it. The day was too nice to be occupied with the people and things she'd stepped away from. She wasn't going to clutter it up with worries. Not when there were so many more appealing things to do.

She stood and slowly walked across the grass toward the fruit trees. The wind blew and she relaxed. Now, this was living. She hadn't appreciated the simplicity when she'd been growing up. But then, there had been nothing for her to appreciate. Neither of her parents had been the least bit interested in ranch work—or work of any kind for that matter. If Shayna's grandfather hadn't willed the ranch to Shayna's mother, they probably would have remained in that rented two-bedroom apartment in Denver.

The ranch had seemed like heaven when her grandfather had been alive. Shayna had enjoyed her all too brief and too infrequent visits with him. She'd run across the vast fields, loving the freedom of the wide open space and the fresh air. She'd spent hours chasing butterflies and rabbits. Her grandfather had planted a huge garden.

Seven-year-old Shayna had loved picking weeds beside him and being rewarded with the sweetest fresh strawberries she'd ever tasted. Life with him had been blissful.

Then he'd died and Shayna and her family had moved in full time. It hadn't taken her parents long to destroy everything he'd worked so hard to build. Life with her parents was completely different than it had been with her grandfather. Before long, the haven she'd found with her grandfather had completely ceased to exist. Maybe she could find another one here with Hank.

A quick inspection revealed that there were more than enough ripe cherries for a pie, so Shayna returned to the kitchen where she grabbed the two wicker baskets she'd noticed in a lower cabinet. That took care of one problem. Now for the other. She needed a ladder. She'd spotted a shed earlier and crossed her fingers, hoping that it held one. It had been quite a while since she'd climbed a tree and her cute floral dress wasn't exactly suitable for the task.

She reached the shed, grabbed the handle and twisted. It didn't move an inch. Of course it was locked. Hank was the sheriff after all. If anyone would be security conscious, it was him. Shayna looked at the tree and then back down at her dress. Climbing the tree would be a last resort. But she did have another option. She could call Hank. It wasn't as if the pie was a surprise. And he did say to call him if she needed anything.

Shayna pulled her cell phone from her pocket and turned it on. She'd turned it off while she and Hank were eating breakfast and she'd chosen to leave it off. As expected, there were nearly a dozen missed calls and texts. Deciding not to listen to the messages, she scanned the texts. Most of them were from her parents. She had no intention of reading them, much less returning them. Paula had texted twice. Her messages were concerned but not hysterical. No doubt her family had called her agent when they couldn't reach her.

Shayna shot off a quick text to let her agent know that she was all right. When she'd first hired Paula, Shayna had attempted to befriend her, but the other woman had shut her down immediately. Paula had been clear that theirs would be a strictly professional relationship. Blurring the lines would only make tough conversations hard to have. They might not be friends, but Shayna respected her and appreciated how hard she worked on Shayna's behalf.

Shayna also reached out to the CEO of her company and let him know that she would be out of touch for a while. He could call her in the event of an emergency, but fingers crossed, there wouldn't be any. And since there wouldn't be a new product launch until November, just in time for Christmas, now was a good time for a break.

Finally she contacted Harvey and let him know that she wasn't up to doing a Broadway show right now. EGOT status would have to wait.

That done, she scrolled her contacts until she found Hank's number. As his phone rang, her heart skipped a beat in anticipation of hearing his voice. She knew that falling for Hank would be a big mistake. Even so, she couldn't control her attraction. Not that there was a chance of something developing with Hank. She'd been around enough men to know when they were interested in having a relationship with her. She wasn't getting those vibes from Hank. But maybe that was a good thing. It kept things clear between them. They were friends. And good friends were hard to find.

"Hi. This is a pleasant surprise. Do you have something you need me to pick up for dinner tonight?"

Shayna smiled as Hank's calm baritone came over the phone. "Yes and no."

He laughed and she could picture the sides of his eyes wrinkling. The image was so sexy that her stomach flipped. *Down, girl.* Wasn't she just thinking that she and Hank could only be friends? "That wasn't a multiple choice question, Shayna."

"But that's the best answer."

"Perhaps you should explain."

"I need a ladder."

"Because…"

"Because I want to make a cherry pie. I need to pick cherries first."

"Hence the need for a ladder."

"Yes. Do you have one?"

"In the shed."

"That's what I figured. The shed is locked. I don't suppose there's a key lying around here somewhere."

"Actually, there is."

There was a long silence.

"And are you going to tell me where it is or do I have to guess?"

Hank chuckled and a shiver raced down Shayna's spine. "Are you kidding? There's pie involved. I'll run home and pick the cherries myself if you need me to."

"That's not necessary. Just tell me where the key is and I'll take it from there."

"There's a mug in the cabinet with the plates. If you

look inside, you'll find a key ring. There are a bunch of keys on there. I have no idea what most of them unlock. I don't think my parents knew either. But they kept them all just in case. I'm doing the same."

She laughed. "That's so illogical and totally unlike you."

"I don't want to be the one who throws away the only key to a lock, then not be able to open whatever it is."

"As long as it makes sense to you." She paused. "How long have you owned this house?"

"Seven years. And my parents owned it for thirty-five years before that."

"I think it may be time to set those keys free."

He chuckled and goose bumps popped up on her arm. Since the sensation wasn't unpleasant, she decided not to fight against it. Not that she stood a chance of winning. Apparently her body had a mind of its own. "Not a chance."

"I see I have my work set out for me."

"What work would that be?"

"To help you break free from the keys."

He laughed again, something he apparently did a lot. "Consider yourself hired."

They talked for a few more minutes before they ended the call. Since she was going to spend a good part of the next hour on a ladder, Shayna decided to change into a pair of shorts and a T-shirt. She thought of the luggage she'd brought. It would be safe to unpack one suitcase. That way she wouldn't have to rummage through her bags every morning for something to wear.

Dragging the biggest suitcase to the bed, she opened it and stared. Then she began to laugh. It was so much worse than she remembered. She grabbed a crushed sequin dress and tossed it onto the bed. It couldn't get any more wrinkled than it was. Not that she expected to wear it anytime soon. She didn't intend to leave the ranch. Next she pulled out a few skirts, blouses and tops. She set aside a pair of shorts and kept searching until she found a colorful T-shirt.

For the most part, Shayna dressed fashionably. Even though she was comfortable in cutoff jeans and cropped T-shirts, she had an image to maintain. Her agent and manager constantly reminded her that she was a fashion icon. She couldn't run to the store in flip-flops and pajama bottoms. Not when every phone was a camera and every person had access to the internet. Not that she went to the grocery store often. She had an assistant for that.

Shayna hung up the clothes that required hangers and then stored her shorts and T-shirts in the dresser. Deciding that she would need clean underwear and pajamas every night, she opened the second suitcase and unpacked that too. Then she changed her clothes, grabbed her phone and went hunting for the keys.

The ring was right where Hank said it would be. There had to be thirty keys on there, including two skeleton keys. She couldn't imagine what they opened. There was no way there were that many locks on this property. Maybe she and Hank could spend a day trying to discover what—if any—locks these keys fit. The notion was intriguing and she was humming as she skipped down the stairs and jogged over to the shed. It took a dozen tries before she found the right key. She cheered softly as she opened the door and spotted the ladder leaning against the back wall. She took it over to the small orchard.

The trees were full of ripe fruit and Shayna wondered what Hank did with it all. She couldn't imagine him allowing it to rot in the field. Nor could she picture him baking. Not after the way he'd reacted when she'd told him about the pie. That kind of enthusiasm couldn't be faked. Deciding to solve the mystery of the fruit at another time, she looped a basket over one arm and climbed the tree.

A sense of peace settled over Shayna while she worked. Though nearly as many cherries made it into her mouth as into the basket, it wasn't long before both baskets were filled with enough fruit to bake two pies and have some left over. When she was done, she descended the ladder, sat on the ground and looked around.

There was nothing but undisturbed nature as far as the eye could see. Birds chirped in the trees and darted overhead with a speed she admired. A freedom she envied. Rabbits looked at her while they nibbled grass seemingly without a care in the world. Squirrels chased each other from one tree to the next in an apparent game of tag. She'd hung out with Hank here a couple of times when they were kids, so she knew there was a babbling brook over the hill and a watering hole some distance away. Even after all this time, the ranch felt familiar. This was what a home was supposed to feel like. Not the house she owned in California that sat empty half the year while she was in some other place in the world. And definitely not the chaotic places she'd grown up in.

"The pie isn't going to bake itself," Shayna said after a while. She returned the ladder to the shed, then took her baskets of cherries into the house. She rinsed the fruit, then gathered the supplies that she would need. The birds' song had kept her company while she picked fruit. Now the kitchen felt too silent, so she turned on her phone to one of her favorite podcasts.

She expertly pitted and halved the cherries and then put them in a saucepan with sugar. When they were ready, she made the crust. Once she'd become a superstar, her world had become increasingly smaller. Though she traveled to some of the most famous cities in the world with lots of exciting spots, she saw very little of them. She couldn't simply wander around like a tourist, a guidebook in her hand, while searching for cozy spots only the locals knew about. Her presence always caused a stir, ruining her attempts at sightseeing. When in Paris, she couldn't wander aimlessly through the Louvre, getting a close up view of the Mona Lisa. Nor could she climb to the top of the Eiffel Tower. She couldn't walk around Times Square in New York while eating a slice of pizza or watch a Chicago Cubs game from the bleachers. Since that was the price of the fame she'd chased after, she couldn't very well complain now.

So she'd looked for hobbies. She subscribed to several YouTube cooking channels and had discovered that she enjoyed cooking. Not only that, she had a knack for it. Over the past few years she'd mastered baking, even becoming an expert at making flaky croissants. She'd also become good at Italian cooking. Now she was teaching herself how to make Nigerian food. Her Jollof rice was pretty good if she did say so herself. She occasionally hosted dinner parties for her closest friends, less frequently now that they were married with husbands and kids that took up their time and attention, but for the most part she ate her meals alone. Her parents would have gladly come over if she'd invited them, but she wasn't that desperate for company. But now, she had Hank to cook for. And she looked forward to making some of her favorite foods for him.

Shayna slid the pies into the oven, set the timer and returned to the backyard, which was becoming her favorite part of the ranch. It was so peaceful. There was a small brick patio with a rectangular table and six chairs around it. Two chaises were placed in the shade of a mature tree. There were no extra throw pillows or potted plants. Like most of the ranch, it reflected Hank's straightforward personality.

She was just settling into a chaise when the sound of a car engine grew near. Her heart stopped as she tried to decide what to do. Hank hadn't mentioned that anyone would be stopping by. But perhaps this was an unplanned visit. Did people simply drop in on him? She had. And he hadn't blinked an eye. Perhaps he extended the invitation to visit his ranch far and wide. But she didn't want anyone to know she was here. This was her chance to figure things out on her own. She was about to flee to the kitchen when Hank's squad car came into view. Her heart rate slowed to its normal pace.

Shayna brushed a hand over her hair. She hadn't bothered to comb it since her tree climbing adventure and she didn't want Hank to see her looking disheveled.

He was smiling as he walked over, a paper bag in his hands. "Well, don't you look comfortable?"

"I was just about to get some sun."

"I imagine that living in California you get a lot of it."

"Yes. But I don't have a view like this." She gestured to the acres of green grass and the fruit trees. It was all so beautiful. "This is magnificent."

He sat beside her and stretched out his long legs, crossing them at the ankles. "You'll get no argument from me."

"Do you spend much time outside?"

"Yes. But I don't sit around and enjoy the view as much as I should. I'm usually on horseback or doing work around the ranch."

"Do you usually come home in the middle of the day?"

"No. But I don't usually have company either. I decided to drop by and make sure that you're okay."

She sighed and glanced at the majestic mountains. They looked close enough to touch. "I'm fine. I'm actually having a great day."

He nodded. "I'm glad to hear it. You aren't getting bored? A quiet Colorado ranch can't compete with the excitement of Hollywood."

Thank goodness. She'd come here to get away from all of that. "I'm actually enjoying the peace and quiet. And the animals have been entertaining me."

"Is that right?" One side of his mouth lifted in a sexy grin that lit a spark within her. "Tell me more about my talented chickens and horses."

"Gladly." She leaned back into her seat, ready to launch into a fanciful tale. The timer on her phone beeped, stopping her before she could get started. "Time to take the pies out of the oven. I suppose that story will have to wait."

He grinned. "Looks like I'm just in time."

"If I didn't know better, I would think that you planned it this way."

"Nah. I'm just living right."

She laughed as they walked into the house. Hank looked so good in his uniform that she had to concentrate on not staring. If there was a chance they could be more than friends, she would put a little extra swing in her hips when she walked over to the stove. Though she felt Hank's eyes on her as she bent over to take the pies out of the oven, she knew he was more interested in the pies than in her.

The aroma of baked cherries filled the air and a sense of pride filled her. She knew the pies were going to taste as delicious as they smelled.

"I wish I would have thought to get some ice cream," Hank said.

"Does Mr. Johnson still own the ice cream shop?"

"Yes. And it still has the best ice cream in the state."

Shayna smiled. "He was always so good to me."

"He's good to everyone," Hank said. "You should stop by and visit him. I know he would love to see you."

"You didn't tell him that I was in town, did you?" Shayna tried to keep the panic from her voice, but given the way Hank was staring at her, she'd failed.

"No. I know you want to keep your presence here under wraps and I respect that."

"Thanks," Shayna said quietly. Hank was eyeing the pies with such longing that she laughed, her worry forgotten. It had been for nothing anyway. "I generally like my cherry pie cold, but if you want, I suppose I could give you a slice now."

"I don't want to burn my tongue. We can let it cool." He opened the brown bag he'd brought with him. "I brought lunch. It's only Italian beef sandwiches and potato chips."

Her mouth watered. "I haven't had one of those in years."

Hank set a foil wrapped sandwich and a bag of chips

on the table in front of her and then took the other for himself. "Really? I'm a regular at What's Your Beef Deli. There's no better Italian beef in the state."

Shayna laughed. "Mr. Smith should hire you as his ad man."

"No way. I have enough jobs as it is."

Shayna took a bite of her sandwich. The bun was the right combination of chewy and soft and the beef was flavorful. "This is even better than I remember."

"It's probably the company."

She grinned. He had no idea just how true those words were. Everything was better with Hank. But that was her secret. "Or it could be the passage of time."

"I guess I had that coming."

"You guess? Seriously though, I'm enjoying your company."

As they ate, they laughed and talked about old times. Though she kept up her end of the conversation, she was frequently distracted by Hank's magnificent body. Each time his muscles moved beneath his uniform, she noticed.

When they were finished with their lunch, Shayna set a thick slice of pie in front of Hank and took a slice for herself.

Hank ate a forkful, then briefly closed his eyes and moaned. "Without a doubt, this has to be the best pie I've had in my life."

"You're just saying that," Shayna said, though she was warm with pleasure.

"You could sell these."

"Like you, I have enough jobs as it is."

He grinned. "Then I'll be the only one who gets to enjoy the deliciousness. That works for me."

"I figured it would."

They finished the pie, then walked to the door. Hank stood close to her and looked into her eyes. A shiver raced down her spine. Would he kiss her? She held her breath in expectation. Instead of leaning toward her, he straightened. "I need to get back. Call me if you need anything."

As she watched him drive away, she realized that he was giving her the one thing she needed now. Time. A part of her wanted even more, but she shut down that thought. She didn't want to risk what she had by asking for more than was on offer.

Chapter Four

The sound of the alarm startled Shayna awake and she sat up immediately. Eyes still closed, she patted the nightstand until she found her phone and silenced it. Sighing, she reluctantly opened her eyes. She tossed the thin blanket covering her legs aside and wandered over to the window, pulled aside the curtain and peered outside. The sky was dark with yellow, red and orange streaks in the east as the sun began making its way over the horizon. It had been quite a while since she'd been awake at this time of day. She wasn't part of the party scene now, but when she'd been in her twenties, she'd stumbled into her house at this hour, just going to bed as opposed to waking up.

She heard Hank moving around in his room. A moment later a door closed and she knew she had to get a move on. She waited until Hank had finished in the bathroom before grabbing her clothes and making her way there. After splashing her face with water, she brushed her teeth and then pulled on her jeans and a long sleeved T-shirt. She was stepping into the hallway as Hank came out of his room.

"What are you doing up this early?" he asked.

"I want to help you with the animals."

"You don't have to do that."

"I know. I want to." Then she remembered that he'd told her that he liked the solitude of the ranch at the end of the work day. Perhaps he felt the same way about the mornings. "Unless you would rather be alone."

He reached out and took her hand. His palm was warm and though it was rough with calluses, his touch was gentle. "I would love the company."

Relief surged through Shayna and she smiled. They walked downstairs, through the house and out the back door without speaking. Though he had released her hand, her skin still tingled where he'd touched her.

Hank led her across the grass to the henhouse. He handed her a wicker basket that was lined with a soft cloth. "Have you gathered eggs before?"

"No. I may have grown up not too far from here, but we didn't have any animals. This is all so foreign for me," she confessed, shaking her head.

"It's not hard. The hens are up and wandering around. Just look in the nesting box. Be gentle with the eggs. And don't be surprised at their color."

Shayna rooted through the loose hay. When she saw a brown egg, she picked it up gingerly. "I feel like such a city girl."

Hank looked up, a tan egg in his hand. "There's nothing wrong with that. City girls have a place in the world."

"But I'm not one. I mean, I grew up on a ranch from the age of ten, albeit a tiny one. But we didn't own any animals. Not one cow or chicken or horse. So, was it really a ranch? And if not, I'm not really a ranch girl."

"I get your point."

"But I didn't grow up in Aspen Creek proper so I

wasn't a townie either. I never really fit in any of those categories."

"Did you feel the need to?"

She nodded. "I would have loved to be anything other than the girl who wore secondhand clothes and whose parents were the two laziest people in the entire county. I was a total misfit."

"I never thought of you that way."

"Of course you didn't. You were the nicest boy I knew. The nicest boy in town." She picked up two more eggs and then continued. "But after I became a star—" she made quotation marks with her hands "—people started to treat me differently. Kids who barely nodded at me when we passed in the hallway suddenly found a reason to talk to me. Suddenly I was invited to the cool kids' parties. The popular girls wanted me to sit at their lunch table. I thought it would make me happy, but it didn't. I knew they didn't really like me. They just wanted to be around me because I was famous. That made me suspicious and insecure."

"I know what you mean. When people change like that, it makes you wonder about everyone you meet. Do they like you because of who you are or because they want something from you?"

She nodded, pleased that he understood her when so many others in her life refused to do so. But then, he'd been a professional athlete. No doubt he'd probably experienced something similar.

"What is your life like now?"

She shrugged. "Can I think about that and get back to you?"

"Only if you want to. You're under no obligation to tell me your secrets or anything you don't want to."

"You're a special man, Hank Morrow. Why didn't we get together in school?"

He laughed. "Let's see, I was busy being big man on campus and dating everything in a skirt. And you were focused on your singing career."

"Trying to become a big star."

"Which you did."

"Thanks to the local TV station airing my performance at the state fair. Lucky for me, that rep from a record company was in town and saw it."

"You would have made it without him. You're too talented not to succeed."

"And you made it in the NFL. I still can't believe that you retired at the height of your career. You could have played for so many more years and won so many more Super Bowls."

"That wasn't guaranteed. Better to quit too soon than too late. There are so many players who don't know when to give it up. Their bodies are wrecked."

Her eyes swept over his body. "You definitely can't be accused of that."

"Nope."

Once they had gathered all of the eggs, Hank showed her how to refill the feeders and waterers and clean the coop.

"You know, this is kind of fun. I think I may get some chickens when I go back home."

Hank managed to hold his smile at Shayna's casually spoken words. Though she had only been with him for a couple of days, he was already getting used to having her around. It was as if she'd always been a part of his life. They fit together perfectly. Yesterday had been great. Starting breakfast with friendly conversation as opposed to listening to the police radio while he ate had been more enjoyable than he had expected. Before Shayna's arrival, he hadn't minded eating alone. In fact, he'd looked forward to his quiet dinners. Now the idea of Shayna leaving him to return to her previous life was disconcerting.

That kind of thinking was ridiculous. He'd been perfectly content with his life before she arrived. And it wasn't as if he lacked female companionship. If he wanted to spend time with a woman, there were plenty of willing ones in town for him to choose from. Yet somehow spending a quiet morning with Shayna was more appealing than having dinner with a date at one of the numerous fancy restaurants in town. And not simply because he wasn't a big fan of tourist hotspots. He could take them or leave them. No, there was something special about Shayna. Something he couldn't quite put his finger on. It wouldn't be overstating things to say that she was one of the biggest stars on the planet, but when he was with her, it was like being with the girl he'd known way back when.

"You might want to spend a little more time with chickens before you make that decision," he said, gesturing to the birds. "Today, they're on their best behavior, trying to impress you. But that won't last. There's a lot more to caring for chickens than meets the eye."

She put a hand on her slender hip and struck a pose. Her cutoff denims were extremely short, giving him an eyeful of her shapely thighs and calves. He knew he was playing with fire, but he allowed himself a second to appreciate her sexy body before meeting her eyes. They shone with mischief. "Are you saying that I don't have the skill to take care of a couple of chickens?"

"That's not what I'm saying at all. I have no idea if you have what it takes to care for chickens. You probably do. But very little of the work is glamorous."

"I'm not only about the glamourous life."

"There wouldn't be anything wrong if you were."

She sighed and her saucy smile faded. "Sometimes that life seems so shallow. It's all about wearing the right dress. Having perfect makeup. Never having a single hair out of place. Being seen at the right events. But I worked hard to create my image and it takes a lot of effort to maintain it. I steer clear of anything that might look like trouble."

"You don't have to worry about keeping up your image around me. Just be yourself. After all, I knew you when weren't the most beautiful woman in the world." He shook his head. "That didn't come out right. You were always beautiful. The rest of the world just didn't know it yet."

"But there's more to me than my looks."

"I know that. But it's also a part of you. And there's nothing wrong with being beautiful." He set his basket of eggs on the patio table and she did the same. "Come on. The horses are waiting."

Shayna's bright smile returned, sending a shiver down his spine. His reaction to her had come out of nowhere. And it didn't make a lick of sense. He'd grown up with her and had never been attracted to her. Sure, he'd always thought she was pretty. Her smile could light up a room. But rather than feel desire for her, he'd always felt protective of her. Even in middle school he'd known that she needed someone to look out for her. Her parents never had. They'd done the barest minimum for her. Their behavior had never crossed the line into neglect, but it had come awfully close. Hank could never figure out why people had children if they had no intention of nurturing and loving them. But once they'd discovered that Shayna could sing, they'd acted as if they'd struck gold. She was the proverbial goose that laid the golden eggs.

Now he found himself noticing Shayna as a woman. The sound of her voice. The curve of her waist. Everything about her appealed to him. Once more, he forced himself to ignore the attraction. A fling was the last thing she needed. And since she wasn't here to stay, a fling was all they could have. Though she hadn't told him why she'd decided to visit him now, he was astute enough to know that something had sent her racing over a thousand miles away. In that case, she needed a friend, not a lover.

Hank opened the stable doors, reached inside and turned on the overhead lights. The familiar scent of hay and animals filled the air, grounding him in the present. A horse snorted and others quickly followed suit. Hank held out a hand to Shayna. "Come on in."

She took a cautious step inside and looked around. Then she sneezed. "Excuse me."

"You aren't allergic to horses or hay, are you?" That would definitely put a damper on things.

She shook her head. "I don't think so. That would be really unfair. It's probably just the dust. What will we do first?"

"The horses need to be fed and given fresh water. They also need to be let out into the corral. Of course their stalls need to be cleaned out, but that's not a fun job. I'll take care of that."

"Did you do that as a kid?"

"Of course. Most ranch kids learn early on to take care of their animals."

"Then that's what I'm going to do. I want to pull my weight around here."

He stopped and turned to look into her face. He saw the worry she couldn't quite mask. The nerves were back again. "Of course you do. You've always been willing to do more than your share. And I appreciate that. But I don't know how many times I need to say it before you believe it, and at the risk of sounding like a broken record, here I go again—you are my guest. You don't have to earn your keep. You don't have to do anything. I'm not going to toss you out on your ear after three days."

"I get to stay four days," she said. Though she laughed, it was clear to Hank that Shayna had no idea how long it would be before he began to think of her as a burden. She just believed that he would.

He took her hands into his and gave them a gentle squeeze, waiting until her eyes met his. "You can stay for as long as you want. I will not get tired of seeing your face or hearing your voice. I like having you here. Okay?"

She nodded and blinked rapidly. He wasn't sure if she was about to cry, but he hoped not. Seeing her in tears would be his undoing. Then she gave him a shaky smile. "I know that I dropped in out of the blue."

"Do you think I'm weak?"

"Weak? No. What a ridiculous question."

"Right. So I had the strength to tell you to leave if I didn't want you around. And yet I haven't. And I won't."

"Thank you," Shayna said, her voice barely above a whisper.

Wanting to give her space to gather her emotions, he grabbed a pair of thick rubber boots and handed them to her. "If you really want to help clean the stables, you're going to need these."

"Thanks." She put them on while he did the same. "How many horses do you own?"

"Six."

"Really?" She raised an eyebrow and he wondered if that number sounded more impressive to her than it did to him. Most ranchers around here had more than that.

"That's not really a lot."

"But it's only one of you."

"True. But it would be cruel to have only one horse. Can you imagine what it would be like for him to be alone in this stable all day and night? To not have another horse to run with in the corral?"

She nodded slowly and there was an emotion in her eyes that he couldn't quite decipher. For a moment he believed that she truly could relate to that kind of loneliness and his heart ached for her. "I'm glad that you have more than one. That way they can be friends."

"Exactly. Although I have to confess that Sinbad is actually the horse that I ride the most." He let the horses into the corral, then guided a wheelbarrow over to her and then showed her how to use a pitchfork to pick up the soiled hay.

"Ah, so you do have a favorite."

"To be fair, Beauty and Beau, my parents' horses, are too old to ride. Now they live the good life, eating and spending the day lazing around in the sun."

"And the other three?"

"They belonged to someone who thought owning horses would be fun." He shook his head in disgust. "You know the type. Wannabe ranchers. People who thought being a rancher would be like it is in the movies. When they discovered that actual work was involved, they picked up stakes, abandoning the horses. There's not an animal rescue around here, so I brought them home."

"That is just like you."

"What do you mean?"

"Always looking out for the underdog. Just like with the town. Aspen Creek needed a protector and you stepped up when others turned away."

"Don't make me into some kind of hero. I'm just a regular guy trying to make it through the day just like anyone else."

She looked at him so intently and for so long that he almost squirmed. "You don't remember, do you?"

"Don't remember what?"

"When we were in fifth grade. My parents hadn't thought to buy me any school supplies because…well, because they were trifling. Anyhow, you shared yours. But you did it in a way that nobody ever knew that I'd come to school without a folder, pen or single sheet of paper. You didn't make a big deal out of it."

"That's because it wasn't. You were my friend. Friends help each other."

"We'd just met."

"How long does it take to become friends?"

"You're doing the same thing now," she said softly. "You welcomed me into your home with open arms. You haven't once asked me why I dropped in without any warning. Why is that? I know you must have questions."

He shrugged. "I figure you'll tell me when you feel like it. And it you don't, that's okay too. Nothing will change. I'm still your friend. I'll always be here for you, just like I promised."

"You have no idea how good it feels to have you on my side."

"You're embarrassing me."

She laughed and leaned closer, staring at his face. "Are you *blushing*?"

"It's the exertion."

"Right." She drew that one word over several syllables, making it clear that she didn't believe it for a second. Since he was lying, she was right to doubt him. "I bet you could pick up twice this much and not break a sweat. You're in great shape. I doubt there is an inch of fat anywhere on your body."

Shayna looked as shocked at her words as he felt. It would be so easy to return the compliment, but then where would they go from there? He wasn't looking to fall in love, so they couldn't fall into his bed. So the best thing to do was dial down the sexual tension. "Thanks. I might have been blushing because of your compliment. But that's not for public consumption, so keep it under your hat."

"It's officially off the record."

"Thanks."

The stable was filled with smells fighting for dominance, but whenever Shayna was near, the pleasant hint of lavender filled his nostrils, testing the bounds of his self-control.

While they worked, he occasionally peeked at Shayna.

She was biting her bottom lip, evidence of just how hard she was concentrating. Her determination to do a good job was impressive. But then, she'd always given her all at everything.

Once they'd put down fresh peat moss for the bedding, he let the horses back into their stalls. Shayna folded her arms on top of the gate and looked at Beauty. "You were right. There's a lot more to being a rancher than I thought."

"It's a lot of work, but totally worth it. If you want, we can go for a ride tomorrow. It's my day off."

"I would like that. But to be completely honest, I haven't been on a horse in years. Not since before I moved to California. It wasn't the best experience."

"Did you fall?"

"No. Nothing like that. I just didn't have a good time. The girls in the in-crowd invited me to hang out with them. I was stupid enough to go."

"Not stupid. Hopeful." His heart ached at the pain he heard in Shayna's voice. He could only imagine how that day had played out for her. "We don't have to ride if you don't think you'll enjoy it. We can always do something else."

"That wasn't what I meant. I just want you to know that I'm not a very skilled rider. I don't want to disappoint you."

"You couldn't disappoint me if you tried. Just spending time with you is all that I need to have a good time." When Hank heard the words coming out of his mouth, he wanted to call them back. But it was much too late. There was no unsaying what he'd said. Even if he could, that wouldn't make the words any less true.

And that was a problem.

Chapter Five

"**P**ut your left foot in the stirrup and then swing your right leg over Sugar's body," Hank said. He stood beside Shayna, trying not to be distracted by the way her faded jeans hugged her curvy bottom. He removed his Stetson and dragged his arm across his forehead, wiping away the beads of sweat that suddenly appeared. It wasn't a particularly hot day and there was a gentle breeze so he couldn't blame the weather for his rising temperature. That was all Shayna.

Shayna giggled and glanced at the stallion. "What made you name him Sugar?"

"I didn't. He came with that name. And what's wrong with Sugar anyway?"

"It sounds like something an old grandma would say. You know, 'Come here, sugar.' Or 'give me some sugar.'"

Hank laughed, something he had been doing from the time he'd awakened. They'd gathered eggs, fed and watered the chickens and horses, then prepared breakfast together. He'd whipped up omelets while Shayna had cut up fruit for a tasty fruit salad. Working beside her had been the perfect start to what he predicted would be a great day.

"My grandmother didn't sound like that and she certainly never called me sugar."

"I don't understand why not. You were always such a sweet boy." Her full lips cured in a sexy smile. "Maybe I'll call you sugar."

"Don't you dare. I'm the sheriff. I'm supposed to be tough."

She stiffened her back, clicked the heels of her boots together and saluted. "Yes sir, sheriff sir."

"Enough stalling. Now are you going to get on Sugar or not?"

"I suppose I will." She looked at him, her rich brown eyes wide. "You aren't going to move, are you?"

"I'll be right here."

"Thanks." She followed his directions and swung tentatively into the saddle. "Wow. This is high."

"Only a little bit."

"I can see a long way from up here. I'm the master of all I survey."

"Is that right?"

"Yep. I declare myself queen for a day."

"All right, your majesty. Do you need any more instructions, or are you ready to go?"

"You just explained everything to me. I know how to start, stop and speed up, so I'm good."

"In that case, let's hit the road." He swung onto Sinbad's back and grabbed the reins. He'd sold off the majority of the land after he'd bought out his parents, keeping only thirty acres for himself. It was small in comparison to many others in the area, but it was no longer a working ranch, so it was more than enough land for someone like him who simply liked the peace and quiet it provided.

"It is so pretty out here," Shayna said after a while.

"I think so. Of course, I didn't appreciate it when I was

a kid. Back then it was just a whole lot of nothing. It was too quiet. And boring. Now I love the solitude. The open space. I can breathe and think."

"What do you think about? If that's not too nosy."

"It's not nosy at all." He sighed and looked out over the expanse. "I think about work a lot. I wonder if there is something more I can do to make the lives of the towns-people better. And of course I think about the path my life has taken."

"So you play the *what if* game."

"Some. I suppose everyone does at one point or an-other." He glanced at her. She'd opened the door so he would walk through. "Do you?"

She sighed. "More often than you can imagine. Es-pecially lately. What would my life have been like if I couldn't sing and didn't write music? Would I still be liv-ing in Aspen Creek? Or would I have married the first jerk who asked me so that I could get away from my fam-ily and the life I was living here?"

"I suppose no matter what path you take, you'll always wonder about the road not taken."

"I used to envy the other people in our class. The girls mostly. Especially when we were in high school."

"You did? But you were making a name for yourself back then. By the time we graduated you'd already had a bestselling album and had been nominated for a Grammy. The first of many that you won."

"But I missed out on so much. Don't get me wrong, it was exciting meeting big stars. And I liked having my picture in magazines for all the mean girls to see. Espe-cially when I was wearing designer clothes. The first time I heard my song on the radio I thought my heart would jump out of my chest. I'd worked so hard and I had actually made it. I'll never forget the first time somebody asked for my autograph." She laughed. "I felt like a star."

"You were a star."

"But I didn't get a chance to be a teenager and do typical teenaged things. I didn't go to school dances or football games. I missed prom. If I hadn't stood up to my parents, I would have missed graduation too. I had to fight with them to be able to go to school at all. They wanted me to drop out so they could homeschool me." She gave a bitter laugh that was nothing like the merry laughter of only a minute ago. "Homeschool. That was a joke. My parents didn't give a hoot about my education. They're barely literate themselves. To them I was just a money making machine. An ATM they could access anytime they wanted."

He'd never known she'd felt that way back then. Never would have guessed it. He'd loved all of the attention that had come from being a star athlete. But then, he'd gotten to enjoy all of the high school activities. And his parents were the best any kid could have asked for. Though it felt inadequate, he needed to say something. "I'm sorry."

"Why? You didn't do anything to hurt me. You were my friend. And my recording career did make me rich. Fame has opened doors that I wouldn't have had the opportunity to knock on otherwise. My cosmetic company is very successful. That's due in great part to name recognition. Again, made possible because of my singing career. And I might not have had that without my parents pushing me when I started to make it big. So I suppose I owe them my thanks."

He thought of the many things that her parents were

owed. Gratitude wasn't among them. They hadn't done anything for her. They'd done it for themselves. "Don't be so ready to credit them for your success. You're the one writing and arranging songs. You're the one performing. And you're the one who created that beauty brand. People buy your products because of the good name you built. Customers know they're getting quality items."

"Thanks for saying that. If I say that, or even think it, it seems ungrateful. Or conceited. Like I think I'm all that."

"You *are* all that."

"Hank…"

"It's the truth. You have a right to be proud of what you've accomplished."

Shayna nodded, but otherwise didn't respond. They rode in silence for a few minutes. Then Shayna turned to him, an unreadable expression on her face. "Can you tell me what life was like when we were teens? I was on the outside looking in for a lot of the time."

"Other people's lives always look better from the outside. But the reality rarely lives up to appearances. To us, you were living the dream."

"Everyone thought that being a singer and performing in front of big crowds was exciting. And it was. I loved it. But the rest of the time I felt like an outsider. I may have been onstage on Friday and Saturday nights, but when I came back to school on Monday, everyone was talking about things that I'd missed over the weekend. It was as if they shared an inside joke that I didn't understand. The girls would talk about some touchdown you threw or gossip about who was dating and who had broken up. Who got caught kissing under the bleachers during halftime. The parties they went to or who they hung out with at the diner. I wasn't a part of any of that. Hearing about it after the fact made me even lonelier."

"That's what I meant about people's lives looking better from the outside. To us, you were a big deal. People were always talking about you. You just weren't around to hear it. And the mean girls didn't want you to know that they wanted to be in your shoes so they tried to make their lives sound better than they were. You were going to parties with celebrities and flying on private airplanes. You were on TV. That was bigger than school dances and football games. Certainly bigger than I was."

"You were the big man on campus. Emphasis on *campus*. You were a part of everything that happened. It wasn't a party until you showed up."

"I wouldn't have imagined in a million years that you felt that way. Life really can be strange."

"You'll get no argument from me."

"Back to your question. You already know we played football games on Friday nights."

"And the whole town shut down so everyone could go to the games."

Hank laughed. "Not even close. A lot of people showed up, but life didn't stop just because Aspen Creek High had a game."

"But there were people cheering for you."

"They cheered for everyone. Even the mascot."

"I can just see it now. I can even hear the roar of the crowd and taste the hot chocolate." Shayna sighed. "What did it smell like?"

"The mascot costume? Considering how hot it was in there, I imagine it smelled pretty awful. Like the body odor of dozens of sweaty teenage boys. But Keith still lives in town so we can ask him."

"That's not what I meant and you know it. Although now I can't get that odor out of my mind. Thank you for that." She pretended to gag. "I was talking about the stadium. Did it smell like hot dogs and grilled burgers? Fresh popcorn?"

"I'm not sure. I was on the field and the food smells didn't reach that far. To be honest, it probably smelled closer to the mascot costume than food. We were working hard down there and doing more than a little bit of sweating even on cold nights."

Shayna laughed as he'd hoped she would. Though there was no way he could go back and change the past, he wished he would have known how lonely she'd been when they'd been in school. But like everyone else, he'd been awed by her seemingly glamorous life. And all the time she'd been envying them.

"Be serious, please."

"You think I'm joking. Picture a bunch of sweaty teenaged boys shoving as hard as they can against each other in order to impress a cheerleader or some cute girl in the stands and multiply that by a hundred."

"Okay. Enough about the stinky boys. Tell me about the girls. What were they wearing? What were they doing? Did they seem to be having a good time?"

He sighed. "That's a harder question to answer. I was the quarterback, so I was focused on trying to make accurate passes and smooth handoffs. When our defense was on the field, my coaches were going over plays with me or I was watching the game. So I have no idea what happened in the stands."

"That's fair. When I was onstage, all I thought about was giving the audience the best performance I could. Back then I didn't have a choreographer or background dancers so all eyes were on me. And I had no idea what individual people were doing."

"I actually went to one of your concerts when you first started out. You were performing at a Mountain Valley High School dance."

"Really? Why didn't you come up and say hi?"

He shrugged. "I didn't want to come across as some sort of stalker or a groupie. Mountain Valley is two hours from here so I couldn't pretend to be in the neighborhood."

"I would have liked to see you, but I guess it's better that I didn't. I don't know how I would have reacted if you went from being a close friend to being a fan. Our relationship was one of the few that I could count on. You didn't change the way you treated me after my career took off. I guess that's why I felt so comfortable coming here after all this time."

He didn't know how to reply. Fortunately he didn't have to because Shayna wasn't finished asking him about what she'd missed. "What about after the game? Did you guys go to the diner for shakes afterwards?"

"For home games, yes. Most of the team and cheerleaders went. A lot of the student body came too, although I'm not sure which ones or how often they came. I was hanging out with my friends and most of them were on the team."

"I guess as the star player you couldn't hang around with the nerds."

"That wasn't it at all. I just hung around the people I knew the best. The players spent most of our time together. Practices started in the summer weeks before school began. During the season we practiced after class. In the offseason we had to work out to keep in shape. It made sense for us to do it together. We weren't excluding anyone. We were just thrown together. Plus we shared a love for the game. But I had friends who weren't athletic and didn't come to one game." It was as if she'd forgotten that they had been friends.

"What else did you guys do?" she asked. "Did you have parties every weekend? The girls were always talking about going to someone's house. They made it sound like so much fun."

"They might have exaggerated the frequency. Probably because they didn't want you to think that you were the only one leading an exciting life. They were more than a little jealous of you."

Shayna grimaced. "The funny thing is that I was jealous of everyone else. You were able to do regular things that I missed out on. You made friendships that lasted a lifetime."

"And what about you? Did you make any lifelong friends?"

She glanced at him, her eyes warm with sincerity. Then she smiled sweetly. "You're my lifelong friend."

His heart thudded. He hadn't expected her quietly spoken words to affect him this way. Now it took all of his strength to not pull her into his arms and hold her tight. But he resisted. They were talking about serious matters. This moment was an important step to them getting to know each other better. "Besides me."

Shayna sighed. Did she really want to get into this? Yes. Wasn't that why she'd come here? Because she wanted to talk about things with someone who knew her. Someone she trusted to be honest with her. Someone she knew had her best interests at heart. Not just someone. Hank. "Not at first. When I moved to California, I focused even harder on my career so I could get to the next level. I took private voice and dance classes. Lessons on how to walk and pose for the camera. I had someone teach me how to do my hair and makeup. How to choose clothes that fit my shape. There were also lessons on how to deal with the media. You name it, I was taught it. Most of the people I met were older and at a different stage in their lives. Some of them had kids close to my age. They did their jobs and then went home to their families."

Hank frowned. "What about later? When you were in your twenties?"

"I became friends with two of the background singers who toured with me. Lisa and Monica were my age and we were at the same stage in life. At least back then. But they fell in love and got married a year apart. Now they have kids. Monica is pregnant again. They gave up touring to raise their children. We keep in touch and get together when we can. Of course we don't see each other as much as before but that's to be expected." She took a breath. "How often do you go riding?"

He gave her a long look and she wondered if he would comment on her abrupt change of subject. "Not nearly enough. I try to ride each of the younger horses at least once a week so they get their exercise."

"Do you always ride alone?" The image of him riding beside a beautiful woman flashed in her mind and the green-eyed monster reared its ugly head. That was ridiculous. She and Hank were only friends. Not one inch of his six foot plus body belonged to her. Until she'd run into him at the reunion, she hadn't spoken a word to him in years. Sure she'd thought about him a lot when she'd first moved to California. She'd missed him. Over time, she'd gotten busy with her life, and thoughts of him became fewer and further apart.

Did she really think that he hadn't been involved with a woman or two over the years? The man had been a major football star. Women had probably flocked to him in droves. Maybe they still did. "I should have asked before now. Do you have a girlfriend?"

He shook his head. "No. I'm happily single. Are you seeing someone?"

"No."

"Good to know. Now, back to your earlier question. Part of being a sheriff is keeping kids out of trouble. If I can prevent crime before it happens, that's a success in my book. So I have an unofficial program where I bring some of the kids to the ranch and let them ride horses. I teach them how to care for horses. They love it. It gives them something constructive to do. And it helps keep them on the path that leads to a successful future."

"Wow." Hank was an even better man than she'd imagined. But then, he'd always been caring and thoughtful. "I can't believe that kids like hanging out with you."

"Really?" He raised his eyebrows.

"I mean because you're the sheriff. Not because of who you are as a person. Can you imagine us doing that as kids?"

Hank barked out a laugh. It was unrestrained and sent shivers down her spine. No matter how many times she reminded herself that they were only friends, she couldn't quite keep herself from drifting into *what if* territory? What if she kissed him? What if she told him that she had dreamed about him last night and had been disappointed to wake up alone? What if she proposed having a short fling while she was in town?

She chased the thoughts away. She didn't have flings, short or otherwise. Besides there was always another *what if*? What if it ended in disaster? They had managed to pick up their friendship as if seventeen years hadn't passed. She liked being around someone from her old life. Someone who knew her before she became a star. She wasn't going to risk that just so she could satisfy her curiosity. She would have to live with not knowing how it felt to be wrapped in Hank's strong arms. The world would keep turning even if she never discovered what it would be like to make love with him all night and wake up beside him. She'd faced disappointment before and lived to tell the tale. This was no different.

"No, Sheriff McLauren was definitely not interested in us kids," Hank replied, answering the question she'd almost forgotten she'd asked. "But then, he was old and not in the best of shape."

"You're quite diplomatic, Hank." The old sheriff hadn't believed in exercise and he'd had the body to prove it. He'd been built like an Oompa Loompa.

"It's part of being a public servant. I can't go around spouting off every thought I have, no matter if it's true. Can you imagine people's reaction if I declared most of the chili in the cook-off inedible?"

"I can picture it, actually. And the image is hilarious. All that pearl clutching. I take it that you're one of the judges."

"*The* judge."

"Oh."

He nodded. "What makes people think the sheriff is automatically the best person to judge cooking contests?"

"I suppose it's because you're honest. You have to be in order to be a lawman."

"Explain to me how that translates to knowing what chocolate chip cookies are best. Especially since I'm an oatmeal raisin guy. Shouldn't a chef or maybe one of the cooks in the diner be better equipped than I am? They cook all the time. Meanwhile I'm a regular at Food Truck Friday."

"When you put it like that, you are the least qualified person to judge. All of the awards are suspect."

"I wouldn't go that far."

"How far would you go?" That sounded suggestive to her, but she couldn't think of a way to clean it up. Luckily, he let it pass.

"I'm not saying I'm not qualified. I just think they could find someone who's *more* qualified. There's another festival in a couple of weeks. One guess who's being pressed into service again."

"What do I get if I guess correctly?" That sounded suggestive again and she spoke again before he could. "What kind of festival?"

"The usual kind."

"Could you be any more vague?"

"Sorry. Aspen Creek now has an events committee. To be fair, they come up with fun activities that everyone enjoys. They range from simple activities like bike races and scavenger hunts to art displays and puppet shows in the park. Every month there's a big festival around a theme. And naturally there's some type of food making contest for the locals. I don't know what it will be this month. Probably homemade jam and pickles."

"Not together, I hope," she said, grinning.

"You're joking but I wouldn't put it past them. I'm starting to believe that somebody on the committee holds a grudge against me and is trying to give me a horrible case of the runs."

Shayna laughed so hard she nearly cried. She actually had tears in her eyes. She couldn't remember the last time she'd had this much fun.

The sound of flowing water reached her and she looked around. "Where are we?"

"We're at the old fishing hole. Do you want to stop?"

She nodded. "Absolutely."

Hank swung down from his horse and she had to force herself not to stare. He looked so natural on horseback, sitting erect in the saddle. So perfectly at ease. But then, he had always been so comfortable in his skin. It had taken her a lot longer to reach that point in her life. She'd felt like a fraud for many years. She'd grown up wearing secondhand clothes, yet now she set fashion trends.

"Do you need help dismounting?" Hank asked, standing beside her horse.

"Nope. I think I can handle it. But don't go wandering off, just in case."

Recalling the way he'd told her to get off the horse, she swung her leg over the horse's back, then slid down Sugar's side. When her feet reached the ground, her legs gave out and she found herself sinking to the soft grass. In an instant, Hank's hands were wrapped around her waist and he was easing her up, pulling her next to him.

She inhaled deeply and got a whiff of his clean masculine scent. He smelled so good that her knees threatened to weaken again.

"Whoa. You were doing such a good job riding that I forgot that you hadn't been on a horse for a while." Shayna placed her head against his strong chest. She could feel the steady beat of his heart. The hard thud was at once comforting and arousing. Tilting her head, she looked into his handsome face. His intelligent eyes were framed with thick dark lashes that most women would kill to have. His cheekbones were perfectly sculpted and his lips were made for kissing. Hank Morrow was temptation wrapped up in six feet plus of muscular man. If he wasn't the one man she could be herself with, she might give in to that temptation.

Sighing, she forced herself to pull away. "I'm better now. I guess my legs were a little bit numb."

"It happens to the best of us."

"To you too?"

He grinned. "Well, no. I was trying to be nice."

She punched his shoulder. It was so hard she nearly hurt her fingers. "That figures. Can we walk around?"

"Sure." He secured the horses close enough to get water if they wanted it, and then held out his hand.

Grateful that he had no inkling of the lustful thoughts that had been popping up in her mind all day, she placed her palm against his. Despite how casual the contact was, she felt an electric shock when he laced their fingers. From there, it raced down her spine all the way to her toes. If he experienced the same sensation, he didn't let it show.

Hank led the way past a tall oak tree and over to the brook. The water didn't appear to be deep, but she knew that looks could be deceiving. A frog croaked and then hopped into the water, making a splash. A few white puffy clouds sailed across the otherwise blue sky. Everything felt so perfect that Shayna couldn't help but sigh.

"Did you catch a lot of fish here?"

"Sometimes. But I never brought them home. My mom's rule was that if you catch it you clean it. That wasn't something that appealed to me."

"Not to mention that you would have to kill it first."

"Exactly. I suppose if we needed to eat the fish in order to survive, I would have done it. But since we had plenty of food, I decided that catch and release was best for me."

"You're just an old softie."

"Who are you calling old?" Hank chuckled and nudged her shoulder with his.

"Since we're the same age, I'm going to say nobody." She turned and looked back across the acres of green hills. "Do you see a lot of deer here?"

"Some. But they keep their distance and I do the same. There's also a fox family living around here somewhere. We have that same policy."

"You don't have bears, do you?"

"I haven't come across any so I'm going to say no."

She gave him a cautious look. In all the time that she'd lived in Aspen Creek, she hadn't heard of anyone being bothered by bears. But times changed. As the town grew and development spread, wild animals were pushed out of their habitats. In California, there were the occasional news reports showing a bear walking around town or swimming with her cubs in someone's backyard pool. "What does that mean? Are there bears or not?"

He placed his hands on her shoulders, holding her gaze.

"I haven't come across any evidence of bears. Nor have I gotten any reports of bear sightings in town or the surrounding ranches."

"That's a relief."

"You don't have to worry, Shayna. You're completely safe with me."

Hank's words touched Shayna's heart. There had been very few people in her life that she'd felt secure with. Hank had always been one of them. Even as a teenager, he'd been a protector. It was his nature to look out for the underdog. Though she was no longer in that category, she knew she could count on him. "I didn't doubt that for a moment."

Chapter Six

Hank stepped into Pins and Needles Craft Store and looked around. Though it wasn't strictly necessary for him to go inside every business, when he was on foot patrol he always did. He'd discovered a long time ago that a little face time went a long way toward gaining trust and building solid relationships. It was also a way to keep his finger on the pulse of the town, a way to address small issues before they became big ones. Not only that, he was a people person and genuinely liked the citizens of Aspen Creek. He liked hearing about the big events in their lives and helping them celebrate.

"Hello, Sheriff," Rebecca Summer, the owner, said as he stepped inside. As always, her smile was warm and friendly.

"Good morning," Hank said, flashing a smile of his own. Rebecca was kind and welcoming, but she was difficult to get to know. He had a feeling that she was hiding something. He didn't sense that it was anything illegal so he didn't press. "How are things going?"

"Great." She unpacked several skeins of yarn from a cardboard box, placed them on a shelf, then walked over to him. "I'm still amazed at how much business I get from tourists in the summer. But then, according to my seniors, real knitters don't take breaks simply because they're on vacation."

"I'm going to take your word for it," he said. "Here's hoping the trend continues."

She raised her hands, fingers crossed. "I second that motion."

"Any issues with anyone? Any problems? Concerns?"

Rebecca shook her head. "Not a one. But there's generally two or three senior ladies in the store from open to close. Nobody wants to tangle with Diana and her crew."

Hank laughed. "The older generation do tend to keep everyone in line. That is when they aren't creating mischief themselves."

"Would you like some coffee? Diana brought in a homemade cake to share with the knitting group. It was delicious and I have a couple of slices left."

Diana Lowrey was one of the best bakers in town. Her cakes were always moist and delicious. Any other time he would have said yes, but Shayna had been baking delicious desserts for him. Tonight she'd promised him a peach cobbler. "Thanks, but no. I'm offered refreshments at just about every business I step into."

"The people in Aspen Creek do like to feed each other."

"It's in the town's DNA."

Four teenaged girls with bags draped over their shoulders stepped inside. They said hello, then walked over to a group of chairs by the front windows.

"My class is about to start," Rebecca said. "Thanks for checking on me. I appreciate it."

Hank nodded and then left, stopping to talk at various establishments until he reached the Aspen Creek Feedstore.

"Hey, Hank," Cole Richards, the proprietor, said as Hank stepped inside. "What's up?"

"Shouldn't I be asking you that?"

"You already know the answer. All is good. But then, what would anyone do with a bunch of tractor parts?"

"You'd be surprised."

Cole offered him a bottle of cold water, which Hank accepted.

"That's a surprise you can keep," Cole said and they laughed.

"Well, it's Sheriff Morrow," Gary Perkins said, walking over. Though somewhere in his mid-seventies, Gary had a sharp wit and didn't miss a trick. He'd owned the feedstore for decades before he sold it to Cole a few years ago. He still lived in the apartment above the store and worked part-time for Cole. "How are things going with the superstar?"

"What?" Surprised by the question, Hank reared back. No one was supposed to know Shayna was in town. He hadn't told anyone and he didn't think she had either. So how did Gary find out that she was staying with him?

"Shayna Givens. Singer and business mogul. How are things going with her? She's staying out at your ranch, right?"

"What makes you think that?"

Gary shook his gray head slowly and fixed Hank with a stare. "You aren't very good at deception, Sheriff. You never have been. I can read you just as easily now as I could when you were an eight-year-old coming into the store with your dad."

Hank sighed. That was the problem with being around

people who'd known you all of your life. It was hard as heck to put anything over on them.

"You know Shayna Givens?" Cole asked with more than a little shock in his voice.

"Of course," Hank said.

"Wow. According to Crystal—who, like teenaged girls everywhere, is into all things Shayna—she has a stalker. At least that's the rumor. But why would she choose to hide in Aspen Creek?"

Hank shook his head. "We've been friends so long I keep forgetting you didn't grow up here. Shayna and her family lived on a small ranch not far from mine. They moved to California after she graduated high school. She came back a short while ago and I invited her to visit the ranch whenever she wanted."

"Is there any truth to the stalker story? If there is, I can be on the lookout for strangers," Cole offered.

"This is a tourist town," Hank pointed out. "It's always filled with strangers."

"True. But if I come across anyone who seems shady, I can give you a call."

Hank could only imagine the chaos that would result if Cole called every time he thought someone looked out of place. "Thanks, but my deputies and I have it covered."

"If you say so. But the offer stands."

Hank turned to Gary. "Shayna wants to keep her presence here under wraps. She doesn't want the press to find out where she is."

The older man pretended to lock his lips. "Her secret is safe with me. Not that it will be a secret much longer with or without me telling anyone. But you can count on the people of Aspen Creek to look out for her. We take care of our own."

"I know. And I appreciate that."

"I hate to cut this short, but I've got a card game to get to. See you later, boss. Sheriff." Gary saluted and then walked out of the feedstore.

After the door closed behind Gary, Cole turned to Hank. "Be honest. Is there any truth to the rumor that Shayna has a stalker? I might not be a cop, but people tend to tell me things. Not as much as they tell Gary, obviously, but I hear things."

"I believe you. And I appreciate your offer. But Shayna didn't mention a stalker, so you and your daughter don't need to worry about that. She just wanted to relax around old friends."

"Friends, plural? Because you seemed surprised that Gary knew she was in town. I think you're the only person who's supposed to know she's here. The only person she wants to relax with. Is there more to the story that you aren't telling me?"

Hank laughed and rubbed his chin. "Maybe I was too quick to dismiss your offer to keep an eye out. You're quite observant."

"Yes. And I've observed that you've done a good job of avoiding my question."

"I *am* the only one who is supposed to know she's in town. She didn't tell anyone."

"And the rest? Is there more to your relationship than friendship? And feel free not to answer that."

Hank shrugged. "Consider this my nonanswer. I'm more concerned with figuring out how someone knew

Shayna was in town. And just how many people know that."

"Could be that someone spotted her driving to your ranch."

"Maybe." Could it be that simple? Not that it mattered. The secret was out. It would only be a matter of time before word spread.

"But Gary was right about one thing. We look after our own. Crystal and I are proof of that. When I moved here, I was a teenaged single father with a baby girl and no one in the world to rely on. The people in this town became the family we needed. And when Andrea came to town and she and I reunited, they welcomed her with open arms. If there is anything I can do, I will."

Hank nodded. "I appreciate that. See you later."

Though he kept his expression calm and his voice level, Hank was concerned. He'd thought that Shayna was keeping something from him. He still did. But a stalker? He was the sheriff. If anyone could keep her safe, it was him. Surely she knew that.

But then again, the tabloids could have it all wrong. That wouldn't be the first time. They weren't known for their investigative journalism. The fantastical stories they printed proved that. They were in the business of selling papers. And stories about Shayna—true or not—did just that.

When he finished his foot patrol, he returned to the office. Christopher was taking a statement from Coral Jackson, the owner of a grocery store in the less prosperous section of town. Hank generally stopped in her store on the days he patrolled by car.

"Good morning," Hank said.

"You should check your watch," Christopher said with a chuckle. "It's afternoon now."

"I stand corrected." Hank glanced at Coral. "Is everything okay?"

Coral frowned. "I was doing inventory and discovered that I'm missing a few items. At first I thought that I had made a mistake when counting. But this is the second time that it's happened. I think someone might be shoplifting so I stopped in to make a report."

"Then I'll leave you to it. And I'll have the deputies drop by a few times, to see if we can catch the perpetrator in the act."

"I hate to be a nuisance."

"You're not a nuisance," Hank assured her. "Serving citizens is literally in our job description."

"It's only small things like chips and juice. A couple packages of lunch meat. Two cans of chicken noodle soup." Coral shook her head. "If they'd asked, I would have given it to them."

"Sometimes criminals start small, just to see if they can get away with it," Christopher said. "They might escalate. No, it's good that you came in now. We'll be on the lookout."

Coral nodded and Christopher continued to take the report.

Hank excused himself and went to his office, his mind split between the shoplifter and the possibility that Shayna had a stalker. A teenager repeating what she'd read in a gossip rag might not be the best source, but sometimes the truth came from unlikely sources. He wouldn't rest until he knew the truth.

There was a rap on his open door and he looked up.

Christopher stood there, the report in his hand. Hank waved him inside.

"What do you think about the shoplifter?" Christopher asked, sitting in the chair across from Hank.

"What do you think?" Hank said, turning the young deputy's question back on him.

"It's not the crime of the century," Christopher said.

"No. But it mattered enough to Coral that she came here to make a report. There's a crime and a victim. So, what do you think is happening? And how do you think we should approach it?"

"I agree with you that we should make more visits to the store. I think it's probably a bunch of bored teenagers acting out. Maybe this is some sort of dare. After all, they only took snacks."

"And lunch meat and soup. We could be looking for someone who's hungry."

"In Aspen Creek?" Christopher said, his tone more than a little skeptical.

"Why not?"

"The people in this town are doing well. Even in that part of the city. They might not be rich, but they aren't poor either. They have good jobs. The resorts are making money hand over fist. They're always hiring workers, so I doubt that it's someone who's looking for a job. No, it's bored teenagers. I'm sure of it."

Hank leaned back in his chair, cupping his arms behind his head. "So, what's your plan? How are you going to catch the shoplifter? And what are you going to do with him when you do?"

"Toss him right into jail," Christopher said emphatically. "The only way to stop a small criminal from becoming a big criminal is to teach him a hard lesson right away."

"Will the circumstances matter?" Hank asked.

"No. I don't think we should coddle criminals." Christopher stared at Hank. "Do you?"

"I'm a small-town sheriff. I'd like to be a friend to everyone. Including troublemakers. I want people to know they can come to me with their problems or concerns. I want them to reach out to me if they need help. I don't want people to hide their circumstances from me because they're afraid of what I'll do. If they do, then I've failed them."

"So you think I'm wrong?"

Hank shook his head. "I'm not making a judgement at all. Let's just see where the facts lead us and go from there. But this is your case. I'm trusting you to handle it in the right way. I'll only step in if you're about to make a big mistake or endanger yourself or someone else."

"I was hoping for something a little more exciting."

"You never know what this will turn out to be."

"True." Chris stood. "I think I'll patrol the area around the store."

"Good idea. And remember…"

"I know. Keep my head on a swivel."

"Exactly."

Shayna listened to the last of her father's ranting voicemails before turning off her phone. She didn't know why she hadn't just deleted the messages without listening to them. It wasn't as if they were any different from the dozens of others she'd received over the past week. The words varied, but the theme remained the same. He'd alternated between feigned concern and genuine anger that she wasn't calling him back. To have him tell it, she'd abandoned them, leaving them high and dry. How were they supposed to manage without her? Or, more accurately, without the extra money they wanted from her. As usual, they'd run through the substantial allowance she provided them each month and were looking for another handout.

Shayna lay back against the blanket she'd spread on the ground beneath an apple tree, dropped her forearm across her eyes to block out the sun, then inhaled deeply. She counted to four and blew out the breath on a count of four, inhaling peace and exhaling stress. After a few minutes she felt calm. Her parents couldn't touch her here. They didn't know where she was. Nobody did.

"But I'm not going to think about them now," she said. What was the point of coming all the way to Colorado to get away from her family if all she was going to do was think about them? She could stress about them at home.

Shayna decided to take a stroll through the fruit trees, her favorite place on the ranch. Simply picking a peach or a handful of cherries lifted her spirits. Once, she'd climbed onto a lower branch and sat there, looking over the ranch, entranced by the acres of green grass and rolling hills. She marveled at the sounds of nature that she had previously ignored. Birds chirped and sang, squirrels chattered and chomped on nuts and geese honked as they flew overhead. The ranch wasn't as quiet as she'd once believed, but it was peaceful. When she'd told Hank about her time sitting on the branch, he'd hung a smooth piece of wood from two strong ropes, creating a comfortable swing.

She was discovering that she enjoyed the simple ranch life. She liked feeding the chickens and gathering eggs with Hank in the mornings. She didn't mind cleaning the stables—although that wasn't her favorite thing to do. But though Hank offered to do it alone, she always refused to let him. She liked hanging around him and feeling as if they were partners.

After walking around and picking a few cherries, she sat on the swing. Immediately her thoughts turned to Hank. Just thinking of him made her pulse race. She remembered how she joked about Hank having a string of women showing up with food. Now it turns out that the person cooking and baking for him was her.

Though she'd long since stopped seeking validation from other people, she was heartened by his compliments. But she knew she had to be careful. Needing validation from others gave them power over you. She was currently trying to regain the power that she'd given to others—namely her parents. It made no sense to turn around and offer that control to someone else.

But then, Hank wasn't asking for it. In fact, he hadn't asked for anything from her. He seemed content to accept whatever she wanted to give. Oddly enough, that made her want to give more.

She pulled a small notebook from her pocket and slipped the pen from its holder. Song lyrics came to her at random times and she kept a pen handy so she could scribble them down in the moment. She also kept a small recorder within reach so she could record any melodies that struck her before they slipped away. But she wasn't planning to work on a song now. She was going to write a list of her goals.

Once the pen was in her hand, she was stuck. She sat there for several long minutes waiting for inspiration to strike. How could she be thirty-five years old and have no idea what she wanted in life? She twisted the pen. There had to be something.

Children. She wanted children. A boy. A girl. Or both. It didn't matter. She just wanted children. So she wrote that down. *A husband. A home filled with love and laughter.* The list didn't have to be strictly serious, so she began to add frivolous things. She wanted to go fishing. She wanted to swim in a swimming hole instead of the heated pools she was used to. She wanted to go to a high school football game and get shakes and burgers at the diner after. She wanted to go to cookouts and camp out under the stars. She wanted to do everything she'd missed out on. She wanted the freedom to do whatever she wanted without worrying about her image.

She wanted to breathe.

Now that she knew what she wanted, she needed to come up with a plan. That was something she was good at. She wouldn't have achieved her dreams of becoming a successful singer-songwriter if she wasn't. And she would find a way to make these dreams a reality too. At least the ones that didn't require other people. Those would be more challenging.

And speaking of challenging, she needed to come up with a way to deal with her family that didn't involve going into hiding. Why hadn't she deleted their texts? More importantly, why hadn't she blocked their numbers? Did she really need them to have access to her? After all, they never reached out just to talk or see how she was doing. They only contacted her when they wanted money.

Knowing that, why she didn't just cut them off? They certainly didn't add value to her life. Was it that important to her to be able to say that she had blood relatives and that she wasn't alone in the world? She didn't know.

Shayna decided not to dwell on it. Leaves were rustling in the trees and birds were singing. The gentle breeze cooled her skin and she let them blow away her concerns. She glanced at the vast mountains against the blue sky. She was in one of the most scenic places in the world. She should be appreciating that beauty instead of walking over paths she'd already trod. She just needed to be patient. The answers would come to her eventually.

Shayna's ears had grown attuned to the sound Hank's squad car made as it drove over the gravel driveway and she could distinguish it without seeing it. Perhaps the skill was a result of her years in the music business where a keen ear was necessary. Or maybe it was because she was on high alert, wary of being discovered. She tried to live a normal life—a private life—but there was always someone out there hoping to snap a photo of her. The worse she looked, the more outrageous the story they could spin. That meant more papers sold or more clicks to their website. Ultimately more money in their pockets at her expense.

Over the years she'd developed a thick skin, but she was still human. She'd told herself repeatedly that it didn't matter if people believed lies because she knew the truth, but that only went so far. The lies and mockery hurt. But she never gave anyone the satisfaction of seeing her pain. Instead, she soldiered on, writing and recording her music and making sure that her cosmetics company ran smoothly.

She heard Hank's footfalls moments before he stepped into the kitchen. Though she'd tried to prepare herself mentally, seeing him in his sheriff's uniform always got her motor running. The white fabric of his shirt contrasted nicely against his rich brown skin. It fit his broad chest and arms perfectly before tapering down to his slim waist and stomach. The way his navy pants wrapped around his muscular thighs made her think of the popular saying, "Thick thighs save lives" and she giggled.

"What's so funny?" Hank asked, a smile on his face.

"Nothing. I'm just happy to see you."

He gave her a disbelieving look, but she would rather he doubt her than know about her lustful thoughts. A woman was entitled to have some secrets. "Well, I'm happy to be seen. And it's good to see you too."

She poured a glass of lemonade and handed it to him.

He took a long swallow and then sighed. "This is perfect. But I don't expect you to wait on me."

"I know. That makes it better. Besides, you do so much for everyone. I like knowing that I can do something for you. Dinner will be ready in about half an hour."

He drained his lemonade and put the glass into the sink. "That gives me time to get out of this uniform and slip into something more comfortable."

Shayna laughed at his choice of words as he no doubt intended. Since it was a lovely evening, she decided to serve dinner on the patio. She was just setting everything up when Hank stepped outside.

"Wow. This looks great."

"Thanks. I found the candles in the back of a cabinet."

"Left over from my mother."

"I figured as much. The wildflowers grow by the drive-way so I picked a bunch. And just like that we had a centerpiece. Easy-peasy."

"It's so fancy, I feel like I should be wearing a tie. Or at least a shirt with a collar."

"Your T-shirt is fine. So are your shorts." In fact, the way the shirt hugged his chest, it was better than fine.

He pulled out her chair and then took his seat. While she plated the chicken cacciatore with fettuccine and sautéed spinach, Hank poured the red wine. Shayna wasn't much of a drinker, but tonight she was in the mood for a glass.

"How was your day?" Hank asked, sincere interest in his voice.

"Good."

"Did you do any writing?"

"No." She was having a hard time thinking of anything to write about lately. For the first time in years, she was suffering from a serious case of writer's block. She supposed she could reach out to other songwriters to see if they wanted to collaborate. She'd cowritten songs in the past. That had always helped to get her creative juices flowing. If she was still facing difficulty when she went home, she'd think about calling someone. But there was no reason for her to burden Hank with her problems. He had the entire town to worry about. "I'm taking a break from all that and giving my mind a rest. This is a real, true vacation."

"Well, there's no better place to refresh yourself than right here."

"I know. It's easy to get lost in nature. The time just flies."

Hank took a bite of his chicken cacciatore. "This is delicious."

Shayna smiled. "You always say that."

"I always mean it."

She took a bite. It was indeed delicious. "I love cooking. When I'm touring, I don't get the chance so this is just as enjoyable for me as it is for you."

"I seriously doubt that," Hank said, scooping a forkful of pasta into his mouth.

They talked quietly as they ate, touching on several subjects, but nothing too deep. Once they'd finished eating, Shayna reached for the dishes.

"Leave them. I'll clean up later," Hank said. "Let's just sit out here and enjoy the evening."

Shayna leaned back, closed her eyes and inhaled the soothing aroma of the mint that grew freely along the back of the house. "I could get used to this."

"There are a couple of things I want to talk about."

Hank's tone of voice unsettled her and Shayna opened her eyes and sat up. "That sounds ominous. Should I be worried?"

"Not at all. I just heard some things in town that you should be aware of."

"Okay." She told herself to remain calm until Hank told her what was on his mind.

He inhaled and then blew out the breath as if suddenly nervous. "Are you running away from a stalker?"

"What?" The question should have been ridiculous, but given the state of the world, it wasn't. Plenty of female celebrities had been stalked over the years. Some with disastrous results. "No. What makes you ask that?"

"That's the word on the curb."

She leaned her chin into her palm. "Is that right?"

He nodded.

"The press likes to make up stories about me. It helps them make money. Trust me, if I had a stalker, I wouldn't have come here."

"Why not?" He sounded offended.

"Isn't it obvious?"

"Not to me."

"You're my friend. The last thing I want to do is bring trouble to your door."

"I'm also an officer of the law and more than capable of taking care of you. In fact, I would dare say I'm better able to protect you than anyone else you know."

"You're probably right." She generally traveled with a security detail. The number of bodyguards protecting her differed given the circumstances. Even so, she doubted that they'd undergone the type of training that Hank had. Nor did they have the weight of the law behind them. "But like I said, I don't have a stalker. What made you think that? I know you haven't been watching those celebrity shows on TV. Have you been reading tabloids in the grocery store?"

He rolled his eyes. "You know better than that. The teenaged daughter of one of my friends heard about it. He mentioned it to me when I stopped by his business today."

Her skin suddenly felt tight. "How did my name come up?"

"Well, that's the second thing I wanted to talk to you about." He stretched his neck and ran his finger along the inside of his T-shirt as if it was suddenly squeezing him. "Do you remember Gary Perkins who used to own the feedstore?"

She shook her head. Her parents hadn't owned any livestock so they wouldn't have had a reason to go to the feedstore. "I don't think I ever met him."

"Well, Gary is a fount of information. Very little happens in this town that he doesn't know about. I don't know how he does it. People just spill their guts to him."

"Like a priest?"

"More like a bartender. There's no expectation that he'll keep what he hears under his hat. That is, unless you specifically ask. Then he's a vault."

"And this concerns me…why?"

"Because Gary knows you're here."

"In Aspen Creek?"

He nodded and gave her a rueful look. "*Here* here. He knows that you're staying here with me."

"How did he find out?"

"Who knows? Maybe someone saw you driving on the road and followed you. Or maybe someone saw you getting gas when you arrived in town. But the result is the same. Your secret is out."

"This is terrible."

"Why? You just said that you didn't have a stalker. Is there anyone else after you?"

Just her parents, but she knew that wasn't what he meant. They were aggravating but they weren't dangerous. And she really didn't want to talk about them now. "I came here to get away from everyone. I want time to myself. Now that the word is out, maybe it's time I went somewhere else."

Chapter Seven

Hank heard the stress and panic in Shayna's voice and he wanted to kick himself. He could have handled this more gently. Instead he'd just blurted everything out like a clod. It was clear from the moment that Shayna arrived that she was struggling with something. If she was given enough time, he believed that she would unburden herself. But she had to trust him first. And she was moving in that direction. That's why he'd told her what he'd heard. He didn't want to keep secrets from her. But he could have eased into it.

"Hold on there," he said, taking her hand and gently tugging her back into her seat. "That's not necessary."

"But if Gary knows, how many more people do? You said this was a tourist town now. Maybe one of them saw me."

"Maybe. But they would think that you're here on vacation. For all they know you could be gone by now."

"I suppose. But I really don't want anyone to know where I am."

"Well, that ship has sailed. The good thing is nobody has bothered you."

"So far. But it could just be a matter of time."

"The people in this town love you. You don't have to

worry about paparazzi showing up here and harassing you. We won't allow it. Our numbers might double because of tourists, but we're just as insular as any other small town. We look after our own."

"I haven't lived here for years."

"That doesn't matter. You grew up here and that's all that matters. You're safe here. We'll protect your privacy."

"What if the press does find out?"

"As long as they leave you alone, I can't kick them out of town no matter how much I would like to. But this ranch is mine. Nobody will be able to intrude here. You can take that to the bank."

Shayna thought about that for a moment. While she did, Hank wondered if he'd really convinced her. He hoped so. He didn't want her to run away in a panic. Who knew where she would go or what would happen? She was better off with him.

He gave her hand a gentle squeeze. "What's going on, Shayna? Let me help. Who are you running away from?"

"It's not so much a who—well, my parents, of course. You remember how they were?" She frowned.

He nodded.

"They haven't gotten better with time."

"But you're an adult. They don't control you now."

She sighed and he had a feeling that he was wrong. They still had a hold on her. She looked at him, her eyes troubled and her shoulders sagged as if exhausted from holding a heavy weight. "It's not just them. It's everything. Everybody wants something from me, every minute of every day. Up and coming songwriters want me to record their music. Companies want me to represent their products. My manager thinks I should do something on

Broadway. Now that I have an Oscar he's all about me reaching EGOT status. He's all about dreaming bigger dreams and setting higher goals. But I don't even know what dreams are coming from inside me and which are being forced on me from other people.

"Then there are the events for product launches. Ad campaigns to review. Rehearsals. Recording sessions. There just are not enough hours in the day to do everything. There are people depending on me to keep it together. And that number grows every day. It used to just be the people who tour with me. Now it includes people who work in the factories and stores. If I go under, I drag them with me."

Her voice grew louder and more panicked with each word. But the dam had broken and the words tumbled over each other in their struggle to be free. "A friend died while I was on tour. I found out the day before the funeral. Not that it would have mattered if I'd heard earlier. I was halfway around the world in the middle of a tour. And despite feeling sad, I had to keep performing. The show must go on and all of that. Everyone was depending on me to keep it together and perform. People are always depending on me. I'm always expected to be strong for everyone else. I know pressure is a privilege but I can't take it anymore."

"Who told you that pressure was a privilege?"

"That's what Billie Jean King says."

"Not to quibble with a legend, but I disagree. Sometimes pressure is just pressure."

Shayna took a deep breath, held it and then blew it out slowly. "Sorry. I didn't mean to dump on you."

"Don't be. I asked because I wanted to know. Because I care. Tell me how I can help."

"Just keep being you."

"I can do that." He stood and pulled her into his embrace. She leaned against his chest and he held her close, rubbing his arms up and down her back. Gradually he felt her relax as the tension left her body. As she pressed her soft body against him, and as her sweet and enticing scent wafted around him, he felt an entirely inappropriate desire growing inside him. She needed his comfort, not his lust. Though he wanted to continue to hold her close, it would be best if he created some physical distance between them. "How about a walk?"

The residue of their unpleasant conversation lingered like a miasma around the table and he wanted to get away from it. Hopefully creating some distance from this space would allow them to recapture the pleasant feelings from before.

Shayna nodded. "That would be nice."

By silent agreement, they headed to the fruit trees—Shayna's favorite part of the ranch. A gentle breeze blew and the sweet aroma encircled them as they walked. Without thinking, he took her hand into his. It felt so natural to link fingers as they strolled. A bit too natural for his comfort. But he sensed that she needed the contact as much as he did.

Hank didn't believe in lying, especially to himself, so he had to admit that his feelings for Shayna were changing into something deeper than friendship. She was so sexy and luminous that it would be unnatural for him not to notice and respond as a man. But what he felt was more than animal attraction.

When Cole mentioned a possible stalker, terror like nothing he'd experienced before in life had chilled him to the bone. It was worse than the iciness he'd felt when he'd known he had to walk away from the sport he'd loved all of his life. The fear had weakened his knees. He'd wanted to race back to the ranch and wrap Shayna in his arms to protect her from all harm. He hadn't truly been able to relax until he'd seen for himself that she was fine. He needed to confirm that she wasn't in danger.

But if he wasn't careful, he would be. They weren't going to have a lasting relationship so it would be best to keep his emotional distance. But that was a lot easier said than done.

As they walked, Hank forced those thoughts from his mind. He'd never been able to control his feelings and it made no sense to try now. "Do you know how to make jam?"

Shayna shook her head. "No. Do you?"

"I never tried. It's just that I have all of this fruit. I don't know what to do with it."

"What did you do with it last year?"

"I had a pick-what-you-want event for the people in town."

"How did that go?"

"Okay at first. Then someone got the bright idea to have a preserve-making contest. And you know who was the judge."

"That's fair. After all, you donated the fruit."

"That's the same kind of logic that Harriet King, one of the members of the entertainment committee, used. Even though I was using a teaspoon and sampling the barest minimum, by the time I'd tasted every entry I had a headache."

"Sugar rush?"

He nodded. "Worse than anything I had ever experienced. I can just imagine how kids act in school after eating a sandwich made with that stuff. Sitting still would be impossible."

"You could always give it away again. There has to be someone in need of food. Someone who would love fresh fruit. Believe me, there are lots of families that are struggling but putting on a happy face for the world. I belonged to one of those families as a kid. And I put on one of those smiles."

"Is that why you always donate to food pantries on your tour stops?"

"It was supposed to be anonymous, but someone working at one of the pantries thought it would make a great human interest story. It went from an innocent social media post to the national news in the blink of an eye."

"I know that you would rather keep your good deeds under wraps, but from what I read, donations increased significantly after the word got out. Radio stations started giving out swag to people who brought canned goods to your concerts."

"That's true. And I'm glad for the additional donations. But I don't need everything I do to be publicized. Sometimes I want to do good in secret." She glanced at him. "Like you."

"Me? What secret good deed am I doing?"

"Other than taking me in?"

"Let me stop you right there. This isn't charity. We're friends. At least, I hope we are."

She nodded. "Yes. Though we'd lost contact, I thought of you often. When things got hard or I discovered that people I thought were my friends were only using me, I reminded myself that there was a time when I had a real friend. *A true friend.* I knew you really liked me, because there was absolutely nothing that I could give you. You had it all."

"I don't know about having it all."

"You had a family who loved and cared for you. If there is anything more important than that, I don't know what it is."

He thought of his parents. His sister. His extended family. "You're right."

"And when you made it to the NFL, I was the happiest person in the world. I had a glass of champagne in your honor."

"Why didn't you reach out? I would have loved to hear from you."

She shrugged and then turned the question back to him. "Why didn't you?"

He gave an uneasy chuckle. "I suppose because you were already a huge star. I wasn't exactly worried that you wouldn't remember me since we had been good friends, but reaching out seemed sort of cliché. Someone from your past trying to worm his way back into your life. It sounds foolish now, but that's how I felt. I wasn't sure that you would want to hear from me."

"I missed you. You were the best part of my life for so many years. You always accepted me. After my career took off, nothing changed. I never felt like you were envious of me the way I felt with girls. Of course, my parents encouraged that paranoia with other female singers. Even with my dancers. If I didn't have any friends, I wouldn't have distractions. I wouldn't have someone telling me that my home life and my relationship with my parents was abnormal." She shook her head. "I can see how messed up it all was. But even now, I'm affected by the way I grew up. Some habits are hard to break."

"Would it help to know that we're all products of our childhood?"

"Not really."

He laughed and put his arm around her shoulders, pulling her close to his side. She was soft and warm and her gentle scent wafted around him, teasing his senses and arousing him in a way he enjoyed though he knew he shouldn't. He wanted to hold her close, all the while knowing that he needed to keep her at arm's length. That was the best way to stick to his plan.

Despite the yearning growing inside him, the longing to discover if her lips tasted as sweet as they looked, he kept the moment light and friendly. "Well, unfortunately, that's all I have. I only took one psychology class in college and I'm ashamed to say I scraped by with a C."

"At least you went to college."

"Did you want to?"

"It was never an option." Shayna ran her hand over her glorious hair before dropping it back to her side. "I shouldn't complain about my life. I hate the whole 'famous girl who wants to be left alone' narrative. It's ridiculous. And I set out to become a big star. If you look at my vision boards from back then, you'll see that was all I thought about. I was determined to make it big. Going to college and furthering my education never crossed my mind. It doesn't make sense to think about what I missed."

"The road not taken."

"Exactly. The choices that I made back then led me to where I am today."

"You have the Grammys and multiplatinum records to prove that you made the right decisions. At least as far as your career goes. But that doesn't mean you have to keep doing something if it no longer works for you. Nothing is etched in stone. You can change your path if you want to."

"And do what?"

"That's entirely up to you."

"How did you decide to become a sheriff? I know your football career was over, but this is such a drastic change. I could understand becoming a college coach or even a sports commentator, but this? How did you know it was right? Do you ever wonder if you should have chosen something else? Did you ever think something else would make you happier but it's too late to change?"

"First, it's never too late to change." He glanced at her and she nodded. "Second, I wasn't kidding when I said that nobody else wanted the job. But it was a job that needed doing. I have a degree in criminal justice so it wasn't that much of a stretch. After I took the job, I joined several law enforcement organizations and enrolled in as many seminars as I could find. I wanted to be qualified. I figured I would serve one term, enough time to give someone else a chance to come along and do the job. But it turned out that I like the job.

"But your path doesn't have to mirror mine. Think of something that interests you and do it."

She shook her head. "You make it sound so simple."

"Really? Because it wasn't. It was actually nerve-racking. Here I was, in my late twenties, with no job and no idea what I wanted to do. I could have raised cattle like my father before me, but I knew I wouldn't be happy doing that. It wasn't in my blood."

"One career path erased," she said dryly.

Hank laughed. "Only for me. There's nothing saying that you can't be a rancher."

"I can barely ride a horse. Somehow I don't think cattle ranching is in my skill set."

"Don't sell yourself short. We'll turn you into a horse-woman in no time."

"Even so, I don't think ranching is in my future."

"How about becoming a baker? You could open your own shop. Your desserts are better than any I've ever had." He gave her a grin. "But don't tell my mother, okay?"

"I don't know. What will you give me to keep your secret?"

"Are you blackmailing me? I am the sheriff. I carry handcuffs."

"Really?" She flashed a naughty look that was hot enough to ignite his blood. "I'll keep that in mind for future reference. But right now, I have the upper hand. I know something you don't want me to tell your mother. So I'll repeat, what will you give me so I'll keep quiet?"

He stopped walking and turned to face her. Seeing the mischief sparkling in her eyes, he placed his hands on her waist and moved close enough for the heat from their bodies to mingle. Her breath hitched and the look in her eyes quickly turned to desire that matched his. "I can think of any number of things. But it would be easier if you told me what you wanted."

"Where would the fun be in that? You might be willing to give me more than I ask for."

"So you're saying you don't want to settle for less."

"Exactly. So what's your best offer?"

"I can show you better than I can tell you." He moved closer. Now their lips were mere centimeters apart.

She tilted her head and stared at him, her eyes dark with desire. "Then show me."

That was all the encouragement he needed. They might both regret the impulse later, but maybe they wouldn't. Besides, he was only a man. And man wasn't designed to resist such enticing temptation. He lowered his head and brushed his lips against hers. Electricity rocketed through him, starting at his lips and shooting through his body. Heat pooled low in his stomach. He'd intended to keep the contact brief and the mood playful, but Shayna had other ideas. She pressed against him, dragged her hands over his abs, up his chest, then looped them around his neck. After that, all bets were off.

Giving free rein to his desires, he pulled her closer, wrapped his arms around her tiny waist and held her delicate body against his. She moaned and opened her mouth to him and he swept his tongue inside. She tasted sweet— a combination of peach cobbler and her own unique flavor. The moment stretched past what was wise, yet he couldn't make himself stop. It was as if he'd been born for this particular moment, created to be with this one woman.

The thought shocked him and he pulled away. That had to be the most ridiculous thought he'd ever had. The most dangerous. Shayna was not going to be here forever. He might not know when, but eventually she would be going home. He couldn't imagine a long distance relationship working between them. But then, she hadn't indicated that she was interested in one. She could simply be scratching an itch.

Regret and doubt began to assault him. Kissing her had been a huge mistake. It would only complicate their relationship. They were friends. Perhaps they could pretend like the past ten minutes hadn't happened.

Unable to completely break all contact, Hank leaned his forehead against hers while he struggled to regain his equilibrium. Shayna was breathing just as hard as he was and the male part of him smiled with satisfaction.

"Wow." Her breath was a sexy whisper that sent shivers down his spine. Resisting her wasn't going to be easy.

"That's exactly what I was thinking."

"So what happens now?" Shayna spoke quietly, so he wasn't able to decipher the emotion in her voice.

"Whatever you want. It can be something or nothing." When she only stared at him, clearly not comforted by his answer, he decided that a bit of comic relief was necessary to ease the tension. "I'm not going to insist that you marry me simply because you've taken advantage of me."

She laughed as he hoped she would. "That's mighty big of you."

"I'm a big guy."

Her eyes widened and she laughed again. "I'm sure you didn't mean that the way it sounded."

"To be honest, I'm not sure how I intended it. But since you're laughing, I'll say that it was a joke."

"It was funny."

"Maybe I settled on sheriff too fast. Perhaps I should have given stand-up comedy a try first."

Shayna shook her head, her glorious hair bouncing

over her shoulders. "It wasn't *that* funny. And one joke doesn't a routine make."

"Ouch. Hey, you could be one of the judges on those talent shows. You're direct enough."

"Nah. I was a guest judge once. I don't think I would be good at it." She started walking again and he walked beside her.

"Why not?"

"Because who am I to step on someone's dream?"

"I've seen a few episodes of those shows. Some of those people are really terrible."

"Maybe. But does that mean they shouldn't dream? They might become better over time. Or maybe they won't. Perhaps they will eventually turn to something else, but I believe it should be at a time of their choosing. I don't know if that is the best attitude for a judge. Maybe it's wrong to encourage people to keep trying when they should just pack it in. But I don't want anything I say or do to be the deciding factor."

He looked over at her. "You have to be the most compassionate person I've ever met."

She smiled. "I could say the same thing about you."

They walked in silence for a while before turning around and heading back to the house. Hank had never felt this content before. He knew Shayna was responsible for the feeling. He also knew that despite his intentions, their relationship was about to become complicated.

Chapter Eight

Shayna's heart thudded so hard as she walked beside Hank that she half expected it to burst from her chest. She couldn't believe it. *They'd actually kissed.* She pressed her fingers to her lips. They were still tingling. Her body was humming, something she hadn't ever experienced before. She wasn't a virgin, but she'd learned early on that she wasn't cut out for casual sex. Her heart always got involved. And since it didn't look like she was going to stumble upon Mr. Right anytime soon, she'd put her physical desires on ice.

Now though, her body was hot and demanding attention. Kissing Hank had been heavenly, but it wasn't enough to satisfy her awakened desires. She wanted more. She yearned for lingering kisses that led to hours of intense lovemaking. But she knew better than to let her body overrule her brain. That would only lead to trouble and eventual heartache.

She'd only had a few serious adult romantic relationships and none of them had ended well. At least not for her. Their demises hadn't resulted in screaming matches or accusations of cheating. But the breakups had been reported in the press ad nauseam. Every person with a platform felt free to dissect the corpse of her dead relationship and say exactly when and why things had fallen apart. The older she became, the more scrutiny her romantic life—or lack thereof—received. Countless screeds had been written about her "failure" to maintain a successful relationship. Was she too successful? Was she too difficult? Were her standards too high?

That had been bearable. Sort of. But what hurt the most was the death of the friendship when the romance ended. A man she'd gotten used to sharing her life with was no longer a part of her life. Instead there was a gaping hole where companionship once had been and she had struggled to fill it.

Though she and Hank hadn't spent time together in nearly two decades, they were friends. Their relationship had deep roots from their childhood that made it possible to pick up that friendship. And she wanted to hold on to it no matter the cost.

Kissing Hank had endangered that relationship. So why had she done it? The answer came quickly. Because she was falling for him. The more time she spent with him, the more attracted she became. But she couldn't ruin the friendship no matter how attracted she was. "So, we never decided what we're going to do about this kiss."

"Shayna, you're overthinking this."

"I need clarity." And she knew that without it her imagination would have her thinking the worst.

Hank sighed as if resigning himself to having this conversation. "I value our friendship. I don't want to risk it by starting a romance that might not work. The odds are stacked against us. So I think we should just stay friends."

"Same. I don't know anyone who went from friends to lovers and back to friends again after a breakup." She'd known lots of people who'd tried and who had even made it work for a little while before giving up. But she knew there was no way of unscrambling the eggs. "We haven't ruined things, have we?"

Hank tilted her chin so that she was looking into his eyes. "No. We're good. We didn't cross that line."

Shayna smiled. The relief she felt battled with the tingling sensation that his simple touch aroused in her. But knowing that he agreed that they should only be friends gave her strength to ignore her stubborn desire.

The sun had begun to set while they'd been walking. Now twilight had passed and bright stars dotted the dark sky. A gentle breeze carried the sweet scent of wildflowers over to them. It was all so romantic. The opposite of what they needed if they were going to root themselves firmly into the friend zone. The rational part of her knew that she should go back to the safety of her room. Alone. But she wasn't ready to be rational.

Tomorrow. Tomorrow she would be sensible and set the relationship firmly back on the friendship side of the track. But tonight she wanted to break free of all restraints. Well, maybe not all restraints. Some restrictions had to remain in place so they didn't cross the line.

When they reached the table, she pulled out her chair and sat back down again. She hoped Hank would join her, but she didn't ask him to.

"Were you hoping for some quiet or do you mind company?" Hank asked.

"I spend the entire day alone. I would love some company." Especially his.

He took his seat and then looked at her. "Are you lonely?"

"A little. Isn't that strange? I came here craving solitude and alone time. The last thing I should do is complain when I get it."

"You aren't complaining. Telling the truth is never wrong. And denying your feelings won't make them go away."

She doubted that he was thinking about the sexual feelings that were currently simmering just below the surface. Controlling her newly awakened desire was a lot harder than she'd expected it to be. "Even so, I should be happy."

"Why?"

"Are you serious?"

"As a heart attack." He stared at her.

"I'm rich. I'm famous. I have my health. Do I need to go on?"

"I get your point. But those things don't change the fact that you are a person. You're just as entitled to experience the whole range of emotions as anyone else without being judged."

Those simply spoken words shot through Shayna as if he had shouted them through a bullhorn. All of her life she'd been told that others had it much worse than she did and that she should be grateful for what she had. So her parents hadn't bought groceries and she had to eat peanut butter and cold cereal again. Kids in other countries were starving and would be overjoyed with anything placed in front of them to eat. The press loved ridiculing the rich and famous who had even the simplest complaint, encouraging their millions of followers to pile on. If you wanted to eat dinner without being disturbed, you were painted as spoiled and unappreciative of your fans who paid for your lifestyle. If you didn't want to take a picture with every person who asked, it was because you were a diva. There was no winning. It was impossible to please everyone and still have a life of your own. Once you had a reputation as being difficult, it was impossible to shake and every interaction was blown out of proportion.

"Then, yes. I love the privacy of the ranch, and I'm enjoying caring for the horses and chickens and wandering in the orchard, but there are times when I'm bored. Lonely even."

"What would help with that?"

"I don't know. Maybe I need to get used to my own company."

"People weren't meant to live in solitude. We need companionship."

"You live here alone."

"Yes. But I don't spend every waking moment here. I see people all the time. I talk to people every day."

"I talk to you."

"I know. But I can't be the only person in your life." He tilted his head in a way that was at once sexy and serious. "You mentioned your friends. Have you been in touch with them?"

She shook her head. "I don't know why I haven't reached out. The best I can say is that I want to keep that life separate from this one."

"Do your friends know you're in Aspen Creek?"

She shook her head. "They don't know about the town. Nobody does."

"So we're your dirty little secret?"

"No. Not at all. When my career took off, my parents created a whole new backstory for me. For our family. They told everyone that I grew up in a ritzy suburb outside of Denver. They didn't mention Aspen Creek at all. They made up a story about how my dad quit his job as an executive to manage my career. Allegedly, my mother homeschooled me. It sounded so much better than saying they were moochers living off the money their teenaged daughter earned.

"Aspen Creek is my own private haven. My slice of heaven on earth. There's no chaos here. Nobody is asking for anything here."

"You know you aren't responsible for everyone simply because they work for you, right? The singers and dancers and everyone else made their choices. They knew the risks when they chose the career."

"A lot of them were just as young as I was when they started out."

"Even so, their career choices and the risks that come with them are not your burden to bear."

She sighed. "A part of me knows that."

"I suppose we just need to convince the rest of you." She laughed.

"I understand that you want to keep your lives separate, but there is still a way to keep you from feeling so isolated."

"What's that?"

"Come to town with me."

She shook her head. "That's not a great idea. There's the possibility that my presence will cause a commotion. Once the press—" *and her family* "—learns I'm here, it's all over."

"I'm not proposing that you take a stroll down Main Street. Some of our high school friends still live in town.

You talked to a few of them at the reunion. At least briefly. If I recall correctly, you had a great time."

"I did."

"Then how about I reach out to a couple of them? I know Veronica and Kristy would love to see you again. I know they get together with a few of the other women in town regularly. I've run into them a few times at Grady's, a club that locals frequent."

"I would love to see them again, but what you're proposing won't work." She stood. "I appreciate what you're trying to do. But I'll be fine here. I really am enjoying my time. So please, forget I said anything."

She went to grab the dishes, but Hank waved away her hands. "You cooked. I'll clean. Remember?"

"Thanks." She went inside and headed for her room where she slipped into a pair of pajamas and climbed into the bed. When she closed her eyes, the memory of kissing Hank filled her mind and she knew that she would dream about a future filled with even more of his kisses.

Too bad that dream could never become a reality.

Hank watched as Shayna disappeared into the house, then leaned back in his chair. He should have known that she would eventually get lonely with only him for company. This wasn't the life for everyone. Heck, it wasn't even the life for him. He'd go stir-crazy with nothing but the animals for company. It had to be a hundred times worse for Shayna.

Hank had no desire to ever be in the spotlight again, but he knew from his football experience that although fans often overstepped, there was a give and take of energy between the team and the spectators. The same applied to musicians and their audience. He hated to admit it, but his power was limited. There was only so much he could do to keep her safe from prying eyes and adoring fans.

Stretching and yawning, he gathered the dishes and went inside. He was loading the dishwasher when he noticed the small pad on the counter. Suspecting that Shayna had written a grocery list for him, he picked it up and scanned it. *Have kids. Go to a football game. Get shakes and burgers after the game. Go to a cookout.*

This didn't quite rise to the level of a bucket list. Those were usually made up of once-in-a-lifetime experiences. Travel goals and the like. But she'd already traveled the world several times, visiting more cities and seeing more sights than most people could ever dream of doing. Maybe doing the ordinary things that most people took for granted was a dream for her. On second thought, maybe this was a bucket list. He read it again, more slowly this time. He might not be able to give her children or a home, but he could host a cookout.

He snapped a picture of the list so he wouldn't forget anything and then set the pad back where he'd found it. Humming tunelessly, he loaded the dishwasher and then headed to his room. He was a man who liked a plan and now he had one. He was going to make Shayna's dream list a reality.

"What are you thinking about?" Shayna asked the next morning as they cleaned the stalls.

He'd been thinking about kissing her again, but he wasn't going to admit that. Not after they'd agreed they would only be friends. "What makes you think I'm thinking about anything?"

"Because you are just standing there." Her eyes narrowed but he could see their sparkle. She placed a hand on her slender hip. "Or are you slacking off, hoping that I'll do more of the work?"

"Would I do something like that?" Hank grinned.

"I never would have thought it of you, but now I'm not so sure. I seem to be the one spreading the hay around while you're just standing there looking good."

"You think I look good?" He dropped the bale of hay he'd been holding, flexed his muscles and struck a pose. His physique was not the same as it had been when he was an athlete who spent hours lifting weights and following a strict diet, but he hadn't gone to seed, as his father was fond of saying. Hank wasn't vain, but he knew he still caught a woman's eyes when he walked down the street. More importantly, he knew that Shayna was attracted to him. He'd caught her looking at him when she thought he was unaware.

"Oh, no," she said, shaking her head. "I think I created a monster. Please don't let that one compliment go to your head."

"There are no take-backs. And I notice that you didn't deny it." Grinning, he walked over to Shayna and playfully nudged her shoulder with his. "Admit it. You like me. You think I'm cute." He sang the last words in a way a tween would.

Instead of denying it as he'd expected, Shayna walked her fingers over his chest, leaving a trail of heat in her wake. Grinning sexily, she looked into his eyes. Hers danced with devilment. Just how far was she willing to take this? How far would he? She leaned in closer and her perky breasts brushed against his chest. "And if I do? What are you going to do about it?"

Her lips were now mere inches from his and when she spoke, her breath brushed against his mouth. Though she was playing, and he'd intended to keep the moment light, he was suddenly hot with desire. He captured her hand and removed her glove. Then he brought her hand to his lips and gently kissed her fingers, one at a time. She wobbled and he felt her shiver.

"Are you trying to get me to mess around with you in the hayloft?" she asked.

"It wasn't my initial plan, but now that you mention it…" He leered at her. "What would you say to that?"

"I suppose you must have done this a lot in your teens."

He shook his head. That wasn't the answer he'd been hoping for, but he supposed it was as good a time as any to disabuse her of that notion. She seemed to have a rose-colored view of everyone else's high school years. "No. This will be my first time. That is, if you say yes."

She giggled. "Sheriff, don't you have to get to work?"

"I don't have to be at the office for hours. That gives us plenty of time to fool around."

"One little kiss won't hurt anything."

"I suppose one kiss is better than none." Before he could stop himself, he wrapped his arms around her waist and kissed her. The kiss started gently but it quickly became hot and intense. Her hands began to rove over his chest and he moaned in response. He let his hands travel up and down her back.

Though he wanted to lead her to the bed of hay so they could take this further, he resisted the urge and pulled back. They'd decided that they were friends. Only friends. It made no sense to muddy the water less than twenty-four hours later.

There was a piece of straw stuck in her hair and he pulled it out. "I have a question for you."

"Sure." She brushed her hands over her shorts, momentarily distracting him. "What is it?"

"I was thinking about having a few people over for a cookout. Nothing fancy. If that's okay with you."

"You don't have to ask for my permission. I'm not the boss of your house."

"But you're staying here, so you get a vote. You'll be mingling with everyone. I was thinking about asking a few of our high school classmates. That way you could hang out with people you already know and like. You can trust them not to tell anyone that you're here. We could ride out to the swimming hole."

"Why ride all the way out to the swimming hole for a cookout? The grill is on the patio."

"I don't have a pool. I thought we could go swimming too. That is, if you brought a swimsuit with you. Or we could hang out here if you prefer. I just thought it would be fun."

Her smile was so bright it could rival the sun. "I love the idea. And I brought a swimsuit with me. Who should we invite? I mean—who are you going to invite?"

"You had it right the first time. *We'll* be hosting, so you get a say in the guest list."

"I really liked talking to Kristy and Veronica at the reunion so we have to invite them. And I know that Malcolm was your friend too."

"Then we can add them to the list."

Her eyes shone with excitement and he could tell that she was getting into the spirit. "Is there anyone else you want to invite? I know that you were close friends with the other jocks. Are any of them still in town?"

"Maybe one or two. But how about we keep this thing small. If you want, we can invite more people over in the future."

"Your other friends won't be upset about being left out?"

He shrugged. "Why would they? I don't get invited to every get-together they have and I'm not offended. I'm sure they'll feel the same way."

"If you're sure."

"I am."

"What should we cook?"

"How about I leave the menu up to you? You just tell me what you want me to grill and I'll pick it up at the store."

Shayna clasped her hands against her chest. "This is going to be so much fun. When should we have it?"

"Today is Wednesday. How about this Saturday? That's plenty of notice."

"Do you think they'll want to come?"

"Why wouldn't they?"

She shrugged and flashed him a shy smile. "Want to know a secret?"

"I wouldn't mind."

"I haven't thrown a party in years. Actually never if you exclude those that were business related. You know, parties with the right people so you can make the right connections."

Hearing that hurt his heart but he kept his voice light.

"Well, since you already know these people you don't have to worry about making connections. You can relax and have a good time. Now let's get back to work."

Though Hank acted naturally as he spread the hay, his heart was cracking. To the world, it looked as if Shayna had everything. Fame. Money. Beauty. But she was missing out on a lot of things he took for granted. He couldn't fix everything that was wrong in her life, and he couldn't change her past or give her a better family, but he could do this. He was going to do everything in his power to make her happy. And if he fell for her? Well, he would deal with that when the time came.

Chapter Nine

"I can't believe you've been in town all this time and didn't tell us," Kristy said to Shayna.

"Neither can I," Veronica added.

They'd driven up to the cookout site a few minutes ago and were now sitting on a log beside the swimming hole, dangling their bare feet over the water while Hank and Malcolm were setting up the grill.

"I was trying to get away from it all," Shayna said by way of explanation.

"Too many paparazzi following you around?"

That was only part of it, but since she didn't want to drag her problematic family into this conversation and cast a shadow over this lovely day, Shayna nodded. "It's so peaceful here. I feel like nothing can touch me here."

"And Hank certainly kept your secret. But now that we know you're here, we can get together in private. If you want."

"I would love to."

"Hank should have invited us sooner," Veronica said. "That way you wouldn't have been stuck out here all alone."

"I asked him not to," Shayna said, coming instantly to his defense—although she probably didn't need to. It was clear that the other women thought highly of Hank. "And he is such a good man. He kept my secret."

"Really," Veronica said, a mischievous grin on her face. "Just how good is he? What's going on between you two?"

Shayna actually giggled. That one sound gave her away and it was too late to pretend not to know what Veronica was talking about. Besides, there was something about the other women that made her trust them.

"So there is something to tell," Kristy said. "I'm going to grab some water from the cooler. Don't say a word until I get back."

Shayna laughed. "I don't know if what I have to say is all that interesting."

Kristy sprinted to the cooler and was back in under a minute with three bottles of water. She'd also grabbed a few cookies that Shayna had baked and doled them out. "If we're going to talk about men, I'm going to need sustenance."

"That sweet tooth of yours is going to get you in trouble," Veronica teased.

"Hey, if you don't want yours, I'll take it," Kristy said. "That's more for me and Shayna. I'll break it in half so we can share it."

Veronica pulled her cookie close to her. "I didn't say that."

Shayna smiled as she watched the interplay between the two women. It was obvious that they shared a special bond and she was pleased that they'd chosen to include her in their circle.

"So," Kristy said, turning to Shayna. "Tell us everything."

"I really don't know where to start."

"With the good stuff of course," Kristy replied. "Is he a good kisser?"

Shayna sputtered and nearly choked on her cookie. "What?"

"You heard me."

"You just dive right in."

"That's a yes," Veronica said, answering for Shayna.

"I don't know," Kristy countered, a sly grin on her face. "It could be a no. That would explain why she's reluctant to answer."

"It's a yes. A definite yes," Shayna blurted out. She couldn't let them doubt Hank's sexual prowess. "Five stars."

Kristy looked at Veronica, a smug expression on her face. "I told you they were dating. Rumor has it that the two of you started dating at the reunion."

"Really? Why do people think that?" Shayna asked, looking from Kristy to Veronica and back again.

"He was so protective of you. He never left your side. Just like in high school. Nobody was ever sure if you were dating back then, but most of us leaned toward yes."

Shayna shook her head. She couldn't believe that the other kids had actually believed she and Hank had been dating. "He was my friend. I didn't have a lot of those back then. I always felt like an outsider. But not with Hank. I always felt comfortable with him."

"Well, maybe you were destined to be with him."

Shayna laughed. "*Destined?* I don't believe in destiny or soulmates or whatever you want to call it. In my experience, people you believe will be together forever break up and people who have no business being together just can't seem to stay away from each other."

"You're not totally wrong," Veronica said, "but you're not totally right either. Malcolm and I went through a lot before getting together. We went from being good friends to not speaking to each other for years. Then we became friends again. Now we're in love and engaged to be married. Was it destiny? It could be. Or maybe we got together because we had a solid foundation based on our earlier friendship."

Shayna smiled. "I'm glad you managed to work it out and now you're in love. That's definitely a happy ending."

"It was a bumpy road. I'll tell you all about it later. I promise. But I'd rather hear about you and Hank."

"I'm happy here with him."

"That's important," Kristy said. "How long are you going to stay?"

"I don't know. Hank said I could stay as long as I wanted. I don't even want to think about leaving." She thought of the texts detailing the opportunities her managers were lining up for her, then quickly shut down those thoughts. She wasn't ready to deal with that kind of stress now.

"You should stay for the rest of the summer at the very least," Veronica said. "There are so many fun events scheduled in town. You'll have a great time."

"Hank mentioned a lot of them and they do sound like fun, but I don't want to be a distraction. That happens when I venture too far outside my usual places."

"You could always wear a disguise," Kristy suggested.

"Like those phony noses and glasses kids wear at Halloween?" For some reason the idea made Shayna laugh.

"I was thinking more along the lines of a wig and a pair of dark sunglasses," Kristy said, "but I suppose a Groucho Marx getup would work too."

"Do you ever do that?" Veronica asked. "I read that celebrities often disguise themselves so they can go shopping. Or they ask the owner to close an entire store so they can shop in peace."

"I've never done either of those things. I think I went the other way and became more of a recluse, staying inside when I'm not touring."

"That adds to the mystique of Shayna Givens," Veronica said.

"But it also makes every sighting that much more of a big deal," Kristy said. "I'm not telling you what to do… or maybe I am, but only because I'm right. You shouldn't hide out here. If you want to go to town, go. If you want to eat at the diner, then do it. You're living with the sheriff. That comes with some benefits. Hank can keep the crowds away. And after a few visits, people will be used to seeing you and it won't be a big deal. You'll be able to come and go as you wish."

"Do you really believe that?" Shayna didn't dare to hope it could be that simple.

"Not entirely. I suppose some people will freak out at seeing you. I mean you are Shayna Givens, one of the world's biggest stars. But the people 'who knew you when' won't. At least I don't think so. And we'll be there with you to keep people from getting too close and making you feel uncomfortable."

"And so will your boyfriend," Veronica said, grinning.

"He's not my boyfriend," Shayna said automatically. She didn't want to start that rumor.

"If you say so," Kristy said with a laugh. "But seriously, you should come to town."

The picture they painted sounded so good. So normal. And if she wore a hat and sunglasses, she might not even be recognized.

"I'll think about it," Shayna said.

"So, you and Shayna Givens," Malcolm said.

"What do you mean?" Hank asked. He flipped the last couple of burgers and then turned to look at his old friend. They'd been talking about the upcoming high school football season, so that comment came out of the blue.

"I couldn't be clearer if I was made of glass. You know exactly what I mean. Your houseguest and you."

Hank shook his head. He should have known that Malcolm wouldn't take the hint and let the subject die. He was going to push and prod until he got an answer. Hank blew out a breath. "She's my friend."

"A friend that you haven't been able to keep your eyes off all day."

"Am I that obvious?"

Malcolm laughed. "I can't believe you actually asked that. Yes. So start talking while we're alone. Unless you want Veronica and Kristy to overhear and put their two cents in."

"Absolutely not." Hank picked up his beer and took a long swallow. Then he placed the cold can against his forehead. "There's not much to tell."

"Have you kept in touch with her all these years?"

Hank shook his head. "No. Before the reunion-slash-goodbye party I hadn't seen her since graduation. To be honest, I was surprised she showed up. But then Mr. and Mrs. Watson were always good to her."

"So what happened between the two of you at the reunion to make all of this happen? I have to admit that I was more concerned about getting back in Veronica's good graces than anything else that was going on that night."

"I remember. You were doing a lot of begging." Hank grinned. "But I can't say that anything out of the ordinary happened. We talked and danced. We did a bit of reminiscing. And before she left, I told her that she was always welcome to come and visit me. Between you and me, I didn't expect her to take me up on it. But one day I came home to find her car in my driveway."

"So where does this relationship go from here?"

"Go? Where can it go? Her life is in California, or wherever in the world she happens to be touring, and mine is here. I'm a small-town sheriff. I'm happy with the life I've built here. This is the life I want to lead. I've had enough of fame and overzealous fans to last a lifetime. And football fans are nothing compared to Shayna's. They've even got a name for themselves."

"It sounds to me like you're trying to convince yourself that things can't work out. I don't want to hear what you think. I want to know how you feel."

Hank stared at Malcolm. "Since when do we talk about feelings?"

"I'm an evolved man. You can give Veronica the credit—or blame—for that." He laughed. "Seriously, I'm much happier now that I've stopped trying to run away from my feelings. You should try it."

"I don't even want to think about how I feel, much less talk about it."

"Why not?"

Hank sighed. "Because when I look down the road, I don't see how a relationship between Shayna and me could work. All I can see is me with a broken heart."

"Wow."

"What?"

"You're falling for her. Maybe you've already fallen."

"I wouldn't go that far," Hank said firmly. "Sure, I like her. Who wouldn't? She's sweet and funny and beautiful. Easy to talk to and even easier to be around. But since there's no future for us, it makes no sense to start something we can't finish."

Malcolm looked like he wanted to argue and Hank steeled himself. Instead Malcolm took a swallow of his beer. "Are you going to keep in touch after she leaves?"

"That's my plan, but it will be up to her."

"Well, I hope you get what you want."

"Me too."

Hank slid the burgers and chicken onto a platter and then called everyone over to the table. Shayna had insisted on going all out with the decor. She'd found one of his mother's cloth tablecloths and matching napkins. She'd filled three mason jars with wildflowers and three others with small candles, creating what she'd called a rustic glamour tablescape. He'd strung white lights in the trees, something Shayna claimed would create the perfect ambience after the sunset.

"Everything is beautiful," Veronica gushed, taking her seat. Kristy echoed the compliment.

"Thanks," Hank said with a wide grin. "Shayna thought it was a little over the top, but I insisted."

Shayna laughed and leaned her head against his shoulder. The scent of her sweet perfume teased his senses, turning his vow of friendship into a challenge. "Nobody is going to believe that. Nice try though."

There was something about the smile on Shayna's face that made his heart leap with joy. In the short time that she'd been around, his feelings had morphed from friendship to desire to something else entirely. Something deeper. He might have denied his feelings to Malcolm, but he knew that he couldn't hide them from himself. He was falling for Shayna. Hard. And there was nothing he could do to stop it. And he wasn't sure he wanted to stop.

It was funny how life changed people. He'd gone from wanting to date every woman who'd shown the least bit of interest in him to preferring to be alone. Until Shayna had shown up, he hadn't even considered settling down and starting a family. Now the notion was beginning to appeal to him. And he knew the type of woman he was looking for. He wanted someone steady who wanted kids and a normal life. Shayna might want those things too, but he couldn't figure out how she could make it work. Not when everything she did made news. He didn't want his kids growing up in that spotlight.

He wanted his kids to have the kind of childhood that he'd had. Getting together with his friends at the diner or hanging out together at the swimming hole had been some of the best times of his life. Riding horses with his friends or just sitting around talking about girls had created bonds of friendship that time and distance couldn't sever.

Still, despite their different lifestyles, he couldn't control his feelings for her. But he knew he needed to make a wise decision. And that required him to consider all factors. But now wasn't the time to try to figure out things. This was a party after all.

While they ate, they laughed and talked and Hank was pleased to see that Shayna was completely at ease. She fit right in with Kristy and Veronica just as he'd known she would. They caught Shayna up on old classmates, telling her who was married and who had moved away. They also told her about the way the town had grown, focusing on the spas and boutiques they liked that he hadn't thought to mention.

"How about a swim?" Hank asked after they'd finished their meals. He couldn't wait to see Shayna in her swimsuit.

"Has it been thirty minutes?" Veronica asked, checking her watch.

"You don't believe that old wives' tale, do you?" Hank asked, rolling his eyes.

"Yes," Veronica and Shayna replied in unison.

Hank looked at Kristy, who shrugged. "I'm staying out of it."

"Anyway, to answer your question, yes, it has been thirty minutes," Malcolm said.

"Why didn't you just say that in the first place?" Veronica asked.

"I guess I just wanted to get you riled up."

"You're playing with fire," Veronica said, stepping closer to Malcolm.

"I can take the heat." He kissed her cheek and then stepped back.

Hank felt an unfamiliar twinge of envy watching the couple. Suddenly he wanted what they had.

"Well, I'm ready to swim," Kristy said.

"Me too," Hank answered, squelching the unwanted emotion. He pulled his T-shirt over his head, toed off his boots and then looked around until his eyes found Shayna. "Who's going to join me?"

Shayna appeared suddenly shy at the thought of undressing in front of everyone. She wore revealing outfits onstage, so her reticence surprised him. After a glance around, she tugged at the bottom of her T-shirt. "I suppose I am."

The other women began to remove their shorts and tops. Veronica looked at Kristy and Shayna. "Come on. The water's not cold. At least I hope not."

That seemed to be the encouragement Shayna needed and she quickly removed her shorts and T-shirt. Then the women raced over to the water and jumped in. Hank and Malcolm quickly followed.

"It's colder than I expected," Shayna said, her teeth chattering. The water reached her waist and she folded her arms over her chest, unwilling to go any farther.

Hank swam over to her. "Just duck under and get your whole body wet. It won't seem so cold after that."

She stared at him for a long moment. The look of trust in her eyes touched his soul. Inhaling deeply, she closed her eyes and squatted until the water covered her head. A second later she pushed to her feet, the water sliding down her body. She shook her head and pulled her hair back from her face.

"Well?" Hank asked.

"I'm still cold, but not as much as before."

They all swam and floated under the sunny sky. Hank thought that he could stay in the water forever, admiring the way Shayna looked in her swimsuit as she glided across the water. She was such a graceful swimmer. More than that, she seemed so happy, floating and talking to Kristy and Veronica. After a couple of hours, they'd had enough and got out of the water. Instead of putting on their clothes, they lay on towels in the grass, allowing the fading sun to dry their suits.

"This is so nice. I miss being able to go to the beach and feeling the sand between my toes. I have a pool, but it doesn't compare to this."

"You know, I never thought of the bad side of being famous," Veronica said. "I imagine it's not all that it seems from the outside."

"I don't want to complain," Shayna said, repeating what she'd told Hank.

"Why not?" Kristy asked. "Everyone has problems that they complain about."

Hank wanted to cheer. He'd said the same thing, but he didn't think he'd convinced Shayna that she was entitled to complain. Maybe she'd believe Kristy.

"Don't you think that it is kind of hypocritical?" Shayna asked. "I did everything in my power to become famous, so why am I complaining about fame?"

"Did you try to become famous," Kristy asked, "or did you try to get people to buy your music and come to your concerts?"

"Aren't they one and the same?"

"I don't think so," Kristy said. "And even if you did want to get famous, so what? You still have a right to privacy. It's okay to want to be left alone."

Shayna nodded. "Hank said the same thing."

Kristy smiled mischievously. "He's not often right, most men aren't, but every once in a while they get it right. You should listen to him this time."

"And you should also come to town with us," Veronica said. "Put on a hat and sunglasses. You'll have a great time."

Shayna glanced at Hank as if seeking further confirmation. Then she smiled. "I guess I will come. I could use a great time."

Chapter Ten

"That was so much fun," Shayna said to Hank later that night when they were alone. Earlier Hank and Malcolm had piled the furniture and grill into the pickup and driven it back to the house while Shayna, Veronica and Kristy gathered all of the dishes. Shayna had insisted that the other women take home the floral centerpieces and they'd readily agreed. After they'd seen their friends off, Hank had suggested that they come back to the swimming hole for a midnight dip.

"I told you it would be," Hank reminded her, a satisfied expression on his handsome face.

"You were right."

"What was that?" He froze and then turned to glance at her, an exaggerated expression of surprise on his face.

Shayna laughed. "Please don't make me say it again."

"Only if you get into the water for that swim we agreed to have."

Shayna pulled her T-shirt over her head and then tossed it onto the ground near her feet. Then, wiggling her hips, she slid her denim shorts down her legs and stepped out of them. She worked out regularly, so she knew she looked good in her one-piece. The suit wasn't particularly revealing because she hadn't wanted to wear anything too sexy around their friends. But now that it was just her and Hank, she wished she was in a tiny bikini. Even so, there was appreciation in his gaze.

"I'm not the only one who's going swimming. Take off that shirt, Sheriff, and get in the water."

"You don't have to tell me twice," Hank said. In one smooth motion, he removed his shirt and tossed it on the ground. Then he held out his hand to her so they could walk into the water together. Grinning, she dodged his hand, then ran and jumped into the swimming hole with a huge splash. Then she swam a few expert strokes before turning back to Hank.

Hank chased after her and jumped in beside her. They swam side by side for a few blissful minutes, moving in sync with each other.

Shayna turned and floated on her back, looking up at the bright stars that dotted the deep, dark sky. A sense of calm and peace filled her. Being here with Hank was better than anything she had ever experienced in life. She let her mind wander and naturally it returned to the kisses they'd shared. Just remembering the feel of his lips against hers as his hands roved over her body made her feel hot and she wouldn't have been the least bit surprised if the water around her began to boil.

After a few minutes, Hank pushed to his feet, then took her hand so she could stand beside him. The gentle waves brushed around her waist, nudging her closer to him. Though she knew she should resist, she allowed herself to be swept along until her body pressed against his. Water beaded on his chest and she reached out and traced a drop down his torso to his sculpted abdomen. His stomach contracted beneath her finger and she heard his swift intake of breath. Water trickled down his face and he swiped it aside, his flexing shoulder muscles immediately drawing her eyes. No matter how often she told herself that her friendship with Hank was too valuable to risk, she couldn't quite tamp down her growing attraction. The steely control she'd mastered over the years was melting under the fire of her desire.

He gently brushed his thumb over her cheek and her knees wobbled. "This is really nice." His voice was husky and it sent shivers down her spine.

She nodded, suddenly incapable of speech. Tonight was everything she had ever dreamed it would be. Unable to stop herself, she pulled his head down and kissed him gently. The kiss was tender, filled with the emotions she didn't want to share. She wasn't even sure she wanted to feel them.

"You know the best thing about today?" she asked.

"My company?"

The answer to that was a definite yes, but admitting that wouldn't help her keep her feelings under control, so she laughed. "I'm not going to be responsible for your ego getting out of control."

"Then what?"

"Knowing that there was nobody with a camera lurking in the background. It feels so good to just be free to be me."

"I don't know how you deal with it. I'm so glad to be out of that life. That was an unexpected bonus to becoming a small-town sheriff."

Hank's words were like cold water dousing her good feelings. Her hope. He'd lived in the glare of the limelight once and had happily walked away. He knew the problems that accompanied a public relationship. Even so, a small part of her hoped that things with him would be different. After all, his experience had given him a perspective many of the men she met lacked. His words were a reminder that he didn't want any part of that life again.

She didn't know why she was so disappointed. After all, she knew that staying friends was the best thing for them. He wasn't saying anything now that they hadn't said before. Even so, his words hurt. But that was her problem.

"Yay you for breaking free," she said, injecting a lightness to her voice. The fact that she was dangerously close to falling in love with him would go to her grave with her.

Hank was giving her a searching look and she wasn't sure she could hide her feelings from him. Needing a diversion, she scooped up some water and splashed it into his face. He sputtered and she laughed.

"I can't believe you did that. Here I was being a gentleman. Well, you know this means war."

"Uh-oh." Shayna knew she only had a split second to make her escape. She turned and took two strong strokes toward the shore. But Hank was taller and his limbs longer and stronger and he easily caught up to her before she reached the safety of dry land. He grabbed her by her waist and lifted her out of the water.

Despite knowing that she was about to be dunked, Shayna giggled. Hank stiffened in surprise at her response and then his laughter mingled with hers. When he started to lower her back into the water, she protested. "Is this your idea of war? I thought for sure you were going to dunk me."

"Really. Well, I'd hate to disappoint you." He swung her back and forth twice and her stomach rose and fell with the motion. On the third swing, he released her and she went sailing through the air before she landed in the water, sinking in over her head. She kicked her way to the surface and swam over to Hank, determined to retaliate.

They dunked and splashed each other for several minutes. Shayna knew that Hank was holding back. Though she was strong for her size, there was no way she could best a former professional athlete unless he allowed her to.

"I give," Hank said, rising from the water like Poseidon. He shook his head, spraying drops of water in every direction.

"So, you're saying that I won? That I'm the champion of the water fight?" She lifted her hands over her head in triumph.

He sputtered. "I wouldn't go that far."

"No?" She cupped her hands, filling them with water. "Then the battle isn't over. Not until you surrender."

He gave her a long look. "That's never going to happen."

"Well, then, there isn't a ceasefire." Before he could move, she tossed the water into his face.

"You're so stubborn. I suppose I can dunk you a couple of times before we head to shore. There are alligators in this water, you know."

She gasped, not sure whether he was joking or not. Unwilling to take a chance, she swam as fast as she could to the water's edge, then jumped from the water, not stopping until her feet were on solid ground.

"I've never seen you move that fast." Hank was chuckling as he stepped out of the water. "I was kidding about the alligators. There are none here. Crocodiles either."

She glared at him. "Only rats."

He picked up his towel and wiped moisture from his torso, then rubbed the towel over his hair. He pulled on his shirt, covering his glorious muscles. Shayna sighed silently. She would have loved to look at his body for a few more minutes.

Hank glanced at her, a grin on his face. "Guilty as charged. But in my defense, I didn't think you would believe me."

"Well, I did. I never expected you to lie to me that way. I don't think my heart has stopped pounding yet."

"I didn't mean to scare you. I thought you knew it was a joke. I apologize. And to show you how sorry I am, you can tell me something scary."

Shayna twisted her hair, wringing out the water as best she could. "That's not remotely how this works and you know it."

He spread his arms. "That's the best I can do."

"Yeah, well, when you least expect it, expect it."

"Oh. I'll keep that in mind."

Shayna dried off and wrapped the towel around her waist. She slipped her feet into her sandals and grabbed her clothes. When Hank held out his hand, she took it automatically.

The ride back to the house was quick and when Hank parked the truck in front of the garage, Shayna sighed. This had been a wonderful day and she would remember it always. She knew that when the time came for her to go home, she would leave a piece of her heart here with Hank.

Hank looked at the broken glass on the laminate floor of the grocery store and shook his head. This was not something he was used to seeing in Aspen Creek. Like every town, they had their fair share of crime. There would be no need for him and his deputies otherwise. Even so, each time he was confronted with proof that his town wasn't the idyll that he wanted to believe it was, a piece of his soul died.

"What happened?" he asked, turning to look at Christopher, who'd been first to arrive on the scene. He'd already taken Mrs. Jackson's statement.

The deputy opened his notebook, glanced at his notes and then turned to Hank. "Mrs. Jackson said the glass was broken when she arrived this morning. She didn't touch anything but instead went outside and called us."

"Has she had a chance to see what's missing?"

"Pretty much the same as before. Lunch meat and snacks. Do you still think this is just some kid?" Christopher asked, a challenge in his voice.

Hank chose to gather more information before answering the question. "Was anything else taken?"

Mrs. Jackson, who had been talking on her phone a short distance away, ended her call and walked over. "No. My computer is still in my office. And they didn't even try to get into the safe. It's untouched."

"What are they going to do with the stuff they took?" Christopher asked.

"Eat it," Mrs. Jackson said as if it were so obvious she couldn't believe he'd asked that question. "They took food that they wouldn't need to cook and something to drink. I'm not happy about the broken window, but I understand. Hunger makes people desperate. And theft is often the result of that desperation."

"Hungry people? In Aspen Creek?" Christopher scoffed.

"You're young so you probably don't remember when this town was struggling. There were lots of hungry people back then. My father always extended credit even when he knew it might be a while before he was repaid. Or if he was going to be repaid at all. But people need to eat. I share his philosophy. If someone is in need and I'm in a position to help them, I will."

Christopher rolled his eyes. Clearly he didn't agree with Mrs. Jackson's position. Or maybe he didn't believe there could be a hungry person in this prosperous town.

Mrs. Jackson turned and looked at Hank. "When you catch this person, bring them to me, okay, Sheriff?"

"Naturally we'll let you know when the person is caught," Hank said.

"And we will catch them," Christopher said confidently.

Mrs. Jackson looked from Christopher to Hank. "How much longer until you're finished here? I'd like to clean up this mess. I called Danny at the hardware store. He's going to come over and replace the glass. He's just waiting for me to give him the go-ahead."

"Did you gather all of the evidence?" Hank asked Christopher.

"Yes. I took pictures and fingerprints."

"Good man." Hank turned to Mrs. Jackson. "You can go call Danny."

"Thanks. I want to be able to open the store this afternoon." Pulling her phone out of her pocket, Mrs. Jackson walked away to place her call.

Hank and Christopher stepped outside and Christopher

turned to Hank. "I don't see how this happened, Sheriff. I watched the place during store hours. I didn't see anything out of the ordinary. It didn't occur to me that a shoplifter would break in. But this is clearly an escalation."

"If it's the same person."

"Do you think it is?"

"Probably. They did take the same things. So let's go with that until we discover something different. Now you need to come up with a plan. I'm going to canvas the neighborhood and interview the neighbors. It's possible that someone saw something and didn't realize it was important. I'll see you back at the station."

Hank watched as his deputy drove away, then started down the street to begin his interviews. He wanted to alert the other shop owners of the break in at the grocery store in the unlikely event that the news hadn't reached them yet. He suspected that Mrs. Jackson was right. They weren't dealing with a professional criminal but rather with someone who was hungry. But there were better ways—honest ways—to get food.

When he finished talking to people in that neighborhood, Hank headed downtown to talk to those business owners as well.

He stepped into the diner and the bell jangled, signaling his arrival. As usual, the restaurant was filled. He took a quick glance around. No one was behaving in a manner that would arouse his suspicion. None of the patrons was eying the door as if planning to make a quick getaway. More importantly, no one looked uncomfortable by his presence, which was often a sign that someone was up to no good.

"What can I get for you, Hank?" Barbara, one of the

waitresses, asked as she approached. She might be a senior citizen but she was just as quick as people half her age.

Shayna had made him a big breakfast that morning so he wasn't hungry. He headed for the bar and sat in a stool at the counter. "How about a cup of coffee?"

"Sure thing. To go or stay?"

"I'll take it here."

Barbara grabbed a coffee cup and filled it, "You haven't been in for breakfast for a while. I was beginning to think that you'd lost the taste for our food."

"No way. The food is just as delicious as always. Just look around the dining room if you need proof of that."

"I know. Then I decided that your houseguest must be a great cook."

Hank shook his head. Gary had warned him that people in town knew about Shayna, but this was confirmation. Of course, very little in town escaped the senior brigade. Their network reached every corner of the town. But their knowledge could come in handy. Perhaps they knew if someone was down on their luck. That could help them find the shoplifter more easily.

"Don't worry. I know. Mum's the word." Barbara pretended to zip her lips.

"Right. Tell me, have you heard about a family that is struggling to make ends meet?"

Barbara grabbed two plates from the window separating the kitchen from the dining room and took them over to a couple seated at a table by the window before returning. "Now, to answer your question. No. I haven't heard anything about that. But I'll keep my ears and eyes open. Do you think that's who broke into the grocery store?"

"I don't know. It's the theory that I'm working with."

"That makes sense. Coral said that only food was taken." Barbara paused. "My knitting group meets later today so I'll ask around. Should I get back to you or to Christopher?"

"You can let him know. And he'll report to me." Hank was letting the deputy run with the investigation, but he was part of a team and they all worked together.

"Good enough."

Hank drained his coffee, then continued down the street, stopping in every business. Word spread fast in this town and most of the people knew why he was there before he said a word. Nobody had seen a thing, but they all promised to keep their eyes and ears open. When he arrived at the station, Mrs. Parks was waiting for him and he squelched a sigh.

"Hello, Sheriff. How are you this beautiful morning?"

"I have no complaints." Other than being roped in to judge every food contest, which was no doubt why she was here. "How about you?"

"Oh, I'm just so busy. Putting the finishing touches on the festival. Before you know it, the weekend will be here. This is going to be the biggest and best ever. We're expecting a great turnout as usual."

Hank nodded. Evelyn Parks might be a busybody, but he had to give credit where it was due. She and her committee always came up with great ideas and fun new activities for each festival. Not only that—they weren't afraid to do the work necessary. He knew they spent numerous hours making sure everything ran smoothly. If Mrs. Parks said that this was going to be the best event ever, Hank believed her. Over the past years, each successive event had drawn more visitors and added more money to the town's coffers than the previous one. Be that as it may, he wasn't looking forward to hearing what was coming next. "With you in charge, that's to be expected."

She didn't let flattery distract her from her mission. She nodded, then glanced at the old-fashioned clipboard that she carried everywhere. "This time we're going to have two different food contests. We'll of course have the apple pie baking contest again. We have even more entries than before. My daughter is competing again."

Hank managed to keep his expression neutral. Evelyn had been matchmaking for her daughter for several years now without any luck. Melanie was pretty enough, but she had an unpleasant disposition, to put it kindly. As the only child of the town's wealthiest family, she'd always been spoiled. Hank could understand bad behavior as a child, but she was a grown woman. Now in her thirties, she should have learned compassion and kindness. Sadly, she hadn't. She was just as unpleasant now as she'd been when they were in school together.

"As you know, the entries are anonymous. I wouldn't want anyone to think that we're playing favorites. What is the second contest?" Hank asked before she could bring up her daughter again.

"Ribs. Every man in town swears that he is the grill master. So, we're going to have a grill-off and determine who is worthy of the title. At least for this year. So far, we have seventeen entries."

"I think that Marty would be a better judge of that than me," Hank said. Marty Adams had grown up in Aspen Creek. His family owned one of the most popular ski resorts in the nation. Rather than go into the family business, Marty had become a successful chef and restaurateur. He even had a line of barbecue sauce that was sold in many stores across the Midwest.

"No. The committee discussed it and dismissed the idea. We don't want some professional judging the cooking. That might prove intimidating and people could back out, taking their entrance fees with them. We want an ordinary person with ordinary taste buds to be the judge. That's you. It's worked in the past, so why reinvent the wheel?"

That didn't make a lot of sense to Hank. Getting tips of the trade from a professional would go a long way toward increasing anyone's self-esteem and improve their cooking. But then, since the entrants all believed they were the best, maybe they didn't think they needed advice. Besides, this was a good-natured contest. Or did this have more to do with Evelyn's reluctance to involve Marty than she was saying?

Party Marty, as he was known around town, was a lady's man. Perhaps Melanie had made a play for him and he'd rejected her. Or maybe they'd had a fling. When Hank realized where his mind had wandered, he gave himself a mental shake. He was speculating about a situation he knew absolutely nothing about. This was the way that rumors were started. He knew from experience—his and Shayna's—how harmful unfounded rumors could be. He wasn't going to travel down that road, even in his own mind.

"If you're sure." At least he wasn't going to end up with a sugar headache from tasting ribs. Now the pie contest… that remained to be seen.

"Of course I'm sure. Same rules as always. Each contestant will be assigned a random number. You'll taste and choose a first, second and third place winner. Easy-peasy. Any questions?"

"No. I've got it."

"Good." Evelyn pressed the clipboard against her bosom, turned and strode out of the office without another word.

Hank heard laughter and looked at Dana. Her shoulders shook with mirth. "That woman is—"

"—a force of nature."

"That's not even close to what I was going to say, but if you prefer that term, I suppose it'll do."

"That's the polite thing to do." Hank paused and looked at Dana. "I don't suppose you would be interested in helping me judge one or both of these contests. You're a deputy with an impeccable reputation."

"And ordinary taste buds?" Dana smirked. "Nope. I'm a vegetarian and I'm not a fan of sweets."

Hank looked at the plate of bacon and toast on her desk. He knew she had a stash of fun-size chocolate bars in her top drawer too. "I suppose that bacon grew on a tree."

Dana just laughed and took a bite. "If Evelyn wanted me to judge, she would have asked me. Make no mistake, I would have said no in a hot minute. Besides, I don't think it's wise to mess with tradition."

"I could always order you to do it."

Dana laughed. "You could *try.*"

Hank laughed with her before he returned to his office and began to work through the pile of papers on his desk. There was a lot more paperwork involved in police work than he'd believed before he'd taken the job, but it was necessary in order to coordinate with various other departments.

He had just finished when Christopher returned to the office. "Do you have time discuss the case, Sheriff?"

"Of course."

"I brought Dana up to speed when I came back. She suggested that I talk to some of the teenagers in town, so I did. They didn't know anything. Or if they did, they weren't willing to tell me. Maybe you would have more luck with them."

"I doubt it. You know how teens can be." Hank still didn't believe bored teenagers were behind this. But then, he hadn't been a teenager in a long time. Christopher was closer to their age and would have a better idea of how kids got their kicks these days.

Dana came in and the three of them tossed ideas back and forth. They decided to continue with their surveillance for a while longer. They would also increase foot patrol in the area. Now that the shop owners were aware that there was a criminal in their midst, they would be more alert. Hank didn't want anyone behaving foolishly and he agreed to speak at an impromptu business meeting tonight. He hated the idea of being late for dinner when he knew that Shayna was waiting for him, but there was no choice to be made. He was the sheriff and this was his town.

He returned to his office, closed the door so he could have some privacy and then called Shayna. While the phone rang, he thought about the day they'd spent with their friends. Seeing how animated she'd been had done his heart good. But it was seeing her in her swimsuit that made him break out into a hot sweat. The suit had been a one-piece, but it had been cut high at the thigh and low in the back, accentuating her greatest assets—of which there were many. Bikinis were sexy, but the one-piece had required him to use his imagination. And he had.

Hank had enjoyed having his friends around, but it was the time he and Shayna had spent alone that had haunted his dreams that night. Just touching her aroused a strong desire in him with an intensity that had surprised him. By now he should be used to the feelings she elicited, but they still caught him off guard. There were so many. When she was sad, he was protective. When she was playful, he was joyful. When she was flirtatious, he was excited. The range of emotions she was able to draw from him was staggering.

Her voice came over the phone and he pushed his musings aside. "How are things going?"

He quickly brought her up to speed on the day's events. Just talking about it with her felt good. He hadn't realized he missed having that special someone to unwind with until Shayna showed up in his driveway. He would miss that when she left.

"Wow. Well, don't worry about being late for dinner. I'll keep everything warm for you."

Hank listened carefully for any hint of disappointment or anger in her voice, but there was none. Instead all he heard was understanding. "I'll make it up to you."

"There's nothing to make up. This is an important part of your job. I understand."

"Still, I want to try."

"How?"

"I have no idea. But I'll think of something."

Her laughter echoed through his mind as he hung up

the phone. Shayna was one of a kind and he was going to do everything in his power to let her know just how special he thought she was.

Chapter Eleven

Shayna glanced at her reflection in the mirror one last time before shaking her head. "This is ridiculous. You're not performing in front of tens of thousands of people. No one is looking at your outfit. You're going to a festival in your hometown. You already know a lot of the people who'll be there. Besides, Hank is going to be beside you the entire time. He won't let anything bad happen to you."

Inhaling deeply, she picked up her purse and draped the strap over her torso. She was dressed casually in a pair of green shorts, a cute green-and-blue top and strappy sandals. She kept her makeup to a minimum, brushing on mascara and lip gloss before calling it a day. Her hair was free around her face and cascading over her shoulders. Everything about her screamed small-town, which was what she intended. She wanted people to treat her as the friend and neighbor she'd been when she lived here, not some A-list celebrity dropping in to spend time with the little people.

There was a knock on her bedroom door. "Are you ready?"

"Yes." Shayna grabbed her hat and dark sunglasses, then opened the door. She took one look and her heart skipped a beat. Though she had seen Hank dressed in his uniform nearly every day since she'd been in town, her pulse still sped up at the sight of him. The uniform gave him an air of authority that she knew was accompanied by an open and warm heart.

They walked down the stairs together and climbed into the squad car. Before Hank started down the driveway, he glanced over at her. "You look just like the girl that I remember."

"That's what I was aiming for. I'm looking forward to seeing some of the old people."

"I'm sure they feel the same way."

"I was going to say I hope they remember me, but I realized how ridiculous that would sound."

He held his thumb and index finger an inch apart. "Maybe a tiny bit."

As they headed to town, Shayna looked out the window at the passing countryside. She'd been so focused on getting to Hank's that first day that she hadn't paid attention to the view. Everything was even more beautiful than she remembered. Red, orange and purple wildflowers grew in random bunches along the side of the road, adding a bit of variety to the green grass. Tall trees grew in clusters, their leaves rustling in the gentle breeze.

They passed horses trotting in corrals and cattle grazing in fenced-in fields. The car windows were open and Shayna inhaled the familiar country scent. A few puffy clouds sailed slowly across the bright blue sky, temporarily blocking out the bright sun before moving along. The day, warm but not oppressively hot, held a promise of great things to come.

When they arrived at the city park, Hank parked on Main Street and they got out. Shayna was suddenly filled with trepidation and she trembled. The people in her wealthy enclave had gotten used to seeing her about and rarely gave her a second glance. But whenever she ventured too far afield, she drew a crowd and was unable to enjoy herself and generally returned to the safety of her house or hotel room. What if that happened today?

Hank circled the car and stood in front of her. He placed his hands on her shoulders and stared into her eyes. His gaze was calm and warm. Soothing. "Take a deep breath. Nothing and no one will ruin today for you."

She inhaled deeply, then blew out her anxiety along with the breath. "You're right. I had a momentary lapse. I'm fine now."

"That's my girl."

Though she knew that Hank hadn't meant the words as they'd sounded, her pulse began to race. Being Hank's girl had once been a dream of hers. Of course it hadn't been more than a fleeting notion that she'd quickly shooed away. Why would one of the most popular kids in school want to be with the poorest girl in town? The girl whose own parents didn't care about her. She'd told herself to be grateful for his friendship. Then, once she'd begun to make records, she hadn't had enough free time to spend with him. When she'd moved, she'd let the friendship fade away. It wasn't until the high school reunion that she realized that he hadn't forgotten about her any more than she'd forgotten about him.

The streets had been blocked to cars and small tents with people selling all types of wares lined the avenue. There were plenty of people about, but she hadn't drawn attention yet. She smooshed the oversize hat on her head and put on the sunglasses. "Do I look ridiculous in this getup?"

He grinned. "Of course not."

Shayna shook her head ruefully. "Talk about a loaded question. Was that like asking if I look fat in these shorts?"

"I'm not sure what the appropriate answer is. Suffice it to say that you look beautiful in that getup and those shorts." He glanced over her shoulder. "If you don't believe me, maybe you'll believe them."

Shayna turned around. Kristy and Veronica were walking toward them.

"I was hoping that we would run into you before it got too crowded," Kristy said.

"Me too," Shayna admitted. "I was hoping to see some familiar faces."

"We're here now. And we can take over as your personal bodyguards," Veronica said.

Shayna looked at Hank, trying to mask her nerves. She knew that he was working today, but she thought he'd be by her side. At least for a while.

He must have sensed her worry because he smiled at her. "I think I'll keep you ladies company for a while."

"Don't you trust us?" Kristy asked with a smile.

"Of course I do. But we just got here. My deputies can handle things for a while. I would like to spend some time with her before things get busy."

"Oh," Kristy sang, mischief dancing in her eyes.

"It's not like that," Shayna said quickly. She had to shut down that notion before even she began to believe it.

"Can we take her with us if we promise not to go far?" Veronica asked. "We promise to call you if we need you. We'll take care of Shayna."

Hank glanced at Shayna. Clearly the decision was hers. Though she was reluctant to separate from him, he did have a job to do. And there weren't many people around yet.

Shayna looked at Kristy and Veronica. They were offering friendship—something she wanted. Inhaling deeply, she nodded. "I'll be okay."

"My phone is on," Hank said, still not moving.

Shayna held Hank's gaze. She wondered if it would be inappropriate to kiss his cheek and decided it would be. He was in uniform and at work. Not only that, they didn't have that kind of relationship. They were friends and friends didn't kiss. Except they *had* kissed. If she played her cards right, they might kiss again.

"Okay." Unable to let him walk away without some contact, she brushed her hand against his, then watched as he turned and walked away.

"Is this where we pretend that there isn't something serious going on between you and Hank?" Kristy asked, her eyes dancing with mischief.

"I don't know what you mean," Shayna said automatically. Despite her denial, she was unable to keep from grinning.

"Really? That's what you're going with?" Kristy said. "The air was crackling with sexual tension."

Shayna giggled. "Okay, there might have been a tiny bit of heat between us."

"A tiny bit? It was hot enough to roast marshmallows," Veronica said, fanning herself.

"I can't help it. He's just so…everything." Shayna sighed. "But we're just friends. We agreed that it was the best thing for us for a lot of reasons. And I'm mature enough to accept it."

"You can always change your mind. And trust me, after seeing how he looked at you just now, it wouldn't take much to change his either," Kristy said. "Just slip into something sexy and let nature take its course."

"You are so bad," Shayna said.

"Don't be so quick to say no," Veronica added. "Malcolm and I were only friends once."

"Didn't you say that you went for years without talking?" Shayna asked.

"Water under the bridge." Veronica waved her hand as if the years of pain were so insignificant that they didn't deserve further comment.

"Maybe. But I don't want to go years without talking to Hank."

"Didn't you already do that?" Kristy asked, arching an eyebrow.

"Yes," Shayna said grudgingly. But it was different now that they'd reconnected.

"Don't worry about it now," Veronica said. "We're supposed to be having fun. There's plenty of time to talk about this later."

Shayna smiled. She was looking forward to talking about Hank with them. Even if nothing could happen between her and Hank.

"Some of our friends are coming this way," Kristy said. "Come on and we'll introduce you to them."

Before Shayna could react, two women had walked over to them. Veronica gestured as she spoke. "This is Savannah and this is Alexandra. They're new to town.

Sort of. This is Shayna Givens. Shayna grew up in Aspen Creek."

Neither woman appeared the slightest bit surprised to see her. No doubt Kristy and Veronica had alerted them to her presence earlier.

"It's nice to meet you," Savannah said and Alexandra nodded and smiled.

"It's nice to meet you both," Shayna said.

"Savannah and Alexandra are married to two of the Montgomery brothers," Kristy said.

"Which ones?"

"I'm married to Isaac," Savannah said, a dreamy expression on her face. "And Alexandra is married to Nathan."

"Wow. I can't believe they got married." Shayna shook her head. "That didn't come out right at all. I didn't know them very well. Mostly by reputation. Nathan was always so serious and Isaac…wasn't."

"They haven't changed much," Alexandra said. "Nathan is still focused on business. But he's a great father and has developed a work-life balance. He's even competing in the grilling contest."

"So is Isaac, but he's not quite as competitive as Nathan. To be honest, I think he entered just to get under Nathan's skin," Savannah added with a laugh. "Heaven help us all if Isaac actually wins. We'll never hear the end of it."

Shayna couldn't help but smile. "Hank mentioned the contest. He's actually judging it, although I'm not sure he's all that thrilled about it. I don't know why he didn't just say no."

Veronica shook her head. "You've been in California

too long if you've forgotten how small towns operate. You don't volunteer as much as you're volun*told*. Evelyn Parks decided that Hank was going to judge the contests and that was the end of that. I don't think even a food allergy could get him out of it. The only way he can escape is stepping down as sheriff. And even that might not work."

"Is her daughter still in town?"

"Yes. And before you ask, Melanie is just as awful as she was in school," Veronica said. "I tried to give her the benefit of the doubt, but there are only so many second chances I'm willing to give a person. And she surpassed her limit a long time ago."

Shayna nodded. "She did her part to make my life miserable when we were in school. I'm going to do my very best to avoid her."

"If that's your plan, you need to get a move on. She's coming this way."

"Where?" Shayna turned around.

"Don't look," Savannah said. She put an arm around Shayna's shoulders and steered her toward the playground. Veronica, Kristy and Alexandra surrounded her, blocking her from Melanie's sight. When they reached the swings, they looked at each other and then burst into laughter.

"That has to be the silliest thing I've done in a long time," Savannah said.

"Really?" Shayna asked.

"Don't believe it," Alexandra said. "She's married to Isaac. Those two are always up to something."

"We like to have fun," Savannah said.

"And if anyone deserves to have fun, it's you," Veronica said.

Before Shayna could ask what she meant by that, a

little girl ran over to Savannah. "Mommy. I was look-ing for you."

"Well, you found me." Savannah scooped the little girl into her arms and settled her on her hip. She turned to Shayna. "This is my daughter, Mia."

"Hello, Mia. It's nice to meet you."

Mia leaned her head against Savannah's chest and smiled shyly. "I'm a big girl."

"You sure are," Savannah said, kissing the top of her daughter's head.

"I can't believe that Isaac is a father," Shayna said.

"Why not?" Isaac had been trailing behind his daughter and now stood in front of Shayna, a mischievous smile on his face. Shayna recognized that look.

She shrugged. "You just didn't seem the type."

He laughed. "I wasn't. Certainly not in high school. And to be honest, I was surprised for a minute or two. But I wouldn't trade my little girl for the world."

The gentle expression on his face as he looked at his daughter and the sincerely spoken words made Shayna smile. Isaac was such a proud father and Shayna had no doubt he would move heaven and earth to keep his little girl safe and happy. Though she knew that good fathers existed in the world, it was especially heartwarming to see someone she'd known as a child succeed in that role. But then, Isaac had grown up with a great dad.

Was that what it took to become a good parent? Did you need to have good parents as an example? If that was the case, then she shouldn't even think about having children. Heaven knew that neither of her parents had been any good. But perhaps marrying someone who'd grown up in a happy home with loving parents would be enough to offset her deficiencies. She immediately thought of Hank and her eyes sought him out. He was talking with one of his deputies. He seemed to sense her gaze and turned in her direction. He paused his conversation and then waved at her. Even from this distance, she felt his warmth.

"How is the grilling going?" Savannah asked Isaac, and Shayna forced herself to look away from Hank before anyone caught her staring.

"We're just getting started," Isaac said. "The kids wanted to play first. We didn't want them getting in trouble so I volunteered to keep an eye on them."

"I'm playing with Chloe," Mia said.

"Do you want to play with her some more?" Savannah asked.

Mia nodded so Savannah set her on the ground and watched as the little girl ran back to the swings. Then she looked at Isaac. "I've got her now."

Isaac nodded.

Shayna couldn't help but notice the way Isaac and Savannah looked at each other. It was evident that they loved each other very much. They seemed to have a way of communicating that didn't require a lot of words. Was there someone in her life that she could be that close to? She instantly thought of Hank. He seemed to know what she was feeling without her having to tell him. To instinctively know what she needed. But she wanted more than to be with someone who knew how she felt. She wanted to be able to return the favor. She wanted to sense when he needed attention or time alone. To know when he needed a listening ear or an encouraging word. A hug or a kick in the pants. And she wanted to be bold enough to act. Secure enough to take that risk.

"I suppose I should check on my daughter too," Alexandra said.

Savannah's phone beeped, signaling that she'd gotten a text. "Jillian and Miles just got here with Lilliana and Benji."

"Are Miles and Jillian married?" Shayna asked.

"Yes. And they have two kids."

"I always knew they would get together," Shayna said. "They were perfect together."

"They took the scenic route," Isaac said. "They each married other people and only got back together a couple of years ago. But I'll let Jillian tell you about that. I've got a grill to man and a blue ribbon to win. It was good to see you again, Shayna."

"You too."

After Isaac walked away, they headed over to the swings. Shayna turned to the women. She was beginning to feel more at ease. "Everyone has been so… normal around me."

The women exchanged glances.

Clearly they were hiding something. "What don't I know?"

Veronica smiled. "Hank."

"What did he do?"

"Group chat. He reminded us how you grew up here and that you were the same person you'd always been. He told us that you wanted everyone to treat you like a regular person. He said we had better act right *or else.*"

"I didn't grow up here and I have to admit that I was

worried that I'd be starstruck, but you're really normal," Savannah said.

Shayna laughed. "I suppose I'm about as normal as everyone else. And since I was a bit starstruck when I met some of my favorite actors and singers, I try to take it in stride. I don't mind when people ask for an autograph or want to take a picture with me. Within reason. But the lies and ridiculous stories the tabloids print annoy me. The exaggerations of every little thing that I do can get under my skin."

"Well, you don't have to worry about that here. At least not with our people. I can't vouch for the vacationers. Although I don't expect many of them to show up here today. Most of them come to town for the outdoor sports," Veronica said.

"Push me," Mia said, pumping her plump little legs. Although she was making some progress, she wasn't going very high.

"Okay," Savannah said.

"Me too," a little girl that Shayna assumed was Chloe called.

Alexandra headed for the swing. "I knew that was coming."

Veronica put a hand on Shayna's arm. "I know you're here to have a good time, and if I'm out of line just say so and we can forget I said anything…"

"Okay," Shayna said cautiously.

"One of your biggest fans lives in Aspen Creek. Crystal is a terrific girl and I know she would love to meet you."

Shayna breathed out a pent-up breath. "Is that all? You had me worried there for a moment."

"Sorry about that. But you should know there are lots of teenage girls in this town and they generally show up for the festivals."

Shayna nodded. "That's fine. They are the least likely group to make up stories about me or to try to find the most unattractive photo of me to post all over the internet. I'll sign autographs and take all of the pictures with them that they want."

Veronica frowned. "Does that happen a lot? Not the autographs and pictures, the mean stuff."

"More than you know. But not just to me. I suppose the public thinks celebrities are fair game. A lot of people seem to get pleasure out of knocking us down. But I have a lot more peace of mind since I stopped reading the rags."

"If it's any consolation, I never did read those things."

Impulsively, Shayna linked arms with Veronica. "It makes me feel great. So, since Hank gave everyone their marching orders, how about you introduce me to some of your other friends. Hank says you're the most popular person in town."

Veronica laughed. "I'm afraid he exaggerated. I'm the children's librarian. I read to them, give them snacks and recommend good books, so naturally they like me. And their parents like me for pretty much the same reason."

"You give them snacks too?" Shayna joked.

"I meant to their kids. But you already knew that."

Shayna was acutely aware when word of her presence began to circulate. It was as if there was a change in the atmosphere. It started out as a low murmur that was soon followed by stares. Instantly she sought out Hank. As if he felt her eyes on him again, he looked up. Their eyes met and he smiled. He was there if she needed him. All she had to do was call and he'd be by her side.

Then, she heard a man's voice call out over the buzz. "Is that you, Shayna?"

Mr. Johnson.

"I'll be right back," Shayna said to Veronica, who nodded. Then, smiling, Shayna jogged the short distance to the older man. "Yes. It's me. I was going to stop by your shop and see you."

"Are you planning on singing for an ice cream cone?" His eyes danced.

His eyes sparkled with the warmth and amusement that she remembered. Feeling unaccountably happy, she hugged him briefly. "I owe you more than a song."

"You don't owe me a thing."

"I disagree. You gave me free ice cream for years. That's a lot of money."

"Do you think you were the only person I gave ice cream to?"

She hadn't ever thought of that. But yes. In her mind, she'd always been the only kid without money. Apparently she hadn't been. "But you gave me more than a single scoop. You gave me banana splits and sundaes. You gave me the same thing that my friends were getting. And you never once made me feel bad about not being able to pay for it."

"There's no reason you should have felt bad. Poverty isn't a character flaw. Everybody needs help every once in a while. And good people help them. Without shaming them. I like knowing that I did my small part to help you have a happier childhood."

"You did. I had a lot of good experiences here in Aspen

Creek." She'd avoided coming back for years. Now she realized what she'd missed by staying away.

"That's what I like to hear. You can keep your money, but I wouldn't turn down a picture with you at the shop to hang on my wall."

"Deal."

Mr. Johnson looked over Shayna's shoulder and his smile broadened. "Here comes another one of my favorite people."

Shayna turned and followed his gaze. A teenaged girl was walking in their direction, a shy smile on her face. When she realized that she had drawn Shayna's attention, she froze as if trying to decide what to do next. Should she keep walking over to them or should she run away?

"Come here, Crystal," Mr. Johnson said. "I want you to meet one of my friends. This is Shayna Givens."

Crystal seemed to think about that and still didn't move. Shayna smiled and held out her hand. "Any friend of Mr. Johnson is a friend of mine. And I've heard quite a bit about you, Crystal."

Upon hearing those words, the teenager unfroze and dashed over to them. "You heard about me? How?"

"We have mutual friends. Mr. Johnson, of course. And Veronica Kendrick. She planned on introducing us today." She pointed to Veronica, who was talking to the other women.

Crystal smiled. "Oh. I used to babysit for Jillian's and Alexandra's kids."

"They're all very nice. So, would you like to take a few pictures?"

"You don't mind?"

"Of course not." Shayna looked at Mr. Johnson. "Would you do the honors?"

"I would love to." He took Crystal's phone from her outstretched hand. Shayna stepped closer to the teenager and put her arm around her shoulder. Mr. Johnson took three pictures and then handed the phone to Crystal. "Check to make sure that you like them."

Crystal looked at each photo and grinned broadly. "These are great."

"Let me see," Shayna said. Crystal handed over her phone and Shayna looked at the photos. She nodded. "They are great."

"Would it be okay with you if I post them on my social media?"

Shayna was surprised by the question. Most people simply posted without asking for permission. "That would be fine."

"My Instagram account is private, so you don't have to worry about stalkers finding them."

Ah. Crystal must have been the source of that misinformation. "Don't worry. I don't have a stalker. At least not one that I know of."

"That's a relief. The sheriff told my dad the same thing. But you can never be too careful. People can get obsessed with celebrities and cross the line."

"Sheriff Morrow is looking out for me so there's nothing to worry about."

"He's really great. He knows a lot about what's going on in town. Not as much as Gary and the old guys, but they usually tell him about important things they hear about."

Shayna smiled. "That's good to know."

Crystal's phone buzzed and she read a text. "My friends are here now. They're fans too. They might want to take pictures too."

"I don't mind. As long as they're as nice as you are."

"They are." Crystal's fingers flew across her phone. A minute later, a group of teenagers came into view. Crystal ran over to them and showed them her phone. As one, they turned and looked over at Shayna. She waved.

"It looks like the secret is well and truly out," Mr. Johnson said.

"I know. So far so good." She glanced around, tamping down on her budding anxiety. She knew that no matter where she was in the park, Hank was nearby, watching out for her. She smiled at him, letting him know that she was okay.

Mr. Johnson nodded. "It's going to stay that way."

Shayna took pictures with the teenagers and briefly talked with them about her career.

She noticed that Crystal and another girl were whispering furiously back and forth. Crystal nudged the other girl. "Ask her."

"She'll probably just say no."

Aggravated, Crystal turned to Shayna. "Livvie wants to ask you something."

Shayna turned to the other girl. "Sure, what is it?"

Livvie pushed her glasses up over the bridge of her nose. When she removed her finger, the glasses slid back down. She inhaled deeply and then spoke rapidly. "I'm the editor of the school newspaper. Could I interview you? If you have time. It's okay if you don't. I understand."

"I have time, so get your questions together."

"How can I get them to you? Do you want me to email them to your agent?"

"No. How about we do an in-person interview."

Olivia's eyes widened. "Okay. But where? The school is closed for the summer and we need somewhere private."

"You can meet in my office," Hank said, coming up behind them, standing beside Shayna.

"Really?"

"Sure. It's private and you won't have to worry about drawing a crowd. Apparently the sheriff's office isn't a destination spot. I can't imagine why."

Shayna laughed.

Olivia smiled and looked at Shayna. "That would work. If you're sure you don't mind. What day are you free to meet?"

"Does sometime next week work for you? That way the festival will be over and there will be a little less activity for Sheriff Morrow."

They agreed upon a time and the teenagers dashed away, their laughter trailing after them.

"You are just as kind and sweet as you ever were," Mr. Johnson said.

"I was just thinking the same thing," Hank said. There was something about Hank's approval that made her heart sing. But she wasn't doing anything special. Although she rarely did interviews with mainstream media—they'd printed too many lies about her in the past and she refused to feed the beast—she always had time for high school journalists. Too many people had helped her when she'd been a kid for her to not do the same when she could.

"I'll leave you young people to it," Mr. Johnson said. "I have to get back to my booth."

Shayna hugged the older man again, promising to stop by the shop to take that picture.

"How about we get something to eat?" Hank asked when he and Shayna were alone.

Shayna nodded. "What do you have in mind?"

"I don't care as long as it's not ribs. Or pie. It has to be something light because I'm going to be judging the cook-off in a few hours."

"I have to admit that the smoke from the grills smells good."

"You could always judge in my place."

"Not on your life. I'll be content to applaud from the crowd when you announce the winner. Besides, I don't want to be the one to disappoint the losers who think their ribs taste the best. I don't want to lose fans."

"Are you saying I don't have to worry about that?"

She raised an eyebrow. "Do you have a lot of fans?"

Hank smirked. "I don't like to brag."

"But you will."

"Maybe just this once."

They laughed together and headed over to the food trucks. They each got a hot dog, a bag of chips and a lemonade and sat at one of the picnic tables. After they ate, they wandered around, occasionally stopping at a booth that drew their interest.

"We have to stop here," Shayna said, pulling Hank toward a booth selling handmade jewelry.

He pressed a hand to his chest. "It's so sudden. Are you going to propose?"

"Not today," Shayna said with a laugh.

They stepped into the booth. Shayna looked at the jewelry, then turned to the young woman standing behind the long table. She was thin and had an expression in her eyes that Shayna recognized from her earlier years. Hunger and a bit of desperation. Shayna doubted that few others, if any, even noticed. "These earrings are really beautiful."

"Thanks." The woman stared, blinked, shook her head and then continued. "I made them myself."

"I'd like a few pairs. And of course I can't get earrings without buying the bracelets and necklaces that go with them." Shayna picked up four pairs of earrings and an equal number of bracelets and necklaces. "I'll take these."

"Really?"

"Yes. How much do I owe you?"

The woman calculated quickly and then gave Shayna a number that she thought was low. Especially for the quality.

"In that case, let me get two more sets." Shayna picked up more jewelry and smiled. "I love a deal."

"Wow. I was worried about not selling anything. You never can tell with these types of events. You've just bought about a third of my inventory."

"Do you have a card?"

The woman nodded, grabbed a card from a bag and then handed it over.

Shayna picked up the first pair of earrings that had drawn her eye. She took off her diamonds and slid them into her purse. "I'm going to swap my earrings for these. If anyone asks where I got them, I'll be sure to point them in your direction."

The woman placed the jewelry in a bag and handed it to Shayna. "I don't know how to thank you. That will definitely help my sales."

"We women have to stick together."

Hank had stood silently by while Shayna and the other woman talked. When the sale was complete, Shayna took his bicep and they walked to the next booth, her mind still on the young woman selling jewelry. Mr. Johnson and so many others had helped her in the past. It felt good to be able to help someone else. But then neighbors took care of each other.

Coming back to Aspen Creek had reminded her of that.

Chapter Twelve

"It's time for the rib taste-off," Evelyn said, striding over to Hank.

"Okay." He huffed out a long breath. He'd known that this moment was coming but that didn't mean he was happy about it. But it didn't make sense to whine about it.

"The contestants are putting their plates on the tables. I'll call you when we need you. Here are the score sheets."

Hank took the clipboard and scanned it. Taste. Texture. Aroma. Appearance. He was supposed to grade each category on a scale from one to five. The same as he'd done with the pie contest an hour earlier.

"Do you have any questions?"

"No." This was the same procedure they always used in contests. The contestants were assigned a random number and they would place their food on the table in front of the space with that corresponding number. Hank wasn't allowed in that area until every contestant was standing in the audience.

Mrs. Parks nodded and walked away, each step filled with determination. She took this contest seriously and Hank tried to do the same.

"Are you ready to judge?"

Hank looked at his friend Marty Adams, who was

leaning against a tree, a broad grin on his face. "You're the one who should be judging this. Not me."

Marty shook his head. "And risk losing restaurant patrons?"

"Like that would ever happen. You're always booked up weeks in advance."

"And I want to keep it that way. Besides, my brothers and a brother-in-law have entered. That's a no-win situation for me. If I awarded one of them, there would always be a cloud hanging over their victory. And if I chose someone else, my family would never let me hear the end of it. No, you're the man for the job."

"So it's okay if I lose friends?" Hank asked, grinning.

"I don't make the rules."

"I guess there's no getting out of it," Hank said, glancing toward the tent. Mrs. Parks beckoned to him. "Wish me luck."

"From where I stand, you're already lucky enough." Marty tilted his head in Shayna's direction. She was talking with Veronica and the other women. At that moment, Shayna threw her head back and laughed. She was so entrancing that all Hank could do was stare. She was positively beautiful. Not only on the outside, although her good looks were unparalleled. He appreciated her inner beauty even more than her good looks.

He recalled the way that she'd been with the jewelry vendor. Hank had no doubt that Shayna's jewelry box overflowed with expensive one-of-a-kind pieces. Yet she'd made quite a fuss over the homemade earrings and matching bracelets and necklaces. He would have expected her to simply buy the jewelry and leave it unworn in the box. After all, she would have done her good deed by supporting a small business. But when she'd swapped her diamond studs for the woven silver hoops, he'd known that Shayna was a woman with a sweet and considerate heart. If circumstances were different, he would pursue her.

He might be lucky—she was his date after all—but he wasn't *that* lucky. One day she would get in her car and drive away from Aspen Creek, leaving him behind. His heart would never be the same. But that was a problem for another day. Right now he'd enjoy the time they had left.

Hank walked over to the tent. Most of the people who'd come to the festival had gathered around to watch the judging.

Mrs. Parks stood front and center, a microphone in her hand, and Hank turned his attention to her speech. "The person who wins today will truly be the grill master of Aspen Creek. The undisputed king or queen of the grill."

The crowd cheered as several people declared that they would hold the title. Hank had to hand it to Evelyn. She knew how to work a crowd. The excitement was palpable.

"And to judge, let's give a warm welcome to everyone's favorite lawman, Sheriff Hank Morrow."

Shaking his head at the applause, Hank went and stood beside Mrs. Parks. There were so many entries that two long tables had been pushed together in order to hold them all. Even from where he stood, the appetizing aromas reached him. Though he would rather not be the judge, tasting the ribs would be a lot better than the time he'd judged the homemade relish contest. He hadn't eaten that stuff once since then.

Hank pulled out a water bottle and took a sip before starting, something he intended to do before tasting each entry. Each contestant had placed four meaty ribs on a plate—two with sauce and two without. He picked up the piece without sauce and took a bite. It was fine. Nothing to write home about. He supposed it was a three. Next he picked up a piece with sauce. It was better but not by much. Maybe a three and a half. Sighing, he marked the paper, grading for appearance, aroma and texture. He took a sip of water before moving to the next plate and repeating the process.

As he worked his way down the line, he felt the eyes of the crowd following him, speculating on the meaning behind his every move. He studiously avoided looking at the contestants. In his years as sheriff, he'd learned to read body language and facial expressions. He could tell when someone was holding something back as well as when they were anxious or excited. He didn't want to accidentally glance at someone when he was tasting their food.

So far all of the ribs were good. He would happily eat any of them at a cookout. That was the problem. He couldn't differentiate one from the other. Oh, they didn't taste the same. Some had more sugar while others had more garlic. But they were all of the same quality. None of them stood out as being especially good or bad. As a result, he'd given them all similar scores. At this rate, choosing a winner could come down to a coin toss.

He moved over to the next table and picked up a rib from the first plate. At the first bite, his taste buds jumped to attention. This sample wasn't simply good. It was outstanding. The seasonings mingled quite nicely, accentuating the flavor of the meat without overpowering it. The meat was tender and practically fell off the bone, but it still had enough texture to chew. Hank took a second bite. And a third. Then he tried the piece with the barbecue sauce. Perfection. He gave it fives across the board.

Though he didn't think he would find another entry quite as good, he finished sampling the remaining entries. Then he retreated to a secluded corner and began to tabulate the numbers. There was a low murmur as people began to talk again. Laughter mingled with conversation as the contestants began to claim that their entries were the best. Gradually everyone headed over to the makeshift stage in the middle of the park where the award ceremony would take place.

When he had determined the winners, he handed the clipboard to Mrs. Parks. Thankfully his part was over. It was her job to match the entry numbers with the contestants' names and he joined the crowd in front of the stage.

When she had finished her calculations, Mrs. Parks exited the tent and joined them. She climbed the steps, walked to center stage and grabbed the microphone. "Well, that was certainly an exciting competition. Let's give all of our contestants a big hand. And let's show our appreciation to our judge, Sheriff Morrow. He told me that in his book, all of you are winners and to feel free to invite him to your next cookout."

"That invitation is contingent on the results of the contest," a voice called out and everyone laughed.

"Well, we'll all know the winners soon. But first we have a few other winners to announce from our other contests." Mrs. Parks started with awards for the youngest contestants. She announced the winners of the coloring contests, the bike decorating contests, the various races and the pie baking contest. The winners had their pictures taken for the *Aspen Creek Weekly.*

Finally it was time to announce the winner of the grilling contest. Hank was just as curious as the rest of the crowd to hear the news.

"Now, it is time to crown the grill master." Mrs. Parks held up the third place ribbon. "Third place goes to Victor Adams. Come up here and get your ribbon."

The crowd applauded as Victor took the stage. He held up his white ribbon and then searched the audience until his gaze landed on Hank. "Third place isn't too bad. I suppose this means you can come to my next cookout. But you can't take a plate with you when you leave."

Hank laughed and called back. "Fair enough."

Mrs. Parks waited until the laughter died down before announcing the next winner. "Second place goes to James Martin, the third. Trey, come get your ribbon."

Trey raced up the stairs. His young face was alight with joy as he took his red ribbon. "I was worried that I wouldn't win, but my mother encouraged me to try. I don't know who came in first, but I'm coming for you. Next year I'm getting the blue ribbon."

The crowd applauded the teen as he took his place next to Victor, still showing off his ribbon.

"And now for the moment we've all been waiting for. The winner of today's barbecue cook-off is—drumroll please—Gary Perkins."

There was a gasp and then applause. Gary walked slowly up the stairs, soaking up every bit of admiration. He grinned and held the blue ribbon against his chest. "That looks good. And feels good." He turned to Trey and Victor. "Congratulations, guys. And, Trey, I'm really happy to see your generation participating in these events. The town needs all of our participation in order to thrive. And it's up to us older people to pass the traditions down to you teens. Again, well done on your second place. But I'll be ready for you next year. I've got a few tricks up my sleeve that you haven't seen yet."

John, the photographer for the Aspen Creek newspaper, snapped several pictures and then motioned for Hank and Mrs. Parks to join them.

Hank made his way to the stage, weaving his way through the crowd. It seemed as if every person he passed had something to say about his judging. He had just stepped on the top stair when he heard yelling and commotion coming from the grill tent.

"Stop right there, you thief. You're under arrest."

Hank jumped onto the ground and then ran toward the tent. He was vaguely aware that the crowd was not far behind. Apparently people were so anxious for excitement that they were willing to run headlong into a situation without knowing if it was dangerous or not.

When he stepped into the tent, Hank saw that Christopher had cornered a youngster who looked to be about fifteen. A boy of about five was holding a piece of barbecue in one hand, clinging to the teen with the other. His cheek was smeared with sauce and his eyes were wide with fear.

"What's going on here?" Hank asked Christopher as he assessed the situation.

"I caught this kid stealing the food."

"It was just sitting there. Abandoned," the teen said belligerently. "So that makes it fair game."

Christopher opened his mouth to reply, so Hank held up a hand, stopping him. He had a pretty good idea of what was going on. He turned to the teen. "What's your name, son?"

The teen jutted out his jaw, silently challenging Hank. When Hank only stood there, his gaze unwavering, the teen lost some of his bravado. "My name is Trevor. And this is my brother, Aaron."

Hank nodded. "I don't think I've seen you around. Are you new to town?"

Instead of answering the question, the teen squared his shoulders. "Am I under arrest?"

"No. Do you want to be? What would happen to Aaron then?"

The kid shook his head. "I've been taking care of him. He was hungry so I gave him some food." He looked back at Christopher and his eyes narrowed. "It didn't belong to anybody."

"Of course you wanted to take care of your brother," Hank said before Christopher could be drawn into another argument. "That's what big brothers do."

"So, can we go now?"

Hank shook his head. "Not yet. We need to get more information from you. And let's get you both something to eat and drink. Okay?"

Trevor looked at his brother and then nodded.

Hank moved closer to Aaron and extended his hand. "Do you want some apple juice?"

Aaron took a step in Hank's direction and then looked back at Trevor, who nodded, giving him the go ahead. Aaron tentatively took Hank's hand. Hank looked at Christopher, who was watching the scene, his face showing his disagreement with the way Hank was handling the situation. The deputy had a lot to learn about community policing. "Let's get my little friend here some apple juice."

Before either of them could move, Mrs. Jackson made her way to the front of the crowd. She looked at Trevor. "Are you the one who has been taking food from my store?"

Trevor held her eyes. The shame was visible in his, but to his credit, he didn't look away. "Yes. I made a list of everything that I took. I planned to pay you back when I got a job. If I can find one."

"And the window?"

His chest rose and fell. "That was me too. I'm sorry about that. It was late and your store was closed. Aaron was hungry. So was I. I'm sorry for the damage. I'll pay for that too." Trevor glanced at Hank again. "Now you know that I did steal something. And broke a window. Are you going to arrest me now?"

"Nobody is going to arrest anyone," Mrs. Jackson said firmly. She looked at Hank and then at Christopher as if daring either of them to contradict her. "You're having a hard time. Trouble knocks on all of our doors at one time or another. If we're lucky, there'll be someone to help us through the worst of it."

"What about the window?" Christopher asked, clearly unwilling to let the matter drop.

"I have insurance. And the damage wasn't that great. The window has already been replaced." Her voice was firm and brooked no argument.

Christopher looked over at Hank as if hoping that he would intercede. But there was nothing Hank could do if the victim wasn't willing to press charges. And in this instance, Hank was in complete agreement with her. He was all about giving people second chances. And if anyone deserved a chance to make things right, it was this young man.

"I still need your information so I can contact your guardian," Hank said.

"We live with our grandfather. He's been sick lately. I've been taking care of him too."

"Let's get you a plate and you can tell me all about your grandfather," Mrs. Jackson said.

Trevor looked at Hank, who shrugged. "Mrs. Jackson isn't pressing charges against you so I suggest you go with her. You get some food for yourself and your brother. And stay with her. I'll be over in a few minutes to get your information."

Trevor nodded. Then he and Aaron let Mrs. Jackson lead them from the tent. Before turning to Christopher, Hank noticed that several of the women—including Shayna—had their heads together. If he knew the people of Aspen Creek, they were already working out a plan to help Trevor, Aaron and their grandfather. Once it was clear that the excitement was over, people slowly made their way out of the tent.

"I can't believe you let him go," Christopher said when he and Hank were alone.

"No? Why not?" Hank asked.

"Because he's a thief and a vandal. You said that I was in charge of the investigation, yet you stepped on me and my investigation. To make it worse, you did it in front of the entire town. You emasculated me in front of everyone."

Hank folded his arms over his chest. He spoke quietly but there was authority in his words. "Is there anything else you want to say, Deputy? We're alone so now is the time to get it out."

Christopher looked at Hank. He wasn't so confident now. It was as if he realized he might have crossed a line and his job was in jeopardy. He sputtered. "No. That's it."

"Good. Then listen. One of the first things an officer does is consider the entire situation. If the kid was shoplifting for fun or broke into the store for kicks and stole the computer, then I would agree we should throw the book at him. But a kid trying to feed his little brother and sick grandfather? I hope that you can see that the two are completely different situations and should be treated differently. Especially when the victim refuses to press charges."

"How do we even know he's telling the truth? Are we just going to take his word for it?"

"Of course not. We'll take him back to his grandfather's house and confirm the facts. If the grandfather isn't able to take care of them, we'll need to step in. But, Christopher, our responsibility to the people of Aspen Creek isn't just to look out for their property and protect them from violence. We are supposed to care about them. All of them. Even people who behave in ways that we don't approve of. And that's what I want to do now."

Christopher blew out a breath. "I suppose what you're saying makes sense."

"I'm glad you agree." Hank frowned. "Now as far as emasculating you in front of the town goes..."

Christopher held up a hand. "I'm sorry I said that."

"Don't be. You spoke your mind. But you need to understand that image isn't everything. In fact, it's nothing. I don't want you to walk around town like you're the all-powerful authority. That's a quick way to lose the respect of the people and to get booted out of here. We are public servants. We aren't the boss of anyone. But we serve *everyone*. And we treat everyone with respect. Including kids. Understand?"

Christopher nodded. "I suppose I got a little carried away. I just wanted to do a good job. So you'd know that you were right to hire me."

"I already know it." He slapped the deputy on the back. "Now, let's go talk to Trevor."

When they stepped outside, they were surrounded by several of the men who'd entered the cook-off. Miles Montgomery, who was generally quiet, spoke up. "Look, I don't want the kid getting locked up because he and his brother ate those ribs. If they're hungry, they can join me and my family. We have more food than we can eat."

"Same," Gary added. "And since I came in first place, I know they would prefer mine."

Hank nodded at the men. "I appreciate that. I really do. But Mrs. Jackson and the rest of her crew has it handled. But if you want to take over some of your ribs, I don't think they'd have a problem with it."

"If the kid is old enough, he can come work with me at the store," Cole said. "I can always find something for him to do."

"Same for me at the dude ranch," Malcolm said. "I always need help."

"And the resort," Henry Adams said. "Between all of us, we can make sure the kid has an income. And when school starts, we can work around his classes and other activities. And we can find someone to keep an eye on the little one if that's an issue."

"Thanks," Hank said. "I'll reach out to you guys if necessary. Right now we just need to gather more facts."

"Keep us in mind," Cole said before the men walked away.

Hank looked at Christopher. "See, that is the way we handle things around here. We help people when they're in a bad way."

"I see. I guess since I never wanted for anything, I didn't believe that there were poor people in town. I couldn't believe that he really needed the food."

"That was your youth and inexperience talking. You have to remember that not everyone has the same background as you do. You have to open your mind to consider all possibilities."

They walked over to Mrs. Jackson's table. Trevor was there sitting across from his brother while a good number of the senior crew hovered around, placing platters of food wherever they could find a spot on the already crowded table.

Aaron was sitting beside Shayna, giving her adoring looks in between taking bites of a hot dog and sipping from a juice box. Shayna was naturally maternal and the little boy was basking under her attention. After a rough childhood of her own, Shayna could relate to what these kids were going through.

Trevor looked a bit shell-shocked, as if surprised by the reception he was receiving from the townspeople. A plate overflowing with grilled chicken, a hamburger, corn on the cob and potato salad was in front of him. Beside that plate was one filled with homemade peach cobbler, cherry pie and chocolate chip cookies. And yet, they kept offering him more food.

"Have some more baked beans, Trevor," Mrs. Jackson said, scooping them onto the plate before he could reply.

"Do you like macaroni and cheese?" Mrs. Fields asked, holding a serving spoon filled with the delicious looking pasta over his plate.

"Yes, ma'am," he answered.

Mrs. Fields found an empty corner of the plate and piled it on. "This is my secret recipe. It was passed to me by my mother. She got it from her mother."

Trevor took a forkful. "It's really good. It reminds me of the mac and cheese my grandmother used to make."

"There's plenty," Mrs. Jackson said, "so you and your brother eat up."

By the speed the food was disappearing from their plates, it was clear that they enjoyed everything. And that they'd been hungry.

A twinge of guilt turned Hank's stomach. How in the world had he been unaware of two hungry kids in his town? Had he been so focused on Shayna that he had fallen down on the job? And just who was their sick grandfather? He always made a point to stop by ranches and check on the families who didn't come into Aspen Creek on a regular basis. They had all been well the last time he'd checked.

"Would you like anything else?" Mrs. Jackson asked after a few minutes.

Trevor looked at his plate. The only thing that remained was one bean and a few bones. "Thank you. But I don't think I could eat another bite."

"Well, I'll just wrap up some for you to take home for later. And some for your grandfather. You and Aaron are growing boys and need lots of food."

"That's not necessary. You've already been very nice to us. Everybody has." He looked around, including all of the women, before looking back at Mrs. Jackson. "Even after everything."

"Don't argue with old people. We don't like it. And you won't win. Just say 'yes, ma'am' and I'll get you some apple pie." Mrs. Jackson stood there, a hand on her hip, waiting for Trevor's reply.

"Yes, ma'am."

Hank pulled out the chair next to the boy. Now that he'd eaten his fill, it was time to get down to business. "What's your last name?"

"Matthews."

Hank thought for a minute. There were no Matthews in Aspen Creek or the surrounding ranches. "Is that your grandfather's name?"

Trevor shook his head. "Grandpa's last name is Ripley."

The name didn't ring a bell either. The town was growing fast and although Hank appreciated the prosperity, he didn't like not knowing everyone, at least tangentially. "I'm afraid I don't know him. Where do you live?"

"Not too far from here. We haven't lived in Aspen Creek long. We just moved here when school got out."

The boy had answered Hank's questions, but had given very little information. Hank had a feeling there was more to the story, but Trevor and Aaron were entitled to their privacy. Hank knew that everyone had the boys' best interest in mind, but that didn't entitle them to know private information. He looked up and the women surrounding the table took the hint and walked away. Only Mrs. Jackson remained.

"It's a white house with a green door. And the address

is 423 River Street. Right, Trevor?" Aaron piped up, a look of pride on his face.

Trevor groaned and nodded slowly.

Mrs. Jackson spoke up. "I know the house. It's been vacant since the Evanses moved out of town."

The Evans couple hadn't lived in town long. In their early forties, they'd come here from Denver looking for a slower pace. Aspen Creek must have been a bit too slow for them because they'd only lasted a few months before they packed up and moved back to Denver. As far as Hank knew, they hadn't sold the house and this was the first he was hearing about renters. But then, what people did with their private property was their business unless they broke the law.

"Well, when we're finished here, I'll take you home and see what we can do for your grandfather," Hank said.

"I'm going to see the fireworks," Aaron said. Now that he'd eaten his fill and had become comfortable with everyone, he was proving to be quite the talker. "And I can play on the slide and monkey bars some more. Trevor said. *Then* we are going home. Not first. Second."

"We might have to go home now," Trevor said. His voice was gentle but Hank could hear the pain behind it. Just how long had this boy been saddled with an adult's responsibilities? He deserved a chance to be a kid.

Hank glanced at Shayna. She'd been forced to take on the responsibility of supporting her entire family when she'd been around Trevor's age. The expression on her face revealed exactly what she was thinking.

"You promised." Aaron's voice held a mixture of disappointment and accusation.

Hank sighed. He would prefer to take care of this now,

but he supposed there was no reason that they had to handle it immediately. The boys' clothes were clean and neat. As were they. There were no signs of abuse that would warrant him jumping into action this very minute. Not after he'd just lectured Christopher about considering the totality of the circumstances.

"There's no reason you can't stay for the fireworks," Hank said to Trevor. "I can trust you not to wander away. Right?"

The teen nodded. "Yes. Grandpa always says a man is only as good as his word."

"He's right. And I'm giving you my word that I'll help you and your family. You can trust me. So go ahead and take Aaron over to the playground. We'll meet up by the stage after the fireworks."

"You can come too, Ms. Shayna," Aaron said, giving Shayna another adoring look as he slid out of his chair.

"I would love to," Shayna said. She glanced at Hank, who smiled back at her. She'd gone from being reluctant to come to town to becoming active in caring for one of the town's newest members.

She stood and took Aaron's hand. "Some of my friends might be over there with their kids. I'll introduce you so you can make some new friends."

"Okay." Aaron swung their hands before holding out his other hand for his brother.

"I'll catch up with you later," Hank said.

Shayna listened as the little boy told her about the fun he'd had that day while they walked to the playground. He'd climbed on the town fire truck and had put on a fire hat and jacket. Then he'd watched the puppet show, sitting in his brother's lap so he could see better. Since she didn't have kids, Shayna hadn't attended either of those events. But there had been so many kids there, she might not have noticed him anyway.

Trevor helped Aaron climb on a swing and then gave him a big push that sent him flying through the air. Shayna could feel the teen's eyes on her as she had while he'd been eating, making sure that she didn't do anything to hurt Aaron. Clearly he took his responsibility as a big brother seriously.

"You're staring," she said.

"Sorry."

"Is there something you want to ask me?"

"Are you Shayna Givens? The singer?"

"Yep." She took off the hat and sunglasses. Most people had recognized her anyway.

"I thought so. What are you doing here? I mean, you're famous and everything."

"I grew up in Aspen Creek. Not in town, but on a small ranch outside of town."

"Oh. I thought you grew up in the Denver suburbs."

She frowned and shook her head. "My parents and record company took a little bit of creative license when it came to crafting my history."

"You mean they lied."

"In a word, yes. I was only a kid and nobody listened to me or cared what I wanted or how I felt. After a while I gave up and just went with it."

"You could tell the truth now," Trevor pointed out.

"Maybe. But it doesn't matter now. And since the press doesn't know about Aspen Creek, I was able to come here and visit my friends without being bothered."

"Don't you care about the truth? My grandmother always used to say that if you told the truth, you didn't have to worry about keeping your story straight."

"Your grandmother was very wise. And I try to be honest in my daily life." She could have told him that she didn't see the point of being honest with people who made up horrible stories about her in order to make a buck, but she decided against it. She didn't want to create a gray area where one didn't exist for him. Besides, it might sound as if she was making excuses for herself.

"What's it like being rich and famous?"

Shayna sighed. It was easy to put herself in his position. She remembered how awful it had felt to not have enough to pay for necessities and either have to go without or depend on the kindness of others to make it through. The embarrassment that she'd felt. "It feels good to be able to pay for what I need. Fame is okay. It was more fun in the beginning. I felt like a star. Important. But I miss being able to be one person in the crowd. Why? Are you considering a career in show business?"

He laughed and his eyes lit up. For a minute, he looked young and carefree. "No. I actually want to be a doctor."

"That's a noble career. What kind?"

"I haven't decided yet. Maybe a surgeon. Or maybe I'll be an emergency room doctor. I want to help people who are hurt in accidents. My parents were in a wreck. If there had been better doctors around, they might have lived. But there wasn't. And they didn't. They died."

"I'm sorry to hear that."

"It was two years ago."

"That doesn't mean it stops hurting or that you stop

missing them. And if anyone tells you that you should be over it by now, they're wrong."

"Thanks." He blinked rapidly and cleared his throat. "You're really nice. I didn't think you would be."

"Because I'm rich and famous?"

He nodded.

"Let me tell you a secret. When I was growing up, Mr. Johnson used to give me free ice cream. He would tell me that I could pay next time. But when the next time came around, I still didn't have money. And he still gave me ice cream. When I started singing, before I made records, he told me that I could sing a song instead of paying. So that's what I did. But even if I couldn't sing, he still would have given me free ice cream."

"People in this town are nice. I thought that the lady— Mrs. Jackson—was going to be mad at me for taking food from her store and breaking that window. But she wasn't. Instead she gave me and Aaron a lot of food. So did her friends. I thought I might burst."

"That's the way people in this town are. At least most of them." She didn't want to paint a false picture for him just in case he encountered someone who didn't have the Aspen Creek spirit. "Just like everywhere else, there are some mean ones. There was a really mean girl when I was in school. She made fun of me all the time."

"I bet now she wishes that she had been nice."

Shayna laughed. "Yep. Once I became famous she tried to be my friend, but I wasn't interested."

"Are you friends with the sheriff?" Trevor asked.

"Yes. We grew up together. He was one of the people who was always nice to me."

"Is he really not going to arrest me? Or is he waiting to do it after we take Aaron home?"

"If he told you that he wasn't going to arrest you, then you can trust him. He understands your situation. He knows that you were trying to take care of your brother and your grandfather."

"Is he going to tell my grandfather?"

"I don't know."

"Grandpa thinks that I bought the stuff. He gave me money at the beginning of the month, but it wasn't enough. I had to buy him medicine. He could barely get out of bed. I had to take care of them."

"You did the best you could in a difficult situation. But you're not on your own now. You have friends who will help you. And you may as well get used to the fact that Mrs. Jackson and the senior citizens are going to be looking out for you. You might not know it, but you just got yourself a bunch of surrogate aunties." She would have referred to them as grandmothers, but she sensed that he had been close to his and she didn't want to offend him with that reference.

"And the men in this town will step up too," she added. "They'll be here for whatever you need. And that includes the sheriff."

"I thought you lived in California in this big mansion. Are you moving back to Aspen Creek?"

Shayna imagined how good it would feel to live with Hank and wake up with him every day. How perfect it would be to know that she would be sharing every day with him for the rest of her life. But that was a fantasy. When he'd told her she could stay with him as long as she wanted, he didn't mean forever. "No. This is just a vacation for me. I'll be going back home when summer ends."

The thought was painful but Shayna had to accept it. When summer ended, she would have to say goodbye to Hank and go back home.

Chapter Thirteen

"**Y**ou're awfully quiet," Hank said as he and Shayna drove back to the ranch later that night.

"I suppose I'm still thinking about Trevor and Aaron," she said, turning to look at Hank. Though she had been staring out the window, she barely noticed the moon and the stars in the dark sky or the silhouette of the trees they passed.

The boys had been on her mind from the moment they'd met. Aaron had decided that he liked her and had been glued to her side for the remainder of the festival. After he'd gotten his fill of the swing, she'd found her new friends and their kids who'd taken an instant liking to him. They'd chased each other around the grass, playing a game with ever evolving rules that she didn't quite understand and she suspected they didn't either. But their laughter had filled the air as they played. They were enjoying themselves, which was all that mattered.

Hank, Isaac and Malcolm had convinced Trevor to toss the football around with them and they'd quickly organized a game of touch football with several other teens and adults. Trevor hadn't believed that Hank had been a professional football player until Hank had thrown a long spiral pass while the teen ran down the field. After that, he'd peppered Hank with questions about life as a professional quarterback, which Hank answered, a slightly amused expression on his face. Trevor had been reluctant to talk to Hank the *sheriff*, but he'd opened up to Hank the *two time Super Bowl champion*.

Once it was dark, they'd headed over to the bandstand to watch the fireworks. Aspen Creek was a small town, but they put on an impressive show. Aaron had sat beside Shayna, and he'd risen to his feet several times as he'd watched the show in awe. After the grand finale, the crowd had dispersed. Assured that his deputies had everything in hand, Hank had led the boys to his squad car. Trevor had taken one look at the vehicle and frozen. Shayna had taken his hand and reminded him that Hank's word was good. Once he'd realized that she would be accompanying them, he'd relaxed and got into the back seat.

When they arrived at the house—a small but neat bungalow—they'd met the boys' grandfather. He seemed to be suffering from the flu, but although he was weak and had a coughing fit when he'd tried to talk, he'd insisted that he was on the mend and refused Hank's offer to take him to see a doctor. Shayna suspected that he didn't have the money to pay the bill, but she didn't butt in. He had his pride and she didn't want to embarrass him in front of the grandsons who so obviously adored him.

Though clearly exhausted, the older gentleman managed to smile and nod while Aaron told him about the fun that he'd had with his new friends and watching the fireworks. Mr. Ripley's eyes widened when Trevor began to pull foil covered pans from a shopping bag. Trevor explained that the ladies had insisted that he take the food and he hadn't wanted to be rude by refusing. Mr. Ripley had agreed that Trevor had done the right thing and told Trevor to put the food in the refrigerator. Shayna knew that Hank wanted a moment alone with the boys' grandfather, so she'd offered to help Trevor. As expected, Aaron had tagged along.

Hank must have been satisfied by whatever Mr. Ripley told him, because when Shayna and the boys came back into the room, Hank said it was time for them to leave.

"Do you want to talk about it?" he asked now.

She shrugged. "I just feel so helpless. I want to write a big check, but I don't know if that would make things better or worse. I don't want to stick my nose in where it's not welcome."

"I understand the urge. But Mr. Ripley explained that the unexpectedly high moving expenses ate into this month's budget. His sickness didn't help. But I don't think you have to worry about the boys going hungry or Trevor shoplifting again. The senior brigade is already setting up a meal schedule to help the family."

"What if Mr. Ripley turns them down? He didn't seem the type to accept charity readily."

"You must not remember just how those people operate. There is no turning them down. They can push and cajole with the best of them. Besides, Mr. Ripley might have seemed a little crotchety, but Trevor says that he isn't normally like that."

"And you believe him?"

"I do. Even the nicest people can get grumpy when they don't feel well. Add the fact that he thinks he failed those kids and it becomes a big ball of grousing. But if it will make you feel better, I'll check on them in a couple of days."

"It would. Thank you."

Hank smiled. "You are the sweetest person I know."

Shayna looked at Hank. "I might say the same about you."

"Sweet? Perish the thought. I'm stern and hard. Masculine to the nth degree. Everyone knows that."

Shayna laughed. "Just keep telling yourself that."

He parked and they got out of the car. "Have you had enough of the outside for the night or would you like to sit out here for a little while?"

"I can never get enough summer nights." Especially when she was spending them with him.

"In that case, I'll grab a blanket and we can lie under the stars."

Hank dashed into the house and was back in a minute with a handmade quilt that his mother had no doubt left behind for him. After he spread it on the grass, they lay on their backs and looked up at the sky. Shayna stared at the brightest star, closed her eyes and made a wish.

"Do you remember that old poem we used to say as kids about making wishes?" Hank asked.

"Believe it or not, I just made a wish."

"What did you wish for?"

"I can't tell you or it won't come true."

"I think that only applies when you blow out birthday candles. It's not the rule for all wishes."

Shayna leaned on an elbow and turned to lie on her side, facing Hank. He did the same. "Once I tossed a penny into a fountain and told someone what I wished. That wish didn't come true, so I'm not going to take a chance."

"Well, I'm going to make a wish and then I'm going to tell you what it is."

"Don't blame me if it doesn't come true."

"I absolve you from all responsibility," Hank said soberly. "Actually you'll have a starring role in my wish."

"Is that right?" She raised an eyebrow.

"Yes." He closed his eyes briefly. When he opened them, they danced with mischief. "I wished for a kiss."

"Did you? There were lots of women at the festival who were checking you out. Perhaps you should have wished earlier when the odds were better."

"There were no stars out earlier."

"Sure there were."

"And I was on duty. I couldn't very well kiss someone while I was working. That would be unprofessional."

"I suppose it would have set a bad example for your deputies."

"It most certainly would have." Hank gave her a sexy grin. "So, can you help a brother out?"

Shayna sighed and tapped her chin, pretending to think about it.

"It might help you too," Hank added.

"How do you figure?"

"The wishing fairies would see you making my wish come true and decide that you're worthy of having your wish come true too."

"I suppose if I don't help you, they might hold that against me too."

"I hadn't thought of that, but they might."

She leaned in closer and put her hand against his chest. She could feel his heartbeat against her palm. It beat in time to hers. "I guess it would be foolish to take that risk."

"Yes." His lips brushed against hers, sending electricity surging throughout her body.

Unable to resist, Shayna opened her mouth to him. When his tongue tangled with hers, she shivered. The kiss was hot and he took his time as he explored every inch of her mouth. His masculine scent encircled her, increasing her desire exponentially. She wrapped her arms around his neck and pressed her body against his. Gradually she became aware that he was pulling back and she moaned in protest before allowing him to end the kiss.

He leaned his forehead against hers as they both sought to slow their breathing. After a long moment, he spoke. "If the fairies were watching, they're guaranteed to grant your wish. Heck, they'll probably grant every wish you make for the rest of your life."

Shayna sighed. "If only it was that easy."

"Is there anything that I can do to help?" He caressed her cheek before dropping his hand.

"I don't see how. I'd have to tell you what I wished and we've already discussed the danger in that."

He lay on his back and then pulled her close. Shayna rested her head on his shoulder. "In that case, I'll wish for your wish to come true. How's that?"

"It's one wish per customer and you used up yours. You really don't know the rules of wishes, do you?"

"Apparently not. But then, I've never been one to bother with the small print."

She laughed. "Since when are rules small print?"

"When they say things that I don't like. Then I just ignore them."

"That's quite an admission from a lawman."

He tapped his finger against her bottom lip. "Let that be our secret."

"Only because I like you."

He shrugged. "Whatever works."

They lay there in silence for a while, content to stare at the stars while enjoying each other's nearness. An owl hooted in the distance, quickly followed by another. A breeze carrying the sweet scent of ripening fruit and wildflowers blew over them, cooling their bodies. Shayna sighed, sure that she'd found heaven on earth.

"I was thinking…" Shayna said.

"About…"

"About this summer."

"What about it?"

"When I was talking to Trevor, I told him that I was spending the summer in Aspen Creek."

Hank nodded. "The two of you seemed to hit it off. And Aaron was totally enamored by you."

"That's not the point I was trying to make."

"So, what point are you trying to make?"

"I know you said I could stay as long as I wanted. Would you mind if I stayed the rest of the summer?" She would have to reschedule a couple of things, but it would be worth it to have more time with Hank.

"I wouldn't mind at all. I love having you here."

Though he'd said the words she was hoping to hear, she was surprised at the disappointment she felt. It wasn't enough. She wanted him to say that she was welcome to stay for the rest of her life. The thought should have scared her—and maybe a few weeks ago it would have—but it didn't. There was something about Hank that made her brave. He made her think about the future. About forever.

She'd give anything to have a deeper relationship with Hank. A romantic relationship. But given their situation, she couldn't imagine a way to make it work. Too bad wishing on stars didn't always make dreams come true.

Hank listened to the sound of Shayna's steady breathing and smiled. They'd been in the middle of a conversation when she suddenly stopped talking. One second, she was telling him about her favorite book, and the next she…wasn't. Her voice hadn't faded out. It had just cut out mid-syllable. She'd fallen into a deep sleep. He knew he should wake her up so that she could get into her bed, but he wasn't ready to release her. She felt so good lying against his chest, the scent of her perfume teasing his senses. She'd shifted onto her side and her right leg was now draped over his.

His smile widened as he recalled their earlier conversation. Shayna wanted to spend the rest of the summer with him. When she'd said that, he'd wanted to cheer. She would be with him for a while longer. Every day he woke up fearing that she would tell him that it was time for her to go home, leaving him behind. Knowing he would get to enjoy her company for several more weeks made him ridiculously happy and he warned himself to tamp down on his enthusiasm. He had to keep his feelings under control or he would end up with a broken heart.

It wasn't going to be easy. He knew that. But that was a problem for another time. She was lying in his arms now, all soft and warm. And now was all that mattered. Who knew what could happen in the future? Being in Aspen Creek was stirring up good memories for her. Memories she might have forgotten. Maybe she could be happy here. With him.

Shayna stirred and he chased his thoughts away. Though she was sleeping soundly now, he knew she would wake up stiff if she spent the night lying on the hard ground. He knew it was time to wake her. Reluctantly, he shook her shoulder and whispered, "Shayna. Baby, it's time to wake up."

"Five more minutes." Her voice was slurred with sleep.

Five more minutes sounded good to him, but he knew how easily five could turn into ten and ten into twenty. The next thing either of them would see was the rising sun waking them. So despite his desire to hold her longer, he tapped her shoulder and spoke a bit louder. "Sorry. No more minutes. It's time for you to get into bed."

Shayna slapped his hand away. Then she heaved out a breath, pulled her head back and looked at him. "You are such a meanie."

Hank only laughed. He was amused to see how grouchy she was. Everyone needed a flaw. He'd begun to believe that Shayna was the exception to that rule. He was relieved to discover that she wasn't perfect. That took the pressure off him. "I may be mean, but I know that you'll be more comfortable in bed."

"I'm comfortable here." She put her head back on his chest as if the matter was settled. She might be willing to spend the night on the hard ground, but he wasn't. Not when he had a perfectly good California king calling his name.

"You're giving me no choice." Before she could answer, if she even intended to, he slid her off his body, stood, then picked her up. She was light as a feather and fit in his arms as if she'd been made specifically for him.

Without opening her eyes, she wrapped her arms around his neck and snuggled closer. Apparently she wasn't opposed to sleeping in bed either; she just wasn't willing to walk to her room.

Deciding to leave the quilt behind, Hank climbed the back stairs, opened the door and walked through the dark house. He'd lived here most of his life and knew the place like the back of his hand, so he didn't bother with the lights. As he climbed the stairs, he wondered what Shayna would do if he took her to his bedroom instead of the guest room. She'd been perfectly happy to lie in his arms on the grass, but would she feel the same about sharing a bed? Though the temptation was strong, he knew it would be unfair to take away her choice. When he reached the second floor, he went to the guest room and gently placed Shayna on the queen bed.

The minute she felt the mattress beneath her, she wiggled around until she found a comfortable position. Then she sighed. Hank removed Shayna's shoes, grabbed a throw from the back of a chair and covered her. Her breathing deepened and he knew that she was sleeping soundly again.

There was no reason for him to remain, so he tiptoed from the room and closed the door behind him. When he was in the hall, he leaned against the wall and blew out a pent up breath. It was becoming increasingly difficult to maintain control over his body. His growing desire for Shayna was making it more challenging to behave as the type of man he'd worked so hard to become.

He and Shayna had decided to be strictly friends and he would stick with that agreement. When the summer ended and she returned to her regularly scheduled life, he would let her go with a smile on his face—even if it killed him.

Chapter Fourteen

"What are you going to do today?" Hank asked Shayna two days later. Now that people knew she was in town and the worst hadn't happened, she felt more comfortable leaving the ranch and venturing into town.

"I thought I'd stop by Pins and Needles Craft Store. I met Rebecca at the festival and she invited me to drop by anytime and check out the knitting club or sit in on a class. Apparently it's all very casual."

"That sounds like fun. You'll be able to catch up on all of the latest news too."

"Really?"

"Yes. See if you can find out what's going on between Gary and Rose."

"I'll keep my ears open. After spying for you, I'm going to stop by the ice cream shop. I promised to take a picture with Mr. Johnson. The rest of the day is open so I'll play it by ear."

"If you make your way to the sheriff's office and play your cards right, I might be convinced to take you to lunch."

Shayna nodded and smiled flirtatiously. "I'll do my level best."

Hank checked his watch and then stood. "I suppose I

should get a move on. As the saying goes, crime and tide wait for no man."

Shayna giggled. "I believe it's *time* and tide wait for no man."

"Whatever. I still need to get going." He put on his Stetson and they walked to his car. "See you for lunch?"

"Yes." The idea of spending more time with Hank was so appealing that she'd rearrange her whole day if necessary.

Once Hank was gone, Shayna quickly straightened the kitchen, then grabbed her purse, phone and keys. She generally kept her phone off when Hank was home. Now she turned it on and checked her notifications. As expected, her parents had been calling and texting nonstop. She was tempted to listen to the messages, but she resisted the urge. Their constant demands for more and ceaseless complaints about what she didn't provide them were guaranteed to wreck her mood. She knew she was going to have to deal with them eventually—this situation wasn't good for her mental or physical health—but she was on vacation and she wasn't going to let them ruin it.

Shoving her phone into her purse, she hopped into her car and headed to town. Thoughts of her parents trailed after her. She'd stopped wishing they'd change and start acting like normal parents long ago. They didn't have it in them to think of anyone but themselves. But why couldn't they be happy with what she gave them? Why did they always demand more from her while giving her nothing in return? She forced those thoughts away—she'd never know the answer anyway—and focused on the majestic mountains in the distance. By the time she reached town, her mood had improved.

Early in her career, she'd guest starred on an episode of a TV show set in a fictional small town. Aspen Creek had a similar appearance, although instead of a fake vibe, the friendliness was real.

Shayna parked on the street in front of the craft shop and went inside. She looked around, taking in the rows of bins filled with colorful yarn. There were also containers overflowing with fabric squares for quilting. She'd never learned to sew, knit or crochet, but she was willing to give it a try. She might like it. And it would be good to have something to occupy her hands and keep her mind off Hank when she went back to California.

"Welcome," Rebecca said as she walked over. Her smile was warm and friendly. "I was hoping you would take me up on my offer to join the group."

"I appreciate the invitation. I just hope nobody minds."

"They won't. We're a friendly group. People come and go all the time as their schedules allow." Two senior women were already there, sipping coffee and snacking on chocolate muffins.

"Well, Shayna, don't just stand there," one of the women said. "Come on in."

Shayna glanced at the older woman. She looked familiar and Shayna searched her mind for a name to go with the face.

"So you and Diana Lowrey already know each other?" Rebecca asked. "Do you know Sheila Fischer?"

Diana Lowrey. How had Shayna forgotten her name? She'd been one of the women who'd given Shayna's parents a stern talking to when Shayna had been in middle school. The lecture hadn't made a difference. It had gone in one ear and out the other. Scott and Wendy hadn't been inspired to get full-time jobs instead of working here and there to earn enough money to keep the lights on. Most of the time. "It's good to see you again, Mrs. Lowrey."

"You too, Shayna."

"I'm afraid I don't remember you, Mrs. Fischer."

"There's no reason why you should. I only moved to town four years ago. But I've heard all about your visit. It's nice to meet you in person."

"Same."

"Get yourself a snack and come over here and join us," Mrs. Lowrey said, her knitting needles flying as she talked. "The rest of the group will be here soon. We're looking for entertainment ideas from a young person. You fit the bill."

Shayna kept the smile on her face. She truly hoped that they weren't going to ask her to sing. Not that she didn't perform for charity. She did. But her time in Aspen Creek had been perfect. With only a few exceptions, she'd been treated like everyone else. Nevertheless, she poured and doctored a mug of coffee, picked up a muffin and took a bite. It was moist and delicious. While she'd been getting her snack, four more women entered. Rebecca quickly introduced them.

Shayna took a chair near the older women and decided she may as well face things head on. "I'll try to help in any way I can."

"Good. We're trying to come up with an event that would interest young people. Sheila thinks a movie night in the park would be good, but I'm not so sure. That sounds kind of boring to me."

"Kids like movies. And they like going to the park,"

Sheila said, clearly unbothered by Mrs. Lowrey's statement. "What do you think, Shayna?"

"What ages are we talking about?" Shayna asked, wondering how she got in the middle of this.

"Young teenagers. The ones who are too young to get jobs. They seem to be more prone to get into trouble and need activities to keep them busy."

Shayna was tempted to tell them that she was the last person they should ask. Her parents had never considered her too young to work. And she'd been responsible for keeping the house clean from the time she was old enough to hold a broom. Instead, she asked clarifying questions. "Are you only planning one event? Is there a committee? Can one of the teens join? I'm sure they would better be able to say what they would like to do than I am."

Diana nodded. "Rebecca, where is Crystal? She's a teenager."

"It's her day off."

"Okay. Well, that leaves you and Shayna to represent the young people."

Three more women joined the group and quickly asked what was being discussed. Once they were up to date, one of the newcomers spoke up. "I was thinking about a carnival. You know, with rides and games. The whole nine yards."

"How about a dance?" someone else suggested.

The ideas flew fast and furious and Shayna's head was spinning as she tried to keep up. While the others talked, Rebecca taught Shayna the basics of knitting. After about fifteen minutes, it became clear that the ladies didn't really need Rebecca and Shayna's opinions. And they didn't appear to reach a consensus. Once they'd exhausted the ideas, the women began exchanging recipes and gardening tips.

"It's like this every time," Rebecca whispered to Shayna.

"So I really don't have to come up with a great idea."

"No. I used to rack my brain for ideas, but I couldn't come up with anything new or earthshattering. And though the women are older, they do occasionally come up with something that the teens like. When that happens they take the idea to the mayor. If he likes it, they form a committee and go from there."

"I see. How long have you lived in Aspen Creek?" Shayna asked. She always felt at a disadvantage when she met new people. They generally knew a lot about her—even though some of what was public record wasn't true—and she knew nothing about them.

"A little over four years. I love this town. The people all care about each other."

Shayna nodded. She hadn't missed the way the other woman expertly shifted the conversation away from herself to the town. But since she often did the same, Shayna let it pass without comment. For all she knew, Rebecca had moved here after going through a horrible breakup. Or perhaps she'd lost a child or a husband and was trying to put a tragic past behind her. Whatever the case, Rebecca's story was none of her business.

"I didn't realize how much I missed it until I came back," she said.

"Are you planning on staying?"

Shayna shook her head. "No. I'm just here for the summer. I'm on an extended vacation."

"You couldn't have chosen a better place."

Shayna nodded and then returned to her knitting, if you could call it that. While the older woman managed to talk and knit at the same time, she needed to give her full attention to making sure the yarn and needles worked together. When Rebecca mentioned that the hour had passed and the meeting was over, Shayna looked at her project. Her lines weren't neat and she had dropped a number of stitches. Even so, she still felt a sense of satisfaction. Knitting might not become a hobby—she couldn't decide whether she liked it enough to keep at it—but she'd challenged herself and tried something new.

The other women grabbed their belongings and headed out, calling goodbye as they went.

Shayna turned to Rebecca. "Thanks for inviting me and making me feel so welcome."

"My pleasure. Drop by anytime."

Shayna nodded. "I will."

Before she stepped outside, Shayna put on her sunglasses and hat, hoping to blend in with the other pedestrians. On her way to the ice cream parlor, she did a bit of window-shopping. Most of the shops she passed were new, replacing the empty buildings of her youth. She wasn't the only one who'd changed over the past seventeen years. The town had done its own glowing up.

When she reached the ice cream shop, she took a look around. It looked just like she remembered. The white brick building with pink trim brought back happy memories of eating ice cream and banana splits with her friends. Four white iron tables with matching white chairs with pink-and-white-striped cushions were spaced on the front patio. Stepping quickly between the tables before anyone could get a good look at her, Shayna opened the door and went inside. There were a few people standing in front of the counter, placing their orders. The way they were dressed and the number of shopping bags at their feet marked them as tourists.

Mr. Johnson glanced at her and winked before continuing to scoop homemade chocolate chip ice cream into a waffle cone. Shayna turned to face the wall, waiting until the patrons left the shop before she took off her disguise.

"I knew that was you, Shayna."

"I know you did. But they didn't. I didn't want to attract unnecessary attention."

"Well, it's just the two of us now." He walked to the door and flipped the sign from Open to Closed.

"You don't have to do that. I don't want you to lose business."

"I'm not worrying about it so why are you?"

Shayna shook her head. She'd forgotten about how straightforward the older generation was. They had a way of reminding the younger generation what mattered and what didn't. People were more important than profits. She hoped she'd be that wise one day.

"Now, what can I get for you?"

"A brownie sundae."

"Coming right up."

While Mr. Johnson prepared her treat, Shayna looked at the framed pictures hanging on the walls. There was one of her as a thirteen-year-old, standing in front of the counter and singing a song. She still remembered that day. Mr. Johnson had said that one day she'd be famous and he'd asked her to autograph the photo. He had no idea how much his belief in her had bolstered her self-esteem. He'd given her the confidence she'd needed to start performing in public. He and his wife came to every talent show she'd entered, sitting front and center and cheering loudly.

Mr. Johnson brought over her treat and Shayna pulled out her wallet.

"You know I don't charge you."

Shayna sighed dramatically. "I *really* want that ice cream. In fact, I've been thinking about it ever since I got to town. But I won't be able to accept it if you won't accept my money."

"Shayna."

"You always said I could pay next time. Well, it's next time."

"You're a stubborn little girl," he said, shaking his head as he took her money. He put a scoop of butter pecan ice cream into a glass bowl. "Don't tell Beatrice I'm eating this."

"You aren't sick, are you? Are you on some special diet?" Shayna couldn't keep the panic from her voice.

He chuckled and patted her hand, then spooned ice cream into his mouth. He swallowed before answering. "No. I'm fine. And Beatrice hasn't got me on some crazy diet. At least not this week. And don't you give that wife of mine any ideas. She just doesn't like me eating ice cream without her. But she's not here."

Shayna laughed and sampled her sundae. Just as good as ever. "I see. Well, in that case, your secret is safe with me."

"So, what did you want to talk about?"

"How do you know that I didn't come here to take that picture like I promised?"

"Oh, I know that's part of why you're here. But you also seem a little bit worried."

Shayna sighed. "You know, it feels so good to be around people who really know me. People who remember what I was like before everyone in the world knew my name and wanted a piece of me."

"I imagine it's hard not to get frustrated with people who have their own agendas."

"Yes." She sighed. "You were such a good friend to me, I was hoping that you could be a friend to someone else."

"I see. And who might that person be?"

Shayna quickly filled him in on Trevor and Aaron.

He raised an eyebrow. "I heard about them and their troubles."

She ran her spoon around the bowl, scooping up a bit of brownie, hot fudge, nuts and ice cream. She ate it before continuing. "I was hoping you could help them the way you helped me and so many others. And, more than that, I want to help him and his family, but I don't want anybody to know about it."

"Even Hank? I thought the two of you were close."

"We are. And he can know. I'm not keeping secrets from him." At least not about important things.

"What did you have in mind?"

"I don't know. I'm still working that out."

"Don't worry about them, Shayna. The people of this town are going to take care of Trevor and his family. They won't fall through the cracks."

"Do you know his grandfather? I think he used to live here."

"Only by reputation. He's had a hard life. He brought a lot of the trouble on himself, but some things were beyond his control. But that could be said about anybody's life if they live long enough. What matters is that we do the best we can in whichever circumstance we find ourselves and hope and pray that help comes when we need it."

"That's true. So many people helped me. I feel like it's my turn to help someone. But I don't want it to be about me."

"You're part of this community. That means that your help will be appreciated just the same as anyone else's."

Shayna swallowed the lump that had materialized in her throat. "You always knew the right thing to say."

"With age comes wisdom."

Shayna thought of her parents. They were in their fifties and didn't seem to have learned any of life's lessons. Since she shielded them from the consequences of their actions, giving them money whenever they held out their hands, she was also to blame. But then it wasn't the child's job to raise her parents.

She nodded at Mr. Johnson. "It definitely did in your case."

"Now that we settled that, what else is going on in your life?"

Shayna leaned back in her chair and spent the next fifteen minutes catching Mr. Johnson up on her life outside the spotlight. He asked a question every once in a while, but for the most part he simply let her talk.

When she finished, he smiled. "It sounds like you still have a good head on your shoulders. I'm proud of you."

"Thank you," Shayna said, warmed by his words.

They talked for a few more minutes and then stood. Shayna posed for several pictures with him, then gave him a hug. "I promise not to stay away so long."

He smiled. "I'll be here whenever you come back."

Shayna was smiling brightly as she headed to the sheriff's office. As she got closer, her foolish heart sped up at the thought of seeing Hank again.

She opened the door and looked around. This was the first time that she'd been in this office. It looked just like she'd imagined. Several neatly organized bulletin boards hung on the white walls. Four gray metal desks, grouped in twos, faced each other on one side of the room. Two empty cells were on the other. A female deputy—Deputy Long according to her badge—was sitting at the desk nearest the door and working at a computer. She glanced up when Shayna stepped inside. Her mouth fell open but she quickly recovered. "Hello. Are you here to see the sheriff?"

"Yes. Is he available?"

Deputy Long shook herself. "Sorry. I'm not usually this unprofessional. And it's not as if I wasn't warned you were in town. That came out wrong." She took a deep breath. "Your music got me through some of my most challenging times. Seeing you in person is well… Anyway, let me get Hank."

"Hold on a minute," Shayna said, halting the other woman mid-stride. "I'm glad that my music helped you. Thank you for everything you do in Aspen Creek. Especially for having Hank's back."

The deputy nodded. "I'll be right back."

Deputy Long walked around her desk and knocked on a closed door before disappearing inside. A few seconds later she stepped back out and beckoned to Shayna. "You can go in now. The sheriff is ready to see you."

Hank was sitting behind his desk, shifting through a pile of papers, his phone pressed between his ear and shoulder. He nodded as if the person on the other end could see him. He pointed to a chair and Shayna sat down across from him, then looked around the office. There were several framed newspaper articles hanging on the walls and Shayna walked over to the closest one. Unsurprisingly, it wasn't about Hank's illustrious football career, but rather about his swearing in as sheriff. Shayna read the few paragraphs, her pride in him growing with every glowing word, then looked at the accompanying picture. Hank looked so strong and powerful in his uniform, his right hand raised as he was sworn into office. His smiling parents stood on either side of him, as proud as any two people could be. Football might have been his career, but being a sheriff was his calling.

Shayna knew there would come a time when her singing career came to an end. Sure she was still winning Grammys and selling out huge arenas, but tastes in music changed. There was always a new artist with a fresh sound coming along. She was amazed that she had managed to stay on top for as long as she had. Most music careers only lasted five or so years, so she'd exceeded expectations several times over. Of course, she worked exceedingly hard to maintain her success. But how much longer did she want to do this? She still enjoyed performing and she wasn't ready to retire now. But when she did, she hoped she could settle into her new life with as much joy and grace as Hank had. She hoped she could find a new calling.

"Sorry about that," Hank said as he hung up the phone, pulling her attention back to him. Not that he was ever far from her thoughts even when she was asleep. He'd actually had a starring role in her dream last night. As he had several nights before.

"Don't worry about it," Shayna said. "Are you free for lunch, or do you have something pressing?"

"I'm free." He stood, straightened his tie, then put on his Stetson. "While we walk I can see what's going on around town."

"I forgot. You're at work twenty-four hours a day."

"I wouldn't go that far, but I take every opportunity to keep my eyes on things. If people want to talk, I always make time. It's like having a few thousand deputies."

"I bet some of what you hear is gossip."

"Some. I try to screen out the talk of who is dating whom. That generally doesn't interest me."

"Unless you're talking about Gary and Rose. I have no information about them to share by the way."

Hank laughed. "That's different. But I have learned to separate the wheat from the chaff so to speak. But sometimes a seemingly minor conversation can break open a case."

"How?"

Hank put his arm around her waist and steered her toward the diner, ensuring that she was on the inside of the walk and away from most eyes. "Let me give you an example. A woman who shall remain nameless complained that there was trash in her can that she hadn't put there. It had happened for three days in a row and she wanted to know what I was going to do about it. Now, she's a serial complainer. I mean she complains about everything from the way the committee decorates the town for Christmas to the birds that wake her up in the morning. Anyway, she went on to say that she didn't know who it could be because there wasn't supposed to be anyone in the house next to hers. She hadn't seen any lights of heard any noises, so as far as she knew the house was empty. Except for the garbage.

"It turns out that there was someone in the house—a wanted criminal from two towns over. He'd been practically invisible for close to a week. He might have made a clean getaway. It was the extra garbage in a neighbor's can that gave him away."

Shayna laughed. "I never would have put two and two together and come up with a wanted criminal. I would have figured it was kids."

They reached the diner and stepped inside. Most of the tables in the front were filled, but they were able to snag a booth in the back. A waitress brought their menus and gave Shayna a long look. One corner of her mouth lifted in a half smile and she winked as if they shared a secret. "Hi, I'm Dora. I'll be your server. Can I get you something to drink?"

Hank and Shayna exchanged glances and he answered. "Water will be fine."

The young waitress smiled at Shayna again before she walked away. Clearly the disguise hadn't fooled her. From the way people at other tables and booths turned their heads to get a look at her, more people than the waitress knew who she was. A few people took out their phones and snapped pictures or short videos.

"Do you want to go somewhere else?" Hank asked.

Shayna shook her head and removed the hat and sunglasses. "No. As long as people allow me to eat in peace, I'll be fine."

"I can guarantee that." Hank tapped the shield on the top of his shirt. "If this doesn't keep them away, I'll give them one of my patented stares."

"And what stare would that be?"

"The one I used on the football field. I had to have a hard stare to intimidate the other team and keep them from tackling me."

"Did it work?"

"Sometimes. But having a great offensive line worked much better."

Shayna laughed. That was one of the many things she admired about Hank. He didn't take himself too seriously. And he always acknowledged the role others played in his success. He'd always been willing to share the credit with his teammates when they won, while shouldering more than his share of the blame when things went wrong. He did the same with his deputies.

"People are keeping their distance, so I think we can dispense with the mean mug for now." Shayna studied her menu. Everything sounded delicious but she ordered the meat loaf. Though she liked to cook, that was one thing she just couldn't get right. Hers tasted good, but it was missing that certain something that would take it to the next level.

"Tell me more about your job," Shayna said.

"There's a lot of relationship building. That's key. Community policing can prevent a lot of crime, but people have to believe that you care about them. So I try to make sure that everyone from the youngest to the oldest knows that."

He looked at her and she nodded.

"Veronica started a program at the library where people from the community read to the primary aged kids. She invited me, so I went. They made a huge deal of it.

There was a big picture of me in my uniform on an easel. And there was cake."

"What did you read?"

"The Little Engine That Could."

"Oh, that's a good one."

"The kids seemed to enjoy it. I brought little train toys to pass out to them as souvenirs."

"Did they like them?"

"Not as much as I liked the cake."

Shayna shook her head. "You are going to have to get that sweet tooth of yours under control."

"Why? It's not hurting anybody. And I have an otherwise balanced diet and I exercise regularly."

"I love the way your defense just rolled off your tongue. It's as if you've had this conversation once or twice in your life."

"My coaches used to harp on it. But I always made weight in training camp and maintained it throughout the season. And I was never one second slower. So a few cookies here and there didn't hurt anything. In fact, if I had denied myself, I would have been resentful. There are some pleasures that I'm not willing to live without and sweets are on that list."

Shayna nodded. "What else are you unwilling to live without?"

He shook his head and his eyes twinkled. "I can't tell you that. Not in the middle of a crowded restaurant. It might make you blush."

"Then you'll have to tell me tonight."

"Under the stars?"

"Yes." They'd gotten into the habit of eating dinner on the patio as the sun set before walking in the orchard.

When they returned, they spread the quilt on the grass. There was something intimate about lying together and talking quietly as the stars made their appearance. Secrets were easier to share then. Problems weren't as insurmountable when she discussed them with Hank. Dreams that she hadn't dared to voice no longer seemed unrealistic. Everything was possible with Hank in her life.

"This is really good," Shayna said as she dug into her lunch. "I wish I knew the secret to making meat loaf this good."

"I think it has to do with the magic wand that Rhonda keeps in the kitchen. She waves it over all the meals she cooks."

Shayna blinked and then laughed. "Rhonda has a magic wand?"

"Of course. What did you think?"

"I thought it came from years of practice."

"Well, in that case, you should ask for the recipe."

Shayna shook her head. "That wouldn't be right."

"Why not?"

"Because I don't want to use my celebrity status to get favors from other people. Favors that they wouldn't do for anyone else."

"Do you think that Rhonda wouldn't share her recipe? You're wrong. Not too long ago, she taught Crystal how to cook a lot of her most popular recipes."

"Really? Crystal, the teenager I met?"

"Yes. Crystal grew up with a single, teenaged father. She and Cole didn't have any family to depend on, so the town sort of adopted them. Anyway, the women decided to teach Crystal things they didn't think she could learn from her father, including how to cook. This was before

Andrea came to town and she and Cole fell in love again. So if you want the recipe, I'm sure Rhonda will give it to you. Not because you're a celebrity, but because you are one of Aspen Creek's very own. I don't know why you keep forgetting that."

"I guess because I wonder why after all this time people still act like I belong. Our family certainly didn't contribute anything to the community when we lived here. If anything, we did the opposite. We were a stain on the town's otherwise pristine reputation. Our house was a wreck and drove down the home values of the property around us."

"You were a child. You weren't responsible for the upkeep of your property. That job fell to your parents."

"Even so, before the reunion, I hadn't been back in years."

"Do you think there's an expiration date on being considered a member of the community?"

"It sounds ridiculous when you say it out loud."

"So maybe it's time for you to stop thinking it. Just look at Trevor, Aaron and their grandfather. Trevor and Aaron never lived here, although his grandfather did for a short time a long time ago. But that didn't stop the community from rallying around them."

"They really are going to be okay."

"Yes. I'm going to invite Trevor to join the youth group and visit the ranch."

"You mentioned the group once before. When do you normally have them out?"

"Once every month or so. It depends on what else is going on."

"So you should be having them out soon."

A sheepish expression crossed his face and Shayna got a sinking feeling. She frowned and stared at him. "Did you cancel because of me?"

"Not exactly."

"Either you did or you didn't. There is no 'not exactly.'"

"I hadn't scheduled anything."

"Because of me."

"You wanted your privacy. You didn't want anyone to know you were here."

"Well, the secret is out now. Everyone knows that I'm in town and that I'm staying at your ranch. And you know what? The sky hasn't fallen. Nor have I been besieged with the paparazzi."

"So what are you saying?"

"I'm saying get the kids together. They need people like you in their lives. More than that, they need the consistency. They need to know that they matter to you. I don't know where I would have been without Mr. Johnson and Mr. and Mrs. Watson. They saved my life."

"In that case, I'll get in touch with them and set up something for Saturday."

"Great. Do you usually feed them? I don't want to intrude, but I can whip up a few desserts."

"I generally throw hot dogs and burgers on the grill. Maybe some brats and corn. And, of course, chips. Nothing special. Just lots of it. They aren't picky eaters but they have big appetites."

"That sounds like teenagers. I'll stay out of the way if you think that's best. I don't want to mess up your plans."

"You won't be in the way. And now that they know you're around, it might seem weird if you didn't at least say hello. You can hang out as much or as little as you want."

"Sounds good." Shayna knew that she was getting tangled in Hank's life, which would make it harder to extricate herself when it was time for her to leave. But she'd worry about that when the time came. For now she was going to enjoy herself.

Chapter Fifteen

"Last chance to back out," Hank said. He glanced at Shayna, who only smiled at him. Dressed in faded jeans that accentuated her slim hips and round bottom, an orange-and-pink T-shirt that clung to her perky breasts, and pink gym shoes, she looked completely at ease. But then, she regularly performed for crowds numbering in the tens of thousands. Entertaining a dozen kids wasn't going to knock her off her center.

"No way. I'm excited to meet your mentees or club members or whatever it is that you call yourselves."

"Unlike your fans, we don't have a name. Even I knew that was too corny to suggest it. And today's group is going to be a bit bigger than normal. Once I put the word out about today's meeting, teens who had previously rejected my invitations told me they would be here. I can't imagine why," he said with a smirk.

"Maybe they heard how cool you are. Or how good you look in your jeans." Shayna's eyes traveled over his body and he actually felt his face getting hot. He needed to knock off that nonsense.

"Seriously though, they know that you're here and want to meet you."

"Everyone keeps telling me that I'm part of the community so I'm going to act like it. Which is why I'm baking up a storm." She looked at the clock on the wall. "You need to get outside and wait for our guests. And I need to finish icing this cake and put the last sheet of cookies into the oven."

"Yes, ma'am." Hank started for the door. As he passed Shayna, he got a whiff of her now familiar perfume. If he lived to be a hundred, he would think of her every time he smelled roses and vanilla. Of course, if the present was anything to go by, he would think of her anyway. Shayna was always on his mind. She was just as much a part of him as his right arm. Or his heart. But that was for him to know and for her to never find out. As far as she was concerned, they were just friends. Buddies. Pals. If he reminded himself of that often enough it had to stick.

A beat-up pickup kicked up dust and gravel as it chugged up the driveway before coming to a stop a few feet in front of Hank. The truck looked like it was held together by duct tape and prayer, but as long as it was roadworthy, Hank didn't have a problem with it.

Jayme Benson tapped on the horn and waved a greeting as her son, Jacob, hopped out of the truck. Jacob was a reluctant and infrequent attendee and he was never the first to arrive. Hopefully the teen would have such a good time today, he would want to come back regularly. Hank hoped that at the very least he would learn something to carry with him this week.

Several more trucks came up the driveway, depositing groups of unusually enthusiastic teens. Hank didn't even pretend that it was because of him. They were Shayna's fans and she was going to be the star of the show, no pun intended.

"Welcome, everyone. It's good to see you."

Where in the past he might receive a grunt that could pass for a reply in a pinch, today he was greeted with wide smiles and hearty hellos. He even received two fist bumps.

"Hey," Billy, one of the teens, said, craning his neck as he looked around as if expecting Shayna to make a grand entrance.

"You could be a little less obvious," Hank said, drily.

"I was visiting my dad when Shayna Givens was in town for the festival."

Hank nodded, not pointing out that Billy never came to the festivals. Most of this group didn't participate in town or high school activities, so their willingness to come to the ranch even irregularly had been unexpected.

"I didn't even want to go to his house. I never do. But he always insists that I come for 'his weekend.'" Billy made quotation marks with his fingers. "Like I'm a puppy or something. I spent two days stuck sharing a room with my six-year-old stepbrother. My dad was hardly there and when he was, he was arguing with my stepmother. I guess she's finally seeing what a jerk he is. And don't tell me that I need to give him a chance, like that's going to make him love me."

"I wasn't going to say that," Hank said. "You know what's going on in your life better than I do. I'm just glad to see you today."

"That's all you have to say?" Billy asked, clearly expecting a lecture.

"It was. Did you want me to say more?" Hank had learned not to give advice unless specifically asked for. Most of the time, the kids just wanted to vent.

"No."

As one, the kids looked over Hank's shoulder, so he turned around. Shayna was standing there and he wondered just how much of the conversation she'd overheard.

"I hear that someone is looking for me," she said, coming over to the group. The smile on her face was so warm that Hank knew she was sincerely happy to meet his teens.

"Wow. It's you." Billy was nearly breathless.

"In the flesh."

The kids talked over each other for a few minutes. Hank watched, waiting until the noise and chaos died out. He'd known that Shayna was a big deal for the teenaged girls who bought the tickets to her concerts and often copied her hairstyles and clothes, but he hadn't expected the guys to be this starstruck.

True to form, Shayna anticipated the boys' wishes. "How about we take a few pictures before we get to Hank's agenda. I'm a bit excited to see what we do today."

"You're going to be hanging out with us?" Jacob asked, a wide grin on his face.

"If that's okay with you." Shayna looked at each teen. "If not, I can stay in the house."

"You can hang out with us," Jacob answered for the group.

Hank watched as Shayna interacted with the youth as they took photos, giving each one of them individual attention. She was a natural. She listened to what they said with clear interest and even joked around with them. Though they were still a bit awestruck, after a few minutes they managed to calm down enough to get with the program.

Once everyone was present and ready to listen—including Trevor, who Hank introduced to the gang—Hank led them to the corral. The ranch kids had trailered their horses over and they led them to the corral as well.

As the kids began to care for the horses under Hank's guidance, he told them stories about growing up on a ranch, sneaking in a life lesson whenever possible. Every once in a while a kid would say something, but mostly they focused on grooming the horses.

When he'd started the program, he wasn't sure that the kids were actually listening to him. They hadn't responded any more than necessary and the abundance of eye-rolling and mocking laughter had been deflating. Someone had even asked why they should take advice from a washed-up football player. But he'd kept at it. Over time they'd become a little less reluctant to talk although they kept information about their home lives under lock and key. But he'd begun to get good reports from their teachers and the principal. Kids in his group were causing less trouble in school and a couple had even become involved in extracurricular activities.

Although Shayna tried to fade into the background, the kids drew her into the conversation. She gave honest answers to questions about her life, pointing out the good and bad parts of fame. She also mentioned the number of performers who'd come and gone, making a big splash only to never be heard from again.

"I know it's easy to make fun of what the sheriff is saying, but he's right. Getting a good education and staying out of trouble goes a long way to being successful. I met a lot of people who lived the fast life and partied their way into debt and bankruptcy." She named a few people that had the boys nodding. "The world can be hard. It's easy to fail. Get that education so you'll have something to fall back on besides the ground. Don't go looking for trouble. And when it comes looking for you, run."

The boys laughed. Even so, Hank thought they'd received her message.

When they finished grooming the horses, they saddled up for a ride. The town kids loved this part of the day. Once they were all astride, Hank led them to a trail where they let the horses trot. Not wanting to hover, Hank hung back, letting them talk among themselves.

After forty-five minutes, they returned to the stables and the kids began to groom their horses, something that Hank had insisted on from the beginning. While he grilled, the kids tossed around a football, then divided themselves into two teams for a game of touch football.

Ricky, the varsity quarterback, threw a tight spiral to Trevor, who caught it, evaded two defenders and scored a touchdown.

"You're really fast. Team tryouts are next week. You should come," Ricky said. "Our best receiver graduated last year and we could use some help at that position."

Trevor shook his head ruefully. "I wish. I have to help my grandfather with my little brother."

"How old is he?"

"Five."

"Maybe he could go to the library. They have lots of programs for kids there. Or maybe you could get a babysitter."

"Didn't you hear him say he had to watch his brother?" Billy said. "Not everyone has two perfect parents like you do. Some of us have single moms and have to get jobs to help out at home. Or didn't it occur to you that he might not have money for sports fees?"

"How about we dial it back a little," Hank said. "Let's try to have a discussion without the anger. It helps communication and keeps misunderstanding to a minimum."

"I was only trying to help by offering solutions," Ricky said.

"How are you going to offer solutions when you don't even know his situation?" Billy said.

"You guys don't need to fight over me," Trevor said. "In fact, I wish you wouldn't. It makes me uncomfortable."

"Sorry," Ricky said to Trevor. Then he looked at Billy. "I'm sorry to you too."

Billy huffed out a breath. After glaring for a minute, he shrugged. "I'm sorry too." He walked over to Trevor and held out a hand for a shake. After shaking Trevor's hand, Billy walked over to Ricky and they shook hands too. With the conflict diffused, the kids resumed their game.

"Impressive," Shayna whispered, coming up to Hank. "I guess they were listening to you."

"I'm more than impressed. I'm shocked. Billy has come a long way. His willingness to solve a problem with his words is huge. And the fact that he apologized and shook hands? That's more than I could have hoped for."

"This is proof that your program is working."

"I hope so."

"Think about it. It can't be easy for the kids to be themselves when they aren't sure who they are. You remember what it's like at that age. Image is everything. And being vulnerable and admitting you made a mistake in front of all of your peers?" Shayna shook her head. "That's hard. And you helped those kids be able to do that."

"Thanks for that. I'm making it up as I go."

"What made you start working with troubled kids in the first place?"

"Statistics. There are way too many kids behind bars. Kids whose lives were made harder because of a mistake they made. I want to show them that there's a world of possibility out there—that if they make wise decisions, they can have a good life. And that they get to decide what that life looks like. I want them to know that at least one person is on their side. That I'm cheering for them. Mostly, I want them to learn to be happy with themselves. That they don't have to prove they are good enough to anyone else."

"Are you sure you didn't take psychology classes in school? Or maybe some counseling courses?"

He laughed. "Positive. Whatever wisdom I have comes from the men in my life. My father and the various coaches that I had taught me a lot. I want to pass on those lessons."

"You're doing a great job."

Hank began to take the food off the grill and pile it on platters before setting it on the table.

"Halftime," Hank called. He'd pretty much tripled the amount that he usually cooked, but he knew there would be no leftovers. As always, the teens descended on the table like a swarm of locusts.

"Save room for dessert," Shayna said. "I didn't know what you guys like, so I made some of everything."

Ricky shook his head. "I can't believe I'm eating food made by Shayna Givens."

The others laughed as if also amazed by the situation. Hank supposed that in their shoes he would be equally shocked. What were the odds of an A-lister hanging out at a small ranch with a sheriff and a bunch of kids who were trying to stay on the right side of the law? But then, he didn't think of Shayna in that way. He never had. To him, she was simply a friend.

"Now the pressure is really on," Shayna joked. "If the dessert is bad, then I suppose I'll be reading about it in the celebrity rags."

"No way," Billy said, staunchly, turning a stern face to the other kids before looking back at Shayna. "We would never embarrass you like that. Nobody likes when people talk all negative about them. And nobody needs the whole world making fun of them."

"Right," Ricky echoed, and the others nodded.

"Besides, you have to be a good cook," Billy added. "Look at how much weight the sheriff has put on since you've been here."

"Hey," Hank said, feigning outrage. "I weigh about the same as I did before."

"Keep thinking that," Jacob said. "Don't look now but you're starting to get a gut. But I suppose that's normal for a man in middle age."

Hank laughed. If the teens felt comfortable enough to roast him, that meant they were starting to feel comfortable around him. Maybe they would turn to him when faced with a tough choice. If the price he had to pay for that was being mocked for his stomach—he still had a six-pack—so be it.

"Anyway," Shayna said, coming to Hank's rescue, "we

have peach cobbler, cookies, a cake and cherry pie. Feel free to eat as much as you like."

Shayna set the desserts on the table and then stood back as the boys served themselves. Though they had mowed through their lunches, Hank wasn't surprised when they piled dessert on their paper plates. As his mother used to say, they must have holes in their toes that let the food leak out.

Shayna placed several cookies and a huge slab of cobbler into a plastic container and set it beside Hank. "This is for Aaron and his grandfather. I already packed up some of the meat."

Unable to stop himself, Hank placed his arms over Shayna's shoulders and kissed her forehead. "You are amazing."

She smiled up at him. "Back at you."

The hooting and laughter had Hank shaking his head as he pulled back.

"Eat your food," Hank said with a mock scowl that had the boys laughing even harder.

They'd just finished eating when the trucks started pulling up. Billy grabbed one more hot dog and a couple of cookies. "Thanks for having me, Sheriff. See you next time."

Hank nodded. "See you next time."

Trevor was running over to his grandfather's car when Shayna stopped him. She held out the container. "This is for your brother and grandfather. There's something in there for you too."

He cleared his throat. "Thanks."

Once the boys were gone, Hank and Shayna began to put the yard back in order. Shayna was singing softly and he leaned in closer. This was the first time that he'd heard her singing since she'd come to the ranch and he didn't want to miss it.

"What are you doing?" she asked, taking a step back.

"Listening to you sing."

"Was I singing?"

At first Hank thought that she was joking, but when he saw the expression in her eyes, he knew she was serious. "Yes. Why are you surprised?"

"I haven't felt like singing in a while. In fact, I haven't even been listening to music. I was tapped out, you know?"

"Maybe you just needed a break."

"I suppose. I have had a couple of notes playing around in my head lately. They have been such short scraps that I haven't paid much attention to them. I didn't even bother to record them."

"Maybe they're the beginning of melodies."

She shrugged and continued to wipe off the table, so he let the subject drop. He didn't know what had happened, but he didn't want to ruin her good mood.

Chapter Sixteen

Shayna stepped into the diner the following Monday afternoon and looked around. When she spotted Veronica sitting at a table in the back, she quickly wove her way through the tables. Once she was seated across from Veronica with her back to the dining room, Shayna removed her ball cap and sunglasses. "I don't know why I keep wearing this disguise. I'm not fooling anybody."

Veronica shrugged. "Better safe than sorry. We may be used to seeing you around, but you can never be too cautious. Don't forget, we get a regular influx of tourists every week or so."

"Good point. I just hate what it does to my hair."

"Oh. You mean you don't want Hank to see you looking anything other than your best," Veronica teased.

"Will you read too much into it if I say yes?"

"I'm going to read into it regardless of what you say."

Shayna laughed. "I appreciate your honesty."

They ordered their lunches and talked about whatever subject came to mind as they ate. Veronica had a wicked sense of humor and Shayna laughed more than she had in years. This was turning into a perfect day that nothing could ruin.

"Shayna."

At the sound of her mother's voice, Shayna knew that she'd been wrong. Two people could ruin this day. And they were standing beside her table.

"Aren't you going to say something?" her father said when she only stared at them. He'd always felt he was worthy of her respect simply because he'd contributed part of her DNA. In Scott's mind, he was responsible for her talent and deserved credit for her career because he'd been born with a great singing voice. But he'd done nothing to develop his talent. He'd lacked the discipline to learn to read music. His time as a lead singer in a garage band had been short-lived because he was too lazy to rehearse. Yet none of those facts had removed his undeserved sense of pride.

"What are you doing here?" Shayna asked finally. Her hands were suddenly damp and she wiped them on her jeans.

"What kind of question is that? You disappear off the face of the earth without a word and you're surprised that we looked for you? You could have been lying hurt somewhere and we wouldn't have known." Her mother wrung her hands and injected just the right amount of concern into her voice, playing the distraught mother for Veronica and anyone else who might be watching. Wendy even managed to manufacture some moisture in her eyes. To anyone who didn't know her, Wendy looked exactly like a worried mother. But Shayna had seen this act too many times to be moved. The guilt her parents always made her feel didn't materialize. Now she was simply annoyed. She knew that Paula had let her parents know she was fine.

Shayna glanced at Veronica, embarrassed to have her friend witness this scene. She'd never told her new friend about her parents. Now Shayna wished she had said something. The last thing she wanted was for Veronica to think badly of her. The expression on Veronica's face was guarded, so Shayna had no idea if she was being fooled by Wendy's act. "As you can see, I'm fine," Shayna said, trying to inject her voice with a calmness she was far from feeling. "So I suppose you can just turn around and go back home. I'll call you later."

Scott frowned and his eyes narrowed. Shayna knew from experience that he was about to do everything in his power to attract the attention of the few people remaining in the diner. Though Shayna didn't look around, she knew they were being watched. No doubt someone was filming the whole scene.

"This looks like a private matter," Veronica said. She grabbed the bill and stood. "I'll take care of this and leave the three of you to talk."

Shayna could only stare in disbelief as her friend practically ran up to the cashier. But then, she would make herself scarce too if the situation was reversed. Once Veronica had completed her transaction, she strode from the restaurant, her phone at her ear. Shayna would follow her if she didn't know her parents would only make an even bigger scene.

"How did you find out where I was?" she asked them.

Wendy frowned. "Aren't you going to ask us to sit down? Honestly, the way you behave, you'd think we hadn't taught you basic manners." Without waiting to be invited, she took the seat Veronica had just vacated. Scott looked at Shayna, who was sitting in the middle of her bench. She knew better than to allow him to block her in.

She lifted her chin, refusing to scoot over to make room for him, so he sat beside her mother.

Wendy pushed Veronica's dirty dishes into the middle of the table and then leaned her chin into her hand and gave Shayna a practiced look of disappointment. "Why haven't you answered any of our messages?"

"Because I don't want to talk to you. I thought that would be clear, even to you."

"Don't talk to your mother that way," Scott snapped. "We raised you better than that."

"You didn't raise me at all." Shayna wasn't sure where her attitude was coming from. She'd never talked to her parents this way. But she was telling the truth. They'd been horrible parents. If anything, the people in Aspen Creek had raised her. Her high school principal and his wife had been her surrogate parents. Mr. Johnson had been the favorite uncle who spoiled his nieces and nephews for no reason other than because he loved them.

"I'm getting tired of your attitude," Scott said and Shayna felt herself shrinking. She knew she had to stand up to her parents, but it was hard. She'd always given in to them in the hopes that it would make them love her.

Don't tell me that I need to give him a chance, like that's going to make him love me.

The words that young Billy had spoken about his father to Hank the other day at the ranch echoed in her mind. Billy had known there was nothing he could do to make his father love him. The boy had been hurt, but he'd also faced reality head on. The truth was the truth and no amount of wishing on stars would change that. If he could face facts at his young age, she could do the same.

"I'm not doing this," Shayna said, sitting up straight.

"I know the reason you tracked me down has absolutely nothing to do with your so-called concern for me and everything to do with wanting more money."

"If it wasn't for us, you would still be living in this run-down little town," Wendy said, looking down her nose. "I can't believe you came here of your own free will. If it hadn't been for a photo on your fan page, we might never have tracked you down."

Shayna grimaced. She knew she should have been more careful. But she'd been enjoying herself and didn't see the harm of snapping a few selfies with her fans. It had never occurred to her that her parents would scour the internet looking for traces of her. She figured they'd focus on the tabloids which her fans hated as much as she did, so she could fly under the radar. But maybe it was for the best. She was tired of hiding from them. She was going to live her life the way she wanted to.

"You obviously haven't been looking around or you would know that Aspen Creek is quite successful now," Shayna said, defending the town and the people that she had come to love. "It's amazing what a little hard work can do." She gave her parents pointed looks that they ignored. Or perhaps they didn't even realize that she was criticizing them. They lived in their own world. Their delusions had become reality and there was no way the truth could ever penetrate the brick walls they'd built to keep it out.

She briefly wondered if they actually believed what they were saying or if they knew the truth and chose to ignore it. Then she decided it didn't matter. They were what they were and they weren't going to change. If they were going to get out of this pattern she had to be the one to change.

"We need more money," her mother said, apparently tired of keeping up the act. "Give it to us and we'll be on the first plane back to California. Otherwise…"

Shayna heard the unspoken threat her mother had left dangling. She inhaled and squared her shoulders. If she was ever going to stand up to her parents, it was now. "You already get a substantial allowance."

"You call that pittance substantial?" Wendy scoffed. "It's barely enough for necessities like clothes and food and regular facials. Forget about entertainment. It never stretches that far."

It was laughable that her mother believed she needed to buy new clothes every month. Especially since Shayna had grown up wearing secondhand clothes. "You could always get a job to supplement that income."

"We had jobs until you decided you were too good for us to be your managers."

Shayna opened her mouth and then closed it. They weren't worth the effort it would take to say the words. It would be easier for her to transfer a goodly sum of money into their accounts just to be rid of them. "How much do you need?"

Wendy and Scott exchanged satisfied smiles. Before they could speak, a shadow fell over the table.

"Is everything okay here?"

Shayna turned and looked into Hank's face. She'd never been happier to see anyone in her life.

"We were just talking to our daughter, Deputy," Scott said dismissively.

"That's Sheriff," Hank said. "And I was not asking you. I was talking to Shayna."

There was something in Hank's tone that was intimidating and Shayna imagined how criminal suspects must feel when they heard it. But she didn't have to imagine its effect on her father. Like most bullies, he crumbled when he was challenged. And in the face of a younger and much stronger man with authority, Scott folded like a lawn chair.

"Surely you don't object to a mother spending time with her daughter?" Wendy said, stepping back into character. "We've been so worried about her."

"Not at all." Hank looked at Shayna. "Do you mind if I join you?"

"Please do," Shayna said, scooting over.

"On second thought, we need to leave," Scott said, sliding out of the booth. "We have calls to make. There are people who would be excited to hear all about what Shayna has been up to lately." He turned to Shayna. "Our cells are on. If we don't hear from you in an hour, well… you know."

Shayna watched, not breathing until her parents left the diner. Then she looked at Hank, who was now sitting across from her. "How did you know that they were here?" *How did you know I needed you?*

"Veronica called me."

"That explains why she ran out of here."

"I decided now was a good time for foot patrol."

"I'm glad to see you." He'd shown up in the nick of time. She'd been about to pay her parents off just to be rid of them. Hank's presence had given her strength. But she knew that the threat wasn't really over. Her parents were not above siccing the paparazzi on her if that's what it took to squeeze more money from her.

"So, what's going on?" Hank asked.

"Do you mind if we talk about it later? I need to get out of here."

"Sure. Come on, I'll walk you to your car."

"That's not necessary. I want to walk around for a while."

Hank gave her a long look. "You know, you can never satisfy bullies. If you give in to their threats once, they'll just keep making them. And they'll keep demanding more."

Shayna nodded. She could probably put up with the paparazzi. But she couldn't do that to Hank. He'd walked away from the limelight. She didn't want him to be dragged back into it because of her. "It's only money."

"Is it?"

Hank's question haunted her as she walked through the town. She knew from experience that her parents would never be satisfied. Hank was right. It was time for her to stand up and say "no more." When she reached her car, she drove to the ranch with one eye on the clock. Would her parents actually sic the paparazzi on her?

The answer to that question came early the next morning. She and Hank had just finished their morning chores and were sitting down to breakfast when his cell phone rang. As he listened, his face grew grimmer with each passing second. When he ended the call, he looked at her, frowning. "Were you planning on going into town today?"

"I hadn't decided. I thought I might go to the craft store and give knitting another try. But my parents are in town and I was hoping to avoid them."

"They aren't the only ones who are here."

"What do you mean?" she asked, although she knew what he was about to say.

"Apparently somebody notified the press—and I use that term loosely—that you're in Aspen Creek. According to Christopher, there are several of them in town."

"Great," Shayna muttered. "They actually did it."

"Your parents?"

"Yes. They said they would." She turned to Hank. "I'm so sorry. I can't imagine how people in town are taking this."

"You don't owe anyone an apology. And don't worry about the town. We're used to all types of visitors. Aspen Creek is a tourist town, remember?"

Shayna blew out a breath. "I don't think of them as tourists. They're more like vultures."

"I agree. I didn't have to deal with the same level of press that you do, but I know how annoying it can be."

"I suppose you need to get to work," Shayna said. "I imagine the deputies can use your help."

"I won't be going in today."

"My parents don't know that I'm staying here so they couldn't share that information with anyone. Besides, you have a town to serve and keep safe."

"You're part of that town. Now let's finish our breakfast. Then maybe we can go for a horseback ride."

Shayna nodded and forced herself to eat her pancakes and sausages. Breakfast didn't taste as good as it had before. Hank didn't appear to be enjoying his food either. She was about to give up the pretense when she heard the sound of cars coming down the driveway. At the same time, Hank's phone rang. He listened and then spoke.

"Thanks for the heads-up. I think they're here now. No, that's not necessary. I can take care of it."

"The paparazzi are here, aren't they?" she asked, dread settling in her stomach.

"Yes. But they won't be for long." Hank stood and gave her shoulder a gentle squeeze. "Stay here. I'll be right back."

He straightened his tie, put on his Stetson and strode out the door. Shayna peered through the open window, watching and listening as Hank stalked down the stairs. Several men with cameras had been heading toward the house. They stopped when they saw Hank. He held up his hand and spoke clearly. Authoritatively. "I'm going to say this one time and one time only. This is private property. And you're trespassing. I'm giving you one minute to get in your cars and drive off. Sixty seconds. And if you don't, I'm going to arrest you and toss you in jail. Now leave."

"Is Shayna Givens living here?" one man called, ignoring Hank's words.

"Are you lovers?" yelled another. Clearly he had more nerve than sense.

Hank checked his watch. "Forty-five seconds."

The paparazzi looked at each other. Hank took a step. And then another. Deciding that he was serious, the men turned, got back into their cars and left. But Shayna knew this was only a temporary reprieve. They were relentless. Now that they suspected this was where she was staying, they'd wait for their next opportunity. They would use drones if they became desperate enough. They'd done it in the past.

When the cars were out of sight, Shayna went outside

and stood beside Hank. He smiled down at her. "They're gone."

"For now."

"Are you okay?"

She nodded, but she wasn't. She blinked back tears. This ranch was Hank's sanctuary. A tranquil place where he could retreat from the world. Because of her, that tranquility had been disturbed. Shayna knew that as long as she was here, the press would be back. She loved Hank too much to put him through that. She'd actually thought she could have a normal life in Aspen Creek, but she'd been deceiving herself. The press would continue to hound her and Hank and all of their friends. She had no choice. She had to leave. She couldn't wait until the end of the summer. She had to go now.

But there was something she needed to handle first. "I have to call my parents."

"Do you want some privacy?"

She shrugged. "All my life I tried to win their love. But that's impossible. My grandfather loved me. And Mr. Johnson loves me. But my parents, the two people whose love should have been automatic, don't love me at all."

"I don't know what to say. I wish I could say that you're wrong, but people who love you don't blackmail you. They don't sell you out to the press without concern for your safety. But that's their problem. There's nothing wrong with you. You deserve to be loved. Protected."

Shayna felt her throat tighten and she fought back tears. "I grew up seeing athletes on TV. After signing a big contract, they'd always say that the first thing they were going to do was buy their mother a big house. I thought that way too. But buying them a house and giving them money didn't change them into better people. And they aren't ever going to change, are they?"

"No."

"I'm a grown woman. In my thirties. I shouldn't need their love or approval. So why does admitting this hurt so much?"

Hank pulled her into his arms and held her close. "Because you are a loving person. Everyone wants to be loved, especially by their parents. That's the way things are supposed to be. I'd be just as hurt as you if my parents didn't love me."

"But I need to accept that and make decisions based on what's true and not what I want to be true."

"It's easier said than done. Somewhere inside you is that little girl who tried everything to win her parents' love. She didn't go away just because you grew up."

Shayna sighed and leaned against Hank's chest. She felt so safe and secure in his strong arms. So loved. "Are you sure you aren't a counselor?"

"I suppose I could add that to my list of jobs."

She chuckled, moved away and picked up her phone. "Delaying the conversation won't change things."

"I'll be in the corral if you need me." Hank lifted her chin and gently brushed his lips against hers. Despite all of the turmoil inside her, Shayna's stomach tumbled.

Once she was alone, Shayna dialed her mother's cell phone. Wendy answered on the first ring. She didn't bother with a greeting. "I suppose you want to apologize now."

"Apologize for what?" Shayna asked.

"The way you treated us. Honestly, Shayna, you can't

just cut people out of your life and not expect them to react."

"You told the paparazzi where I was. They showed up at Hank's ranch this morning. That was uncalled for."

"We warned you what would happen. I suppose Mr. Tough Guy Sheriff wasn't happy."

Shayna sighed. Why did she even bother? There was something broken in her parents that she couldn't fix. "No. But then he isn't the one you have to worry about making unhappy."

"Meaning?"

"Meaning I'm not giving you any more money. I don't just mean this month. I mean that your allowance is gone. When I hang up this phone I'm calling the bank and ending the automatic deposit. And I'm cancelling your credit cards. I'll pay the balances because… Well, just because. But that's it. The house was a gift so you can keep it. I hope you're able to pay the taxes and the upkeep. If not… Well, that's not my problem."

Wendy sputtered. "Wait a minute. Maybe we overreacted by calling the press, but we've been so worried about you."

Shayna scoffed. "You were so worried about me that you sent the press to hound me. Well, I'm fine. And I'm going to stay fine. I hope you'll be the same. But your welfare is no longer my concern."

Wendy was still attempting to justify her behavior when Shayna hung up. Then she immediately blocked her parents' numbers and followed through on her threats. It was sad and disappointing, but she had to protect her peace of mind. Part of being an adult was setting fantasies aside and accepting reality.

And that applied to her relationship with Hank too. Her heart broke at the realization that she had to leave him now and she rubbed a hand against her chest in a futile attempt to soothe it. Tears filled her eyes and she blinked them away. She had fallen deeply in love and leaving him would hurt. But she had to face facts. He couldn't be happy sharing her spotlight with her. Sadly, there was no future for them.

It was time for her to say goodbye.

Hank knew something was bothering Shayna the minute she walked out to the corral. He wasn't sure if things had gone wrong with the conversation she'd had with her parents, or if something else had caused the sorrow that was radiating from her. Hooking his foot on the bottom rail, he silently cursed her parents. They'd really done a number on her. If he would have had his way, she would have kicked them out of her life a long time ago.

"What's wrong?" he asked, closing the distance between them.

She inhaled deeply and slowly blew out the breath. "It's done. I've officially cut them out of my life."

He took her hands in his. "I'm sorry."

"Why? You and I both know they didn't love me. I'm better off without them."

"They're your parents. Taking this action might be necessary, but it still has to hurt."

"You're amazing. Do you know that?"

"It's been said from time to time." He gave her a searching look. "But there's more that you want to say, isn't there?"

She nodded and his heart fell. "It's time for me to go

home. I ran away from my problems. You provided a sanctuary, but now that I've dealt with my parents, I need to get back to my life. I left a lot of things undone there."

"So you aren't going to stay for the rest of the summer."

She shook her head. "I've had the time of my life, but it's time to get back to reality."

He managed to keep his voice light. "So, when do you plan on going back to California?" He couldn't say the word *home* because in his mind *this* was her home. She belonged here with him.

"Tomorrow."

"So soon?" He realized too late that his voice had been filled with panic. Anxiety. He didn't want to add to her stress when it was clear that she'd been under pressure for far too long. It was what had sent her running here.

She nodded. "I'm going to miss you. But I realize that I have just been carried along in my life like a raft on the waves. I can't think of the last time that I sat down and planned my next move. My life followed the path that I put in place as a child. I haven't really taken the time to question whether I want to continue along this path."

"And you can't do that thinking here? You yourself mentioned how peaceful and quiet it is."

"It was. Until the press found out I was here. Thanks to my parents." He didn't miss the anger and pain in her voice. Then she shook her head. "But the truth is that I have to figure out my life while I'm living my life. I have to see how the changes that I make work in that environment. Does that make sense?"

He nodded. She was holding something back from him. The thought disappointed him. Though he didn't like the idea of her leaving now, when there were weeks of summer left, it might be for the best. He'd been falling more in love with her every passing day. The more time they spent together, the harder it would be to let her go. He knew that she needed to decide for herself what she wanted her life to look like. Just as he had.

Hopefully there would be a place for him in her life.

"I want you to know that you will always be welcome here." He was tempted to tell her that he loved her, because he did, but that smacked of emotional blackmail. She'd dealt with that from her parents.

"I know that. And this isn't goodbye forever. It's not as if we won't keep in touch this time. I know I disappeared in the past, but I won't do that again."

"Well, since this is your last day here, what would you like to do? We can do whatever you want. Just name it."

"I'd like to go for a ride on Sugar. Do you think we could ride to the swimming hole? And I would like to walk in the orchard."

"Absolutely." He didn't know if she realized it, but it was as if she was saying goodbye to the ranch as much as to him.

After the ride and stroll through the orchard, Shayna excused herself to go pack. Hank checked in with Christopher and Dana. Even more press had arrived. Apparently a rumor was circulating that he and Shayna were planning to elope or some such nonsense. Hank hadn't seen any press around the ranch after his initial encounter, but he didn't put it past them to try again. Christopher and Dana assured him that they had the town secure and promised to contact him if the situation changed.

The odd thing was, he wished he and Shayna *were*

engaged. But the chaos that surrounded her life was just too much for him. He had gotten off that merry-go-round and he wasn't interested in hopping on that ride again.

Chapter Seventeen

"I guess you're all wondering why I called you here today," Shayna said, laughing as she looked at her closest friends. They were sitting in the sunroom off of her kitchen, relaxing on overstuffed furniture. She had a view of the infinity pool from her chair. That had been a selling feature when she'd bought the house. Now it didn't compare to the view of the mountains from Hank's ranch. It also lacked the fragrant air from the orchard. "I've always wanted to say that."

"As long as we could help," Lisa said, feeding a morsel of roast chicken to her toddler. Stevie opened his mouth like a baby bird. Once he chewed and swallowed his food, he turned and walked away on chubby legs, shaking a plastic tambourine.

"I wasn't wondering at all," Monica said, her arms resting on her pregnant belly. "But I don't want to steal your thunder. I just suggest you get to it before this kid decides to make his grand entrance."

"You aren't in labor, are you?" Shayna asked, suddenly panicked. She wanted to be there for the baby's birth, but she'd been envisioning being in the waiting room while medical professionals did their thing. Not catching the baby as it was born.

Monica laughed. "Relax. That was a joke. I have two more months to go. Two *long* months. I was just trying to get you to stop beating around the bush. Just get to it."

Shayna nodded. The three of them had spent a lot of time together when they'd toured. After performances, they'd hang out in one of their hotel rooms, talking or playing board games. On off days, they'd even occasionally convinced Shayna to wander around whichever city they happened to be in, shopping before getting something to eat. They'd become friends. But while Lisa and Monica had progressed to the next stage in life, Shayna had stayed in the same place. She continued to record and tour while they'd married and had families and were blissfully happy. She knew everyone's path was different and she shouldn't try to emulate their lives. Even so... "How did you know when it was time to stop performing and move on?"

Monica and Lisa exchanged looks. Lisa spoke first. "For me, there was no decision. I got pregnant and had the worst morning sickness in the history of the world. Then I got pregnant twice more in three years. I was sick both times. I suppose if we'd needed the money I would have kept touring. But we didn't. I'm happy with my career as a studio background singer."

"For me," Monica said, "I just got tired of the grind and wanted to do something that didn't require me to be in a different city every three or four days. Teaching voice and piano works better for me. Even with one and a half kids, I'm able to satisfy my love of music and spend quality time with my family."

"But that's not why you called us here today," Lisa said, tossing her curly hair over her shoulder. "You don't want to talk about our lives and the decisions we made. You want to talk about the changes you're considering making in yours."

"Does it have anything to do with that gorgeous and ferocious looking lawman you were living with?" Monica asked, her eyes dancing with mischief.

Shayna grinned. When the paparazzi hadn't been able to get a photo of her, they'd snapped several of Hank. Dressed in his uniform, a stern look on his gorgeous face, he'd looked like something out of central casting. They'd dug into his background and discovered his NFL career. Shayna's smile faded as she recalled how the press had hounded Hank for a week after, dredging up old photos and stories about his days of dating a new woman every month.

"What happened? You went from happy to depressed in the blink of an eye," Lisa said.

"Yes, it has to do with Hank. I fell in love with him. But he doesn't want to have anything to do with the spotlight. He suffered through it while he was playing in the NFL. He told me more than once how much he enjoys the quiet small-town life. The tranquility. Because of me, that peace was destroyed. Now there's renewed interest in him, which I know he hates."

"Hold on a minute," Monica said, holding up a hand. "Let's rewind to the part where you said you fell in love with Hank. You kind of glossed over it, but we need to talk about that some more."

Shayna sighed. "I grew up with Hank. He was one of the best friends I ever had. After high school, I moved here and we lost touch until I went back to Aspen Creek for a class reunion. He invited me to visit and when things got too rough for me here, I took him up on that invitation. And things…well, progressed pretty quickly from there."

"Until your parents ruined everything," Lisa muttered. "I hope they're somewhere living the miserable lives they deserve."

"Amen to that," Monica added.

Despite everything, Shayna smiled. There was nothing like loyal friends who always had her back. "I don't know how they are. I haven't spoken to them since I got back here almost two weeks ago. And I have no intention of changing that."

"Good. Now back to being in love with Hank," Monica prompted.

"We had a great time. In Aspen Creek I was able to enjoy the simple life. Now, I'm not saying that people weren't starstruck on occasion. They were. But after a while I was able to blend in. I became a member of the community. I even took a knitting class."

"You might want to take a few more classes," Monica said, and they all laughed. Shayna had shown them the scarf she'd been making for Hank. It was a tangled mess of yarn and needles.

"That would be nice. But I can't."

"Why not?" Lisa asked. "They teach classes everywhere. I bet YouTube has a few channels."

"But you're thinking about Aspen Creek," Monica said. "Why can't you go back there?"

"Because I have a spotlight following me everywhere I go. Hank doesn't want to live that way. And it would hurt too much to be there and not be with him."

"Even the most obnoxious paparazzo will get sick of

following you around eventually. Live your life the way you want," Monica said emphatically.

Shayna smiled. "That's what Kristy and Veronica said."

"We're going to pretend that you didn't try to replace us with other people," Lisa said. "We're just going to be happy that you made other friends."

"Speak for yourself," Monica said. "I need to meet them before I'm willing to go that far."

Shayna laughed. "You'd all like each other."

"But really, don't let your fear of how other people might act control what you do," Monica said. "You'll only make yourself miserable."

Her relationship with her parents was proof of that. But she wasn't going to think about them now. Or later either. "What if he doesn't want to be with me? He told me he didn't want to deal with fame and all the hassles that went with it."

"When did he say that?" Monica asked, her voice gentle.

"When I first arrived in Aspen Creek. Maybe a few times after that. Why?"

"He might have felt that way in the beginning, but it's possible that he changed his mind. Maybe he fell in love with you too and decided it was worth the hassle to be with you."

"He never said that."

"Did you tell him that you were in love with him?"

"No."

Monica gave Shayna a knowing look. "Well, then."

"Do you think it's possible?" Shayna whispered, not daring to hope.

"Of course it is," Lisa said. "You changed. So did your feelings. It's possible he's also changed."

"I hadn't even allowed myself to consider that." Shayna looked at her friends, her mind racing a million miles a minute. Was she really going to make that big a change to her life? Would she actually move to Aspen Creek? There was plenty of place for her to build a recording studio like the one she'd built here. That is, if he let her. And she could help start a food pantry for the needy. "Is there anything you miss about touring?"

"I miss room service and not having to make beds," Lisa said.

"Ditto," Monica added. "And I miss laundry service. I could be happy never having to wash another load of clothes. But life is full of trade-offs. You'll have to make sacrifices in order to be with Hank. He'll have to do the same. But I have a sneaking suspicion that you've already decided that you're willing to make them," Lisa said.

"I am. I just wanted to be sure that I wasn't making a big mistake."

"It's never a mistake to follow your heart," Lisa said.

Monica sighed. "Go get your man."

Hank heard the car coming over his driveway and heaved out a breath. He wasn't in the mood for company or another well-meaning person asking if he was okay. And definitely not a paparazzo. One had parked at the edge of his driveway for two days after Shayna had driven off, while the rest had made nuisances of themselves in town. Once Shayna had been spotted in California, they'd all scuttled away like rats. Of course, that was only after they'd dredged up every ancient story they could find about his previous relationships. Suddenly there was renewed interest in him and lots of unwanted speculation about his future with Shayna. Unnamed sources—code for people who didn't exist—gave fabricated details about him and Shayna that bore no resemblance to the truth.

Now that the press was gone, things in his town were settling down and returning to normal. Shayna's parents had been invited to leave the B and B and they too had left town.

Even though things were quiet again, the past two weeks had been difficult for him. Lonely. He and Shayna had talked on the phone every night. He loved hearing her sweet voice. After they hung up, he missed her even more. Last night she'd sounded happy and more at peace than ever. And he wanted her to be happy. After the hell her parents had put her through, she deserved every ounce of joy she could find. So he didn't say the words in his heart. *Come home.*

Last night she'd confided that she was beginning to write music again. The words were flowing out of her so fast she could barely keep up with them. The few notes that had been playing in her mind while she was in Aspen Creek had turned into an entire melody. Apparently going back to California had been the right thing for her. Too bad it was all wrong for him. It was as if they were on a seesaw. She was flying high while he was down in the dumps.

He saw her everywhere he went on the ranch. He'd ridden Sinbad to the swimming hole and immediately recalled the night they'd gone swimming together. The kisses they'd shared. If he closed his eyes, he could practically feel her body brush against his as the waves nudged them together. When he walked through the fruit trees, he saw her sitting in the swing, gliding through the air. He'd told himself to take it down, but he hadn't been ready to cut that connection to her.

How in the world was he supposed to live the rest of his life without her?

That was a question for another time. Now he had to deal with whoever it was who had decided to bother him this early on his day off. He spread the last of the hay on the floor for the horses, opened the doors between the corral and the stables, then headed outside.

Cole was just getting out of his car when Hank reached the driveway.

"Cole. You're out and about awfully early. I'm not expecting a feed delivery today. Or did I get my dates mixed up?" Given the fact that he had been out of sorts these past two weeks, that wasn't entirely out of the question.

"Nope. This is an intervention."

Hank looked around. "Doesn't an intervention usually involve more people? Or are you hiding the others in your truck?"

Cole grimaced. "You're funny. Sort of."

Hank smiled as he recalled how Shayna had told him that he wasn't quite ready for a career in stand-up. "I'm still working on my material."

"Can you work on it another time? I brought fresh coffee cake."

"I suppose you want me to supply the coffee."

"That would be nice."

Hank shook his head. "Come on in."

Hank poured the coffee while Cole cut them each a huge hunk of coffee cake. Neither of them spoke. When he finished his pastry, Hank looked at Cole. "You know, if this is an intervention, you need to start talking. This is my day off and I don't want to spend it staring at you."

Cole laughed. "Then I'll get to it. You're miserable. When are you going to get things back on track with Shayna?"

Hank huffed out a breath. "Her life is in California and mine is here."

"That's the rumor," Cole said dryly. "But have you asked her to come back?"

Hank shook his head. "I can't do that."

"Why not?"

Hank didn't feel right telling anyone about Shayna's parents. She'd had enough of her privacy invaded without him doing the same. "She needs to put herself first."

"And she can't do that here?"

"No."

"Where does that leave you?"

Lonely and miserable. "What would you give up in order to be with Andrea?"

Cole didn't hesitate. "Everything. She's the love of my life. I'd do anything it takes to make her happy. I'm not going to lie—I let my pride and anger at her for leaving me and Crystal get the best of me for a while. But now that I have her in my life again, I'm never going to let her go."

"I hated being hounded by the press. But you know what I hate more? Waking up every day and knowing that I won't be seeing Shayna. Walking through this ranch alone. I guess I can deal with the press and her fans if that's what it takes for us to be together."

"So does that mean that we're going to lose you as sheriff?"

"I hope it doesn't come to that. Shayna seemed happy

here so hopefully she'll think about moving here perma-nently. But if that's not an option for her and the only way I can be with her is to move, then yes."

"So, what are you going to do?"

"I'm going to California and putting it all on the line. And I'm not coming back until I win her heart."

Hank spent the rest of the day making plans. Two of the teens from his program had agreed to take care of his horses and chickens for him until he came back. The deputies assured him that they could provide coverage for the town. If necessary, they could request help from a neighboring town. Hank had two weeks of vacation time banked. Hopefully it wouldn't take longer than that to convince Shayna of his feelings.

He paid an exorbitant amount on an airline ticket for a flight leaving first thing in the morning. It was nearly nine o'clock when he set his suitcase by the front door. He heard another car coming down the driveway. Now who was it? It couldn't be Cole again. He'd agreed with Hank's plan. He'd also planned to update their other friends, so he didn't think any of them would be coming here this late.

There was only one way to find out.

Hank was walking down the porch stairs as the car came to a stop. Then Shayna stepped out. His heart skipped a beat and began to race as he looked at her. He could barely believe his eyes. "Shayna."

She smiled. "Hi. I suppose I should have called first."

"You always have an open invitation. You know that."

Her smile wavered and then disappeared. He didn't know what had brought about the change in her mood, but he wanted to bring back her smile.

"I'm sorry about the press. I saw some of the articles

they wrote about you. I can't believe the way they dredged up your past or the way they followed you around. I know that you must have hated that."

"I did." It had been annoying. But standing here with her, looking into her beautiful face, all of that faded into nothing. He shrugged. "But I got over it."

Her smile returned and she took a step in his direction. Her voice trembled. "I missed you."

"Not nearly as much as I missed you."

He took a step. Then another. She did the same. In a moment, they were practically running toward each other. Then he was holding her in his arms, breathing in her sweet scent. It seemed like years had passed since he'd felt her soft body against him. He pressed a kiss against her cheek. "Oh, Shayna. I can't believe you're here."

She turned her face so their gazes met. Her eyes were filled with tears. "I've dreamed of this moment."

So had he. But the reality was even better than he could have ever imagined. Though they had a lot to discuss, he couldn't help himself. He leaned in close and kissed her. Instantly, he was filled with desire, but he didn't try to rein it in. It was too powerful to stop. She tasted so good—so sweet. He could have kissed her forever. But there were things he needed to say to her first. After reluctantly ending the kiss, he placed his hands on her waist and looked into her eyes. "I just made arrangements to come to California. My flight was for tomorrow."

She gasped and her eyes widened in surprise. "You were? Why?"

Shayna held her breath as she waited for Hank to reply. She was coming to believe that he loved her, but that didn't mean that he was willing to change his life for her.

"Why do you think?"

"I don't want to hope."

He lifted her chin. "I was coming for you. I want to be with you."

"But you hate the spotlight."

"I do. But I'm willing to deal with it."

"Why?"

He took a breath. The confident man who she loved so much looked ill at ease. Worried even. "I guess it's time for me to put my cards on the table. I know your fame comes with some hassles. But I'm willing to put up with the fans and the press. The interruptions at dinner and the requests for photos. All of it. Because I love you. And I want to be with you."

"You love me?" Her heart skipped a beat and her knees wobbled. She'd longed to hear those words from him for so long. Now that he'd said them she could hardly believe it.

"With all my heart."

"That's the first time you've said that to me." She smiled, suddenly feeling shy. "I was hoping you felt that way."

"Why?" A dimple flashed in his cheek. She'd never get tired of seeing his smile.

She leaned into him. "Because I love you too. That's why I came here. I was hoping that you felt the same and that we could make our relationship work. I know we'll both have to compromise. I'm willing if you are."

"You already know the answer to that. I was on my way to California. To you. I'll do whatever it takes. Just tell me what you want and I'll do it."

Shayna smiled and looked at the dark sky. Stars were

beginning to pop out. She sighed. "I know there's a lot to discuss. But for tonight, I'd like to get that quilt and lay under the stars with you."

"I can't think of anything better." Hank took her hand and led her to the yard. "Welcome home."

* * * * *

Get up to 4 Free Books!

We'll send you 2 free books from each series you try
PLUS a free Mystery Gift.

Both the **Harlequin® Special Edition** and **Harlequin® Heartwarming™** series feature compelling novels filled with stories of love and strength where the bonds of friendship, family and community unite.

YES! Please send me 2 FREE novels from the Harlequin Special Edition or Harlequin Heartwarming series and my FREE Gift (gift is worth about $10 retail). I may cancel anytime by emailing ReaderServiceInfo@Harlequin.com or by calling 1-800-873-8635. If I don't cancel, I will receive 6 brand-new Harlequin Special Edition books every month and be billed just $6.39 each in the U.S. or $7.19 each in Canada, or 4 brand-new Harlequin Heartwarming Larger-Print books every month and be billed just $7.19 each in the U.S. or $7.99 each in Canada, a savings of 20% off the cover price. It's quite a bargain! Shipping and handling is just 75¢ per book in the U.S. and $1.75 per book in Canada.* I understand that accepting the free books and gift places me under no obligation to buy anything—they are mine to keep for free no matter what I decide.

Choose one:

☐ **Harlequin Special Edition** (235/335 BPA G3CD)

☐ **Harlequin Heartwarming Larger-Print** (161/361 BPA G3CD)

☐ **Or Try Both!** (235/335 & 161/361 BPA G3CE)

Name (please print)

Address   Apt. #

City   State/Province   Zip/Postal Code

Email: Please check this box ☐ if you would like to receive newsletters and promotional emails from Harlequin Enterprises ULC and its affiliates. You can unsubscribe anytime.

Mail to the **Harlequin Reader Service:**
IN U.S.A.: P.O. Box 1341, Buffalo, NY 14240-8531
IN CANADA: P.O. Box 603, Fort Erie, Ontario L2A 5X3

Want to explore our other series or interested in ebooks? Visit www.ReaderService.com or call 1-800-873-8635.

*Terms and prices subject to change without notice. Prices do not include sales taxes, which will be charged (if applicable) based on your state or country of residence. Canadian residents will be charged applicable taxes. Offer not valid in Quebec. This offer is limited to one order per household. Books received may not be as shown. Not valid for current subscribers to the Harlequin Special Edition or Harlequin Heartwarming series. All orders subject to approval. Credit or debit balances in a customer's account(s) may be offset by any other outstanding balance owed by or to the customer. Please allow 4 to 6 weeks for delivery. Offer available while quantities last.

Your Privacy — Your information is being collected by Harlequin Enterprises ULC, operating as Harlequin Reader Service. For a complete summary of the information we collect, how we use this information and to whom it is disclosed, please visit our privacy notice located at https://corporate.harlequin.com/privacy-notice. Notice to California Residents—Under California law, you have specific rights to control and access your data. For more information on these rights and how to exercise them, visit https://corporate.harlequin.com/california-privacy. For additional information for residents of other U.S. states that provide their residents with certain rights with respect to personal data, visit https://corporate.harlequin.com/other-state-residents-privacy-rights.

HSEHW2603